W9-BNG-587

Praise for *A Summer without Dawn*,
winner of Prix Jean d'Heurs, at the Centre Mondial de la Paix in France—
Salon du Livre d'Histoire

"In this sweeping, well-crafted historical… recreates the 1915 Armenian genocide through the eyes of a young family… this richly textured work is exciting and horrifying, infused with lust, betrayal, vengeance, and plenty of bloody mayhem."
—*Publishers Weekly*

"This is a remarkable, unforgettable novel of survival based upon the true story of the ethnic cleansing by the Turkish government during the First World War… well-written with fascinating and memorable characters… I highly recommend this book…"
—*Historical Novel Review*, Editors' Choice

"Armenia's *Gone With the Wind*… Saga of the 20th century's first ethnic slaughter is a page-turner…"
—*The Gazette* (Montreal)

"Not since Pasternack's *Doctor Zhivago* and the works of Kundera have I found a novel as moving and significant."
—*Voir*

"A captivating novel… The characters are real heroes of a type seldom seen, larger than life…"
—*Le Droit*

"A gripping read…. A fascinating and cinematic novel, written from the gut."
—*The Independent* (London)

"*A Summer without Dawn* is a penetrating examination of man's inhumanity to man. This strangely fascinating novel is hard to put down."
—*The Ottawa Citizen*

"*A Summer without Dawn* is in the tradition of thick novels that exercise the same effects as a drug, the reader loses all sense of time and becomes completely immersed in the central couple, Maro and Vartan."
—*Le Soleil*

"The material which forms the basis of this spectacular novel is a treasure trove of adventure and emotion… A novel to discover…"
—*Le Canada Français*

"Through fictional characters and a highly romantic plot, this mosaic keeps the reader in suspense, and demonstrates just how far inhuman folly can drive the forces of consolidation and the threat of power."
—*Châtelaine*

"The storytelling talents of the author and the romantic plot that is developed with such superb skill combine to endow them with an undeniable fascination... One quickly becomes attached to this young family... Whose chaotic path the author persuades us to follow, with utmost realism and the most beautiful of feelings to the very last page. The spirited writing, the vivid style, and the frequent twists of plot, all play a part in keeping interest at the boiling point. I got swept along by it myself... I found myself unable to put it down until I finished it."
—*La Tribune*

"*A Summer without Dawn* is a... captivating book."
—*Le Devoir*

"The publication of this great mosaic is an important event... a great beautiful story, which will provide a great many people with long hours of intermingled pleasure and anxiety."
—*La Presse*

"A novel to supersede Werfel's *Forty Days of Musa Dagh* has at last been written. *A Summer Without Dawn* is an epic which assiduously faithful to history, shows that events will always create their own momentum, that atrocities, even if brushed under the carpet and condemned to oblivion, will invariably surface and cry out... The characters are masterfully drawn and elicit immense empathy from the reader; when they love, they love truly; when they collapse, they cry out for a Simon of Cyrene; and when they bleed, their blood drips from the page..."
—Morris Farhi, MBE, Fellow of Royal Society of Literature

"Extraordinarily evocative in terms of sense of place and time..."
—BBC, London

"Agop Hacikyan's gripping novel, *A Summer without Dawn*, an Armenian epic is not only a great read, but is a wake-up call to the truth of the 20th century's first racial cleansing..."
—*The Examiner* (Westmount, Quebec)

# The Young Man in the Gray Suit

Agop J. Hacikyan

Interlink Books

An imprint of Interlink Publishing Group, Inc.
Northampton, Massachusetts

*To the memory of my parents*

First published in 2013 by

INTERLINK BOOKS
An imprint of Interlink Publishing Group, Inc
46 Crosby Street, Northampton, Massachusetts 01060
www.interlinkbooks.com

Copyright © by Agop J. Hacikyan 2013

**Library of Congress Cataloging-in-Publication Data**

Hacikyan, A. J. (Agop Jack), 1931-
The young man in the gray suit / Agop J. Hacikyan. -- 1st American ed.
p. cm.
ISBN 978-1-56656-907-1
1. Lawyers--Turkey--Fiction. 2. Family secrets--Fiction. 3. Armenians--Fiction. I. Title.
PQ3919.2.H224Y68 2012
843'.914--dc23
2012032329

Cover image Copyright © Morpheusm | Dreamstime.com
Book design by Pamela Fontes-May

Printed and bound in the United States of America

To order or request our complete catalog,
please call us at 1-800-238-LINK, e-mail: info@interlinkbooks.com
or visit www.interlinkbooks.com

# Acknowledgments

With gratitude to my wife, Brigitte, who tolerates my work habits and excessive concerns and provides the most helpful reads of my manuscripts;

With gratitude to Rebecca O'Connor, poet, writer, and editor/publisher of the *Moth* magazine, for her dedication, critical eye, and expert suggestions;

With gratitude to Kitty Burns Florey, novelist, nonfiction writer, editor at Interlink Books, for her brilliant copy editing and I'm delighted to have had the opportunity of working with her;

With gratitude to all the indefatigable bibliophiles at Interlink Publishing, devoted to changing the way people think about the world, for believing in my stories;

With gratitude to Moris Farhi for his unfailing friendship, dedication to and love of justness for all;

With gratitude to my dear guru, John Milhail Asfour, poet, scholar and a dear friend, who has "a hundred worlds to create and has lost only one of them";

With gratitude to Ana Afeyan, a friend, humanitarian, and chronic reader, for giving her precious time to peruse the draft manuscript and for her frank, helpful comments;

And I am immensely grateful to an extraordinary team of enthusiasts: Sandra, Pierre, Levon, Harry, Seti, and Mike, for their sincere incentives, promotion, and expedient suggestions.

# Prologue

There is a legend on the banks of the Bosporus that over the centuries the miraculous air has restored the sickly and revived the dead. The myth still persists, and rumors of epic proportion circulate.

The people adore these tales. They fuse them with equally fanciful legends and myths, especially with one of the many stories about Zeus:

The ruler of Mount Olympus falls in love with Lo and transforms her into a white heifer to avoid detection by his beautiful wife Hera. But Hera discovers the ruse, and Lo is forced to flee the afflictions contrived by the jealous goddess, eventually crossing the straits dividing Europe from Asia. The waters have been known ever since as the Bosporus, or the Crossing-Place of the Cow.

There are hundreds of other tales about enchanted sultans and spellbound sultanas who have been betrothed and impregnated under the gusting spell of the straits. Myths and phantasms lie thick as sea fog over the Bosporus and pass from one generation to the next like precious family heirlooms.

Over the centuries, the legend has enticed the rich into building extravagant yalıs, waterside residences, along the European and Asiatic shores. These venerable estates are spread out under lofty cypresses and linden trees and shielded by the towering Anatolian and Rumelian ramparts. When they were first built they were the solitary monarchs of the majestic seacoasts; they stood out against the green backdrop of wooded hillsides and, in spring, they were aligned with the fiery bloom of the Judas trees. They are now surrounded by small cottages, fishing piers, and rambling commercial streets with taverns and restaurants. And yet, when people stroll down the garden alleys of these imposing estates, they have no sense of the graceless mass of summer bungalows crowding the hills behind but only of the all-curing breeze, the sun, and the boundless waterway.

*Part* **one**

# 1

On the evening of 6 September 1955 a savage roar rose over Istanbul. It boomed, relentless and frenzied, devouring all other sounds, expunging all that was peaceful, sweeping away the harmony that had reigned since the declaration of the Turkish Republic in 1923.

The roar had nothing human about it. An infinite mob of ruffians, distorted faces, each with dozens of fingers and tentacles and nails, plundered the stores and shops. They burnt churches, synagogues, and consulates, and gorged themselves like vultures on non-Muslim flesh. The police watched on helplessly. The frantic horde multiplied, doubled, tripled. La Grand'rue de Péra shook. The store signs came down. The fanatics besieged the city, and the past, like a chronic ailment, rose from its decaying slumber... the massacres of 1896... the 1915 Armenian genocide... the burning of Smyrna in 1922... the Kurdish rebellion a decade later...

◆

The afternoon was overcast. Dusk fell early. The violet twilight slashed the sky. The plush suburb of Yeniköy along the European shore of the Bosporus changed color: from sky-blue to lavender and then to dark purple. Nour Kardam, a thirty-two-year-old lawyer and the youngest heir to the Kardam Empire, was still working in his study at his family's *yalı*. An invigorating breeze scattered the papers on the desk. He couldn't finish the report he was preparing for the next board meeting. His mind was elsewhere—with the bestial horde of the day before—looting, burning, bulldozing...

Nour had watched everything from his seventh-floor office window in the old city. He could still hear the outcry, the clamor of broken glass crushed under the feet of the marauding mob. He was struck by a sudden spell of disillusionment. He thought ruefully of his homecoming after long years of study in the United States: first Harvard Law School, then his years in a Philadelphia law firm. How happy he was to return home, to live and work in a country that would soon occupy a warranted place among the Western democracies. While in the States, he had written to his father that he wished to be part of the new Turkey. But Turkey had reminded people that conflict, prejudice, and bigotry were permanently ingrained, like malignant tumors that nobody dared to remove.

Since the retirement of his father, Rıza Bey, Nour had been put in charge of Kardam & Sons Tobacco International. This had caused a great deal of jealousy among his brothers and sisters, who thought their father had always favored Nour over the rest of his children

The telephone rang. It was Metin Bey, the company's marketing director. Nour's face darkened. He wanted to hang up on the man, but he just said, "Yes? What is it?"

"Who are you to teach me how to handle my clients?" Metin Bey rasped.

"I'm your boss. And I'm warning you for the last time," Nour said bitterly. "My secretary brings me dozens of complaints from our clients every day."

"Do you mean you're dissatisfied with me?"

Nour was aware that behind the deceptive voice there was a mind like a steel trap. The man was stubborn. He would never admit that he had used his authority to cover numerous shady dealings. Only recently he had diverted huge orders of high-grade tobacco to an unknown client in New York instead of shipping them to their long-standing American customers.

Only a few weeks before that, Nour had had another serious wrangle with Metin and had fired him. When Nour informed his father about the incident, his father simply said, "I rehired him."

After listening to Metin Bey's long-winded arguments, Nour said, "You know as well as I do you've screwed up the company's reputation."

"I think you're forgetting that your father made a lot of money because of me, *Küchük Bey.*"

"Damn it, Metin. I forbid you to call me that again!" A vein in his forehead began to throb. "Listen, you bastard! As of today you are history."

Nour might have been young and inexperienced, but he would not give in to any old hand, let alone one who was out to get him right before his father's eyes. This latest incident would create serious tension between father and son, but Nour didn't care.

Nour put Metin out of his mind. He had trouble thinking about anything but the violent events of the night before. How desperately he wanted to believe that what he had seen was fabricated by the hungry mob, and that the government had had nothing to do with it. He wanted to believe that those who pillaged were a bunch of ruffians, probably stewed to the ears. The order, though, had come from the top: to provoke the crowd and foment violence.

And now there was his father, finding paltry excuses to justify Metin Bey's actions. What was behind his father's leniency toward a man who was—to say the least—so undeserving?

He poured himself a glass of whisky and gazed through the tall bay windows at the waterway: the lights of the glass factory on the Asiatic side glittered intermittently, as if synchronized with the beacon that floated between the two shores. A breath of sea air cleared his mind. He loved the sea like an old sailor. Over the years, better roads had shrunk the distance between Yeniköy and the metropolis. Many who had once resided in this seaside resort only during the summer months now lived here all year round. The *yalı* was his favorite retreat; he much preferred this palatial retreat to his flat in the city. He had nostalgic ties to the place, having always spent his summers here. Every room, every piece of furniture, even the tooting of the steam-ferries shuttling between the European and Asiatic shores brought back tender memories.

In town Nour moved with a fast crowd, all of them young and rich. He loved going to parties, the movies, concerts, and night clubs, especially when accompanied by attractive women—all of whom, he knew, considered him a potential husband.

He decided to finish his report, so he would be free to enjoy his guests' company over the weekend. Several friends were coming to visit him, among them Esin Ozan, a young pediatrician. Nour had met her not long ago at his cousin Rani's dinner party. Rani had placed Esin next to him at the dinner table. Her reputation as a matchmaker was legendary among the socialites of Istanbul: they called her Turkey's Wingless Cupid. Nour hated his cousin's meddling in his love life, and he often declined her invitations.

This time, though, Rani was gratified by the attention her young cousin paid to the budding physician. After everyone had left, she said to her husband, "Old customs never die, my dear Ismet. You just have to keep trying."

Nour had arranged to meet Esin again at the fashionable Marquise Tea Room on Grand'rue de Péra, then for a third time at Yekta's, not far from Rani's Nişantaşi penthouse.

Her image returned to him unbidden: oval face, black eyes with large pupils, generous mouth, small nose. The last time he saw her she was wearing a light blue woolen dress with a strand of pearls whose milky lustre set off her dark brown hair and tanned complexion. But her sense of humour and unpretentious conversation had impressed him almost as much as her beauty.

He went back to his report, but anger heaved again inside him, directed more toward his father than toward Metin. Rıza and Metin Bey had worked together during the First World War. They had been involved in many official missions, the details of which his father never properly disclosed. Nour had always wondered...

Unable to concentrate on the report, he pushed aside his notes. Kerim would soon come to announce dinner was ready. He'd get back to work later.

Nour was four years old when Kerim and his wife, Aysha, came to work for the Kardams at the *yalı*. They were both from Ordu, a little Turkish province on the Black Sea. They lived on the property year-round and took care of the estate. Aysha, a talented cook, was in charge of the kitchen. Coming from a coastal town, Kerim knew a great deal about the sea. He taught Nour the secrets of fishing, tidal waves, the winds, and mooring. Despite his advanced age, he treated the young boy with the utmost respect, never forgetting the gulf between himself and the future *bey* of the Kardam clan.

Kerim knocked at the door at exactly eight o'clock. He was wearing his usual black frock coat. He bowed to Nour, as he did to all the adult members of the family.

"Dinner is ready, Beyefendi."

"I'll be there shortly, Kerim Agha. And please, how many times do I have to remind you that you shouldn't bow to me every time you want to say something."

"Yes, *Beyefendi*, I shall bear it in mind." And the old servant bowed yet again and left.

Rıza Bey was a stickler for protocol. Kerim, despite his old age, would never violate it. Even Rıza's children used formal titles of address when speaking to their parents. The maidservants still performed the graceful *temenna*, a sign of deep respect in which the right hand touched the heart, the lips, and the brow in turn. These little marks of esteem and propriety were reminders of the family's glorious past. For Nour that past was no more than an interesting chapter of Ottoman history. He criticized his father for attaching so much importance to obsolete conventions even decades after the empire had ceased to exist.

He was getting up from his desk when the phone rang. He hoped it was not Metin again.

"Hello? Nour?"

"Who is it? I can't hear you." The line faded out and then came back more clearly. "Altan, is that you?"

"Yes. I've been trying to reach you all afternoon." He sounded troubled. "I tried to call the office, then your flat. I couldn't get through."

"What's the matter, Altan?" No answer. "Altan, are you there?"

"It's father, Nour. He had a heart attack. We rushed him to the hospital but it was too late."

"No, it can't be true. I was talking to him only two days ago." Nour was thunder-struck. A father who was the embodiment of health... Tears welled up in his eyes. "I told him I was coming next week."

"I know. He was looking forward to your visit, like a child."

"What happened?"

"He was with your mother, in her room." Altan's voice choked. "Suddenly Aunt Leila ran downstairs, shaking and crying, yelling that her husband was dead."

Now Nour regretted his clash with Metin Bey. Guilt only made his anguish worse. "Altan, let me talk to my mother, please."

"She's in her room. She refuses to talk to anybody."

"Altan, please, go tell her I want to speak to her."

Nour had never imagined losing his father so unexpectedly. He loved the old man dearly, despite their frequent clashes. He remembered the untimely death eight years ago of Aunt Makboulé, his father's second wife, the long weeks of mourning.

"Hello, *jijim*." His mother's small voice trickled down the wire. Nour was jolted back to painful reality. He fumbled for his handkerchief to wipe his tears.

"Hello, Mother. Altan told me everything. This is awful. Are you all right?"

"Nour, my soul, the apple of my eye," she said. "Don't worry. Remember what Father used to say? We must accept Allah's will." Despite her words, he could hear the tears in her voice.

"I'll be there with you tomorrow," he said. "I love you, Mother."

"I love you too, my son. Don't worry. I'll be all right."

Nour wanted to say more but he had run out of words. He returned to his chair and sank back into thought. He always found his father enigmatic. It was only recently that he had begun somewhat to decipher the old man, who had become a legend because of his riches and his former political activities. And now he was gone.

Kerim came back to remind him that supper was still waiting. "Kerim, my father's dead," Nour told him. "I'm leaving early in the morning. Thank you, Kerim. I won't have dinner."

The old servant stood speechless. Finally he uttered a few incoherent words of condolence and hobbled to the door. For once, he forgot to bow.

# 2

The Kardam mansion along the Bosporus had been built in the mid-1840s for the Grand Vizier Kibrisli Mehmet Pasha. Years later, at the outbreak of the Great War, the pasha's heirs had sold the *yalı* to Rıza Bey, who was then the governor of the Province of Aïntab.

When the governor took up residence, he modified and refurbished the interior to suit his own taste, a mixture of East and West. The property had twenty-eight rooms: elegant bedrooms and boudoirs, dazzling drawing and dining rooms, reception halls, and an immense library. Over the years, the *yalı* was meticulously maintained, allowing the Kardam family to spend idyllic summers miles from the stifling heat of Aïntab.

The opulence of the past had gradually disappeared and with it the empire, the sultanate, and the caliphate. The Great War devastated the world. The Turks lost their empire. Thanks to their liberator, Mustafa Kemal, they were now a free and independent nation. The old guard— the Young Turks and their cronies — had either resigned in disgust or gone into self-imposed exile. Others, like Governor Rıza, had survived with their fortunes and positions intact, despite rumors of their notorious roles during the war.

Rıza Bey was a seasoned politician with a keen intelligence and a sharp tongue. During the Great War, he embodied every available form of authority: he was the principal statesman of the district, commander-in-chief of the regional forces, and supervisor of the refugee convoys of Armenians heading to the Syrian Desert. Besides his political responsibilities, he occupied the role of feudal lord, overseeing hundreds of thousands of acres of pistachio, date, cotton, and tobacco plantations.

Rıza Bey knew how to manoeuvre, even under the most precarious of circumstances. His good fortune, political cunning, eloquence, and education helped him to emerge from his questionable past unscathed. The Grand Assembly's agreement to abolish the caliphate and vote for the immediate expulsion of the sultan triggered Rıza Bey's unexpected resignation and swift departure to Geneva. No one questioned his sudden disappearance. The Turks were busy building a new country and trying to salvage their ruined reputation as a nation.

Rıza Bey was also a shrewd businessman. He created a new, interesting circle around him in Geneva. His impeccable French, refined manners, and fierce hunger for accumulating wealth helped him become friends with many tycoons and members of the White Russian community, also exiles from the past. Although separated from his wives and children, he fully enjoyed his self-imposed exile, which ended as soon as the political turmoil in Turkey subsided. By then the old rebels of the new Turkey were declared national heroes. There were no unpleasant surprises awaiting Rıza Bey, who had already tripled his fortune in European money markets.

On a cool spring day in 1926, Rıza Bey, the ex-governor of Aïntab, alighted from the Orient Express at the European railway terminus of Sirkeci in Istanbul. He rushed through the crowds of passengers straight to the quay and hired a caïque to row him across the water to the Haydar Pasha station for his Asiatic connection to Aïntab, which was by then renamed Antep, or Gaziantep.

Nothing had changed for Rıza Bey. With him were his respectable wives, obedient children, and servants, and before him were unlimited opportunities in a newly independent country.

But despite his enviable wealth and lavish lifestyle, there seemed to be always something missing. His first wife, Safiyé, had her suspicions, but her frequent references to his former love affair with Maro, a beautiful Armenian refugee, elicited no response.

# 3

The twin-engine Turkish Airlines DC-3 descended through a turbulent sky to land at Gaziantep Airport. Nour Kardam, in his gabardine suit and Panama hat, was the first off the plane.

He spotted his brother Altan standing just behind the barrier. They embraced, patting each other on the back as though each was somehow seeking to alleviate the other's pain.

"Good to see you, Altan."

"How was the flight?"

"Bumpy, but at least on time. It's hard to believe. I was coming to see Father next week. Now I'm here for his funeral."

Seeing how distressed his brother was, Altan quickly changed the subject. "You should've seen my son's big smile when he heard you were coming."

"Poor Ilhan! I know how much he loved his grandfather. Tell me, Altan, did he ever have any heart complaints before?"

"Not that I know of. He came to see me just two days ago, to inspect the fields, and we had lunch together. He seemed perfectly normal. And he was so happy you were coming."

Behind Altan's trembling tenderness Nour suspected a twinge of bitterness, knowing he was Rıza Bey's favorite—the intelligent, educated son. But no, this was probably only in Nour's mind. Unlike his older brothers, Altan had never been jealous of Nour. Heartsick, perhaps, because his father's biased attitude created an opportunity for the others to resent Nour.

"Let's go. Your mother's waiting impatiently for you. The doctor gave her a sedative. I went up to see her this morning. She looked rested."

"You're a good man, Altan."

Altan, in his late thirties, was about six feet tall and heavy-set, with a strong physique. He was an introvert, shy and solitary. He had already

13

taken care of all the funeral arrangements, as he was the only one of Rıza Bey's children on the premises that day.

Nour's luggage tumbled onto the outdoor carousel. A porter stacked the suitcases on a trolley and pushed it to the parking lot.

Altan had driven there in his vintage 1936 Hudson Terraplane—his pride and joy. As happened frequently, the old automobile wouldn't start. Nour had to leap out and turn the hand crank until the car rocked and got going.

Rıza Bey's mansion was about thirteen miles outside the city limits. On the way, Nour explained about his upsetting experience with Metin. "I had no choice but to fire the son of a bitch."

"I'd have kicked him out a long time ago."

"Yes, but Father always protected him. I fired him before, but he rehired him the next day."

"I've only met him two or three times, but it's not hard to see how obnoxious he is."

"I never understood why Father gave the guy so much leeway."

"I didn't either."

Nour pulled a pack of Lucky Strikes from his pocket, shook one out, and offered it to his brother before taking one himself. "Just between you and me, Altan, there are times I suspect the worst."

"Meaning?"

"Participation in war crimes."

Skepticism greeted Nour's remark. "Quite an accusation, Nour!"

"I'm judging from the stories still circulating years after his return from Switzerland."

"They're only rumors."

"I hope so."

"You know that many of his colleagues have been either removed from their posts or assassinated."

"Our father had a tremendous talent for keeping several irons in the fire. Judging from what I've heard in bits and pieces from him and others, he was apparently very accommodating toward the Allies. He probably hoped to obtain a plum post if the Great Powers remained in the country."

Nour's words filled Altan with trepidation. He had always had similar questions about their father. He said, "Metin is a bloody dangerous man. Our brothers will no doubt blame you."

Nour shrugged and blew a stream of smoke out the window. "What difference does that make, Altan? It's not the first time I'll be blamed."

They rode in silence for a while, and then Altan broke into Nour's thoughts. "The family's going to clash over the will."

Nour felt a pang of depression at the prospect of new quarrels between his brothers and sisters. "Let's not worry about it until we have to."

"We carried the body to the mosque," Altan said. "Father had told my mother that when he died he didn't want anybody to see him before the funeral prayers. That's what happened when Aunt Makboulé died, remember?"

"Yes, but I didn't exactly understand why."

"I asked my mother. She said Father considered it bad luck for the ones left behind. You know how superstitious he was."

"If you ask me, he simply wanted to make it easier on everybody. Don't forget, Altan, in spite of his rash moments, Father loved his family."

"Unfortunately, it won't be possible to bury him within twenty-four hours. A huge crowd is expected at the funeral."

"We do our best. Allah will consider the circumstances."

Altan snorted. "Since when have you become so knowledgeable about religious matters?"

They were crossing the ugliest part of the city, the business section. This was where the Middle East made room for shoddy, European-style buildings. Cold, massive blocks of stone, pitted and blackened by pollution, rose from the paved streets.

The ugliness of the city center stood in sharp contrast to the elegance of the paternal mansion. It stood in a large expanse of parkland and was surrounded by olive groves and large fields of cotton and pistachios. The stone mansion, still known as the governor's *konak*, carried an aura of Arabian architecture, situated in a valley littered with ancient Assyrian, Persian, and Seljuki ruins.

Homecoming had always been a joyful event for Nour. His mother, Leila, would wrap her arms around him in a grand performance of extravagant affection. Then, convinced he had lost weight, she would overfeed him. Nour's father had always been more reserved. He welcomed his children with few words but with happiness in his eyes.

But homecoming was terribly sad when a beloved family member had died. It was like going to group therapy, where each patient was expected to alleviate the pain of the others. First it had been his grandmother, the Validé Hanim, when the entire city of Antep shared the family's grief. Then it was their old nurse, Eminé, the sweetest soul in the whole world, who had brought up Rıza and many of his children and loved them all as if they were her own. Next was Makboulé, his father's second wife. Then there was the tragic incident that people referred to as the harem homicide: Vedat, the *hodja*'s twenty-year-old son, who had been carrying on with one of the chambermaids in the old harem, was found dead one morning in a cotton field.

And today, it was his father, the head of the Kardam dynasty and the benefactor of hundreds of workers and their families. The entire city would mourn the death of its beloved son.

Altan parked the car in the inner courtyard. The front door to the house was wide open. The sound of loud conversation, male and female voices, young and old, awoke in Nour a whole swarm of sensations and memories. He was reluctant to go in.

"The entire clan must be here," he said.

Altan looked at him sympathetically. "Don't worry. Everything will be fine."

As soon as the two brothers stepped into the hall, they were deluged by a tide of brothers, sisters, mothers, and relatives, moaning and crying, clamoring for a hug. Some put on elaborate displays of grief. They reminded Nour of hired mourners at important Ottoman funerals with their ritual drums and tambourines, emitting long tremulous shrieks to stir up the sorrow of the other mourners.

Altan's mother, Safiyé, the first wife and matriarch of the house, was sitting on a divan in the drawing room, surrounded by her grandchildren. She possessed a perfect simplicity that everybody liked. Her dry sobs stopped as soon as Nour approached her to kiss her hand.

"Oh, my sweet Nour, the core of my soul, we lost our *bey*. This is the darkest day of my life."

"It's a dark day for all of us, Aunt Safiyé."

"And how are you, my sweet Nour?"

"I'm crushed, Aunt Safiyé."

"It was very sudden, my boy. One minute here, the next minute gone. Allah gives, and Allah takes. That's the way of the world."

Nour looked for Leila; she was nowhere to be seen. "Where's my mother?"

His niece Oljay jumped in. "Aunt Leila's upstairs, sleeping. She wasn't expecting you so early."

"Thank you, angel," he said, and smiled at her. "Look at you! I can't believe my eyes—you've become a real woman."

Oljay blushed to the roots of her hair and lowered her eyes.

Turning to the others, he said, "Excuse me, I'm going to see my mother."

Nour had already had enough. If it hadn't been impolite, he would have covered his ears to shut out the constant barrage of condolences.

Aunt Nili, Rıza Bey's sister helped him escape. "Leila's dying to see you, my sweet. Let him go," she said to the crowd. "Let him get through."

Nour had always been fascinated by this aging woman. Her progressive views made her a shameless revolutionary in the eyes of the family. He gave her a look of gratitude, hugged her warmly, and rushed up to the women's quarters.

His mother was alone in the antechamber to her bedroom. It was a sweltering afternoon, and she didn't hear his knock over the constant hum of the fans. He tried again.

"It's me, *annejiim.*"

Leila was at the door instantly. "Oh, Allah be praised! *Jijim.*"

She leapt at her son with a feline agility and covered him with kisses. Nour embraced her tightly instead of giving her the usual kiss on the hand. When he stepped back, he saw that her eyes were red and swollen. Leila self-consciously removed the black silk scarf she had thrown over her head, revealing a wave of black hair streaked with gray. She tried to smile but the strain of her husband's death was too much. She broke into tears.

Nour put his arms around her again, pressing her head against his chest. He dried his eyes against her curly hair. "I wish I'd seen him one more time before he died."

"It was too quick, my son. You can't move the clock back. May Allah welcome him to paradise." Then she examined her son. "Good God, as you grow older, you look more and more like your father, only more handsome."

"Father looked so healthy, so full of life the last time I saw him." He led her gently to the sofa so she could sit down.

Leila covered her face with her hands and shook her head violently. "I don't want to talk about it. I don't even want to remember it," she cried, as if suffering a sudden attack of unbearable pain. "I *killed* your father, my son."

"What do you mean, Mother? You know that's not true." The idea was ridiculous. Leila had worshipped him all her life. "You could never have killed my father."

"All the same, I'm responsible for his death. He died peacefully in my arms. Believe me, my son, your father was twenty years older than me, but he made love like a young man in his prime—virile, energetic, savoring every sensation. We cared for each other, we wanted each other." Her confession filled her with humiliation. "And so he—"

She was unable to go on. Nour was relieved, but it was a strange situation all the same: a mother confiding in her son how her burning passion had stopped her husband's heart.

"You don't think I murdered him, do you?"

"No, Mother, no."

"When I saw that he was choking, I decided to dress him first before running out of the room for help. I didn't want anybody to know what we were doing." After a short pause she said, "If I hadn't wasted time dressing him, perhaps he would have survived."

"I'm sure it made no difference, Mother," he said quickly, though in fact he wondered.

"Really?"

"Yes. Of course. Mother—have you told anybody else about this?"

"Of course not. I told them he died in his sleep."

"You did well. It should stay a secret between you and your husband. What you did was out of love. Don't blame yourself. Don't heap self-reproach on top of your grief." He took her hand. "Think of it this way. He died happy."

Leila blew her nose and managed a smile. "You've always been such a big comfort to me, my son."

"When things are settled," he said, "you must come and stay with me in the city."

"I wish I could, my soul, but you know that I've got to stay here for a while."

"If you come, I promise to introduce you to your future daughter-in-law."

Leila was thrilled. "No! I don't believe it."

"I don't either," he said with a grin.

"Tell me about her," Leila's face was glowing.

Nour hemmed and hawed and eventually admitted he had only seen her three times.

"But where there's smoke there's fire, *jijim*," Leila said impishly.

"I do like her," he said. "She's nice. Intelligent. Very pretty." Then he changed the subject, "Come and stay with me in Yeniköy. Remember how you used to say the Bosporus could cure all ailments, even forlorn and broken hearts?"

"Yes, even broken hearts," Leila repeated sadly. "I can't leave right away, but when I can, I'll come and visit you."

He knew she was dreading the week of mourning, when she would receive the condolences of countless relatives, friends, politicians, employees, and town officials who had worked for Rıza Bey. Among them there would also be the gossips who'd pay their visits to scrutinize the widows and make cynical remarks.

For now, though, she was calm, dignified, and a little reserved, the opposite of her normal self, which was outspoken and impulsive. Nour was pleased he could appease her pain and guilt a little, even at the cost of increasing his own; the images of his mother and father *in flagrante delicto* were more than his mind could comfortably handle.

"Mother, let's go down. I still haven't had a chance to talk to anyone."

"I'll be ready in a minute," she said and disappeared into her bedroom.

Out on the balcony Nour breathed in the scent of camellias and lemon trees. His glance swept over the old *caravanserai* out in the fields—those old walls, darker than the night, with their shattered broken lines. For a moment he felt the panic he had experienced there as a child, when his older brothers, Ramazan and Touran, had taken him to the *caravanserai* on horseback and left him there alone for hours. Rıza Bey had punished the two boys and forbidden them to ride for two months. Nour never forgot the feeling of abandonment, the sudden terror when he realized they were gone.

As usual, his mother's minute stretched out to a good half hour. She would try on three or four dresses, examining herself in the pier glass for a long time before convincing herself that she was presentable enough.

Nour went back into her room, also full of memories. The velvet armchairs, the silk tapestries on the wall, the magazines and books lying about on the floor. There was a pile of official papers on the top of a chest of drawers, and next to it lay a Moroccan-bound photo album. He had seen the album before. His grandmother had kept it with the rest of the albums, neatly arranged on rosewood shelves in her sitting room. He would have liked to page through it, but just then Leila walked in. She was dressed in black and wearing a silk veil over her face.

"What's that, Mother?"

"To still the wagging tongues, my son. Westernization hasn't reached the provinces. I have to obey the old rules."

"What a waste, hiding yourself behind that horrible screen! Let people jabber as much as they want, let them go to—"

"Are you coming or not, Nour? We mustn't keep our relatives waiting."

# 4

The funeral would take place before the noon prayers. It was another scorching day, sizzling brains in skulls.

Phaetons, cars, horses, and camels cluttered the tree-lined road that led to the family mosque, next to the governor's mansion. From the carriages and cars stepped government officials, the top brass of the region, business colleagues, and acquaintances. Some of the Kardam employees had left their plantations early in the morning to make sure they would arrive before noon. Although these peasants described the distance between the plantations and the mosque as a stone's throw, it was a good two-hour walk under the broiling southern Anatolian sun.

Rıza Bey's first wife, Safiyé, decided to have the entire service outside in the quadrangle. Because of the suffocating heat it was impossible to follow the usual tradition and go inside the mosque for the *namaz*. The change didn't surprise anybody. It was the funeral of a man of power. The crowd jammed the quadrangle and spilled out into the street.

As a sudden silence fell, they could hear the cool and familiar splashing of the ablution fountains around the marble reservoir in the middle of the courtyard. All heads turned toward the open pine casket, borne by Rıza Bey's sons. The wives and daughters followed in order of age and seniority. Behind them walked their relatives and close family friends. After placing the coffin on the *musalla,* the sons stood together off to one side. The middle-aged imam, with a solid black beard, wearing a darkly glistening brocaded silk kaftan and with his head swathed in a full, wide Turkish turban, read the first prayer in Arabic. He read it melodiously, with the traditional resonances of the teaching of the Koran. The crowd, eyes fastened on the ground, hummed in unison and began the *namaz* on the prayer rugs spread out for them.

In spite of her seniority both in rank and age, Safiyé, the first wife, stayed with Leila instead of standing with her daughters. Safiyé, who was getting on toward her mid-seventies, was dressed in black, with only her eyes visible above her veil. She had always been kind to Leila, who was much younger and more beautiful. She gazed at her husband, peacefully sleeping in the open coffin. Then she looked at Leila, who expressed her appreciation that Safiyé had stayed with her: "Thank you, Safiyé," she whispered emotionally, without turning her head. Despite occasional fits of jealousy when her husband crept into his first wife's bed instead of her own, she loved Safiyé.

Leila followed the prayers, completely oblivious to her surroundings. She was uncertain about what the future had in store for her, and an immense loneliness enveloped her.

Touran and Ramazan, the elder sons, were resplendent in their military uniforms. Nour looked haggard and ill at ease. He made a conscious effort to avoid any wrong move that would betray his limited knowledge of religious rituals. Many eyes were on him, the eminent but estranged member of the family.

The weather was so hot that the imam shortened the prayers. Every two or three minutes a mist gathered on his glasses, and he had to take them off and wipe them with his handkerchief. He asked the funeral gathering solemnly, in a deep baritone voice:

"Was the deceased an honest person?"

"Yes, he was," the congregation responded.

"Was the deceased a godly person?"

"Yes, he was."

"Was the deceased a charitable person?"

"Yes, he was," they all replied.

The imam, satisfied with their answers, didn't bother to ascertain whether the deceased had been a good man, or a hard-working, loving, and abstemious man, and went on with the prayers. Safiyé and Leila felt a sudden pride listening to the unanimous replies of the public.

As the assembly of friends and relatives knelt one last time, murmuring in unison after the imam, they heard thunderous sounds from afar. Dark clouds filled the sky and it started to rain heavily, accompanied by thunder and lightning.

"This is a bad omen, Leila," Safiyé said, tears streaming down her cheeks.

"There's a curse on the family," Leila confirmed, removing her veil with trembling hands.

Nour bit his lip in fury and, without uttering a word, ran back to help his brothers carry his father's body to the family mausoleum behind the mosque. Nour stared down at the lifeless corpse; it had already begun to decompose in the stifling heat, and the decaying body gave off a foul stench. Fortunately the thundering shower had driven away the black flies hovering above it... his disintegrating face... the soiled, wet shroud... the crying and wailing of women behind their veils... the burial... the inability of the imam to remember his lines...

At the end, as the body was lowered into the grave, Kenan tossed in a rose. The imam, standing close to the edge of the grave, leaned forward to see where the flower fell. He lost his balance, and if it hadn't been for Touran he would have landed head first on Rıza Bey's shrouded body.

Nour closed his eyes and repeated the final words of the imam: "Out of primordial chaos came order. Without order there can be no world."

The unexpected thunderstorm and the imam's blunders upset the entire family. And predictably, many later blamed Nour for having fired the marketing director.

Nour was infuriated by the biased stance of his brothers. "The man was a crook!"

"Metin Bey did the company a lot of good," Ramazan said.

"And brought in hundreds of excellent sales," Kenan agreed.

"He also acted irresponsibly, which is why I fired him," Nour shot back, exasperated.

"You really let your power go to your head," Ramazan barked. "Who the hell do you think you are to decide such things all by yourself?"

"Am I the director of the company or are you?"

"He was a close friend of your father," Safiyé interjected in her soft voice, attempting to take the heat out of their dispute. "And he was his close associate during the war."

Safiye's remark was loaded. Was it because of this close association that Rıza couldn't kick him out like any other employee accused of felony? If yes, then it must have been a very special association. Why had his father never mentioned this relationship? What was so special about this hideous man that he enjoyed the generous protection of the Kardams?

# 5

*T*he sky was clear and washed-out after the storm of the day before. Two hours before Counsel Nourettin Borahan's arrival, Rıza Bey's children were gathered in the library for a family meeting. The veteran lawyer, who had looked after Rıza Bey's legal affairs for thirty years, was coming to read his client's last will and testament.

The library was on the main floor. Despite the ornate trellises on the windows, it commanded splendid views of the gardens and the long pebble mosaic path leading to the main gate of the estate. A gigantic Isfahan rug covered most of the floor. The furnishings reflected Rıza Bey's eclectic taste. A massive carved oak desk, with equally massive velvet armchairs, occupied the study section. The two rows of locked drawers on each side of the desk had always been a source of mystery to the children. According to rumors, Rıza Bey kept his guns there. Others said they contained stolen maps to hidden treasures.

The Kardam children were oddly assorted. Kenan, Makboulé's son, was an insignificant person with a permanent vacant stare, unmarried, easily influenced and with a voracious appetite for jewelry and precious stones. Makboulé hadn't succeeded in finding a suitable bride for Kenan, despite her frantic search. To his mother's frustration, the man never showed a spark of interest in any eligible girl. Some even suspected that he might be homosexual but dared not mention it openly. Today, Kenan was examining the books neatly arranged on the shelves, not so much for their contents as for their rare, gilded Moroccan bindings.

Colonel Ramazan, the eldest of Rıza Bey's children, was seated at his father's desk. He was a handsome man, and, although he was of average height, everything about him seemed oversized: his hands, his chest, his voice, his eyes, which inevitably drew people's attention. He always wore well-cut suits when dressing in civilian clothes. Today, because of the weather, his jacket hung on the back of his chair, and his shirt cuffs were carefully rolled back. He sat sullenly, the effects of last night's quarrel still in evidence, gazing at the silver-framed photos arranged on top of the desk: snapshots of the children when they were young. It was difficult, as usual, to guess what was on his mind.

Although Altan and Erol were only half-brothers, and there was a difference of nine years between them, they bore an uncanny physical resemblance, both heavily built, with dark brown eyes. Their characters, though, weren't alike. Altan got his way by smiling rather than frowning. He was compassionate and generous. Erol was the opposite. They came in together, and, after their *merhaba*s, they sat on the leather sofa facing the desk.

As for Colonel Touran, he was of an altogether different breed—a belligerent, narrow-minded professional soldier. Today he was in civilian clothes, chatting with one of his brothers-in-law, exuding his familiar severity. It was unusual for him to be out of uniform; he was convinced that the uniform gave him the authority he dreamed of.

The three sisters, Shahané, Emel, and Zehra, were the only women asked to the meeting. They came in with their husbands. Zehra, the youngest sister, had already given birth to two sons. She looked washed-out, fragile, coyly dismissive. Emel, the middle sister, was an innocuous soul who read love stories all day and dreamed of far-off lands to which her husband would never take her. Because she was tiny and slim of figure, she was often mistaken for the youngest of Rıza's offspring.

Shahané, the oldest of the daughters, was the same age as the oldest son of the family. Although she had been brought up in a world of women, she had refused at a very early age to accept the restrictions imposed on her sex. She was the chain-smoking, outspoken rebel of the clan.

Nour was standing with his arm resting on the mantelpiece, smoking, pondering Rıza Bey's portrait. It was majestically mounted in an antique gilded wooden frame hanging behind the desk. The governor of Aïntab, in his late forties, wearing an officer's uniform heavy with medals, peered down with a portentous smile. Nour was feeling something entirely new to him: an acute reluctance to face the family directly, to confront them with his beliefs and intentions.

According to centuries-old Ottoman tradition, in prominent families the eldest son took over as head of the family following the father's death. It was a coveted position, but could be obtained only as a birthright. Ramazan, at forty-five, was the eldest, and the purpose of this gathering was to give him the opportunity to officially accept his responsibilities.

Ramazan, growing impatient, called everyone to attention. "Thank you, Mother, Aunt Leila, brothers and sisters for being here this morning, after the funeral of our beloved father." Ramazan talked as if addressing his troops. "As you all know, it's time for one of us to assume responsibility as head of the family. And, as we all know, it's expected that I, the eldest son, will accept that obligation."

Nour knitted his brow; his brother's monotonous tone and formal speech got on his nerves.

"I'm a professional soldier," Ramazan continued. "As a colonel in the Air Force, I'm often away on missions far from home. I'm told I shall soon be promoted to Brigadier-General and posted to our embassy in Bonn as military attaché. Under the sad circumstances of the last couple of days, I didn't have the chance to tell anyone but my mother about this."

"Congratulations, *Aghabey*! We're proud of you," Erol said enthusiastically.

"Congratulations! You deserve it," Touran said a bit resentfully.

"Your turn will come, Touran," Shahané observed, but Touran didn't appreciate the remark.

"Thank you all, but let me finish what I have to say. Under the circumstances, after giving the matter a lot of thought, I've decided to relinquish to someone else the honor of heading the family."

They checked each other's expressions questioningly. No one showed any surprise.

"We're pleased to hear your good news, but disappointed to lose you as head of the Kardams, Ramazan *Aghabey*," Kenan said. "I think everyone would agree that we should offer the honor to Touran *Aghabey* who is next in line." He stopped, seeking approval from the others.

Ramazan said, "Well, it's up to you, but I find Kenan's suggestion most appropriate."

Touran remained silent. Altan glanced at Nour, who looked as if he might flare up at any moment. Their eyes met, and Altan raised his eyebrows in a signal that he should not meddle.

Shahané Abla, eldest sister and recently self-appointed leader of the Muslim women's rights group, was itching to say something, but her husband, Sefer, warned her with a discreet kick to mind her own business. This interplay between husband and wife didn't escape Nour's attention.

"You've something to say, Shahané Abla?"

After throwing a charming, helpless expression at her husband, Shahané waded in: "I'd like to know if we women may be considered for the honor, since our senior brother has declined it."

Touran, who was showing signs of nerves, cut in: "My dear little sister, you know as well as I do that my mother, Safiyé, as the oldest wife of our father, is the *Büyük Hanim* of the house. How do you expect to be considered for a title that already belongs to someone else?"

Shahané's husband looked at her as if to say, didn't I tell you to keep your big mouth shut?

Ramazan got up from the desk and walked over to turn on the big fan in the middle of the ceiling. It was evident, he was ready to burst with anger. Incapable of restraining himself any more, Nour broke the silence: "Anyone listening to us would think we were feudal lords, left over from the Middle Ages, quibbling about seniority, disregarding women, refusing to elect the person most qualified—"

Touran's face flushed scarlet. "How kind of you to chip in with your piece of shit, my little half-brother. Are you insinuating I'm not the most qualified? Or now that Father is gone would you like us to hand the reins of the family over to you, so you can make an even bigger mess of things than you already have with Metin Bey?"

"Nour saved the family a lot of trouble, Touran *Aghabey*. Why are you picking on him?" Shahané grumbled.

"Mind your own business, sister. Stick to your lesbian friends. Let the men make the decisions, as we've always done."

She stood up in a rage."You, *Aghabey*, you are a pig-headed ass. I think the seeds of your inflexibility were sown the day you entered the military academy. Your place is with your square-headed officers, not at the head of our family." Her face was so flushed, and a million more words fought their way to the tip of her tongue. But all she said was, "I don't think you deserve my presence here any more," and left the room.

Sefer ran after her furiously. Her sisters started to do the same, but their husbands grabbed their arms and pinned them to their seats.

Nour stood up. He forced himself to smile, took another cigarette from the silver case and said, before lighting it, "You're totally mistaken if you think I had myself in mind. Nothing could be further from the truth. I'm ashamed. Before our father has grown cold in his grave, we're all insulting each other." His heart was beating fast, but outwardly he appeared composed. He blew out smoke, then turned to Altan, who was sitting on the sofa, nervously tapping his fingers. "I wonder if it's still wise in this day and age to burden one person with all the responsibilities of a family of our size. If you all insist, however, I'd like to propose our brother Altan. He has always been generous, and has handled things for all of us so conscientiously."

Erol heaved a profound sigh, and the two sisters thought, Thank God, we still have one sensible head among us.

Altan was taken by surprise. He looked at Nour gratefully and was ready to say something, but the sudden piercing ring of the telephone broke the silence. Ramazan answered it.

"It's for you," he said, holding the receiver out to Nour.

"Excuse me." Nour took the phone. "Hello. Yes, speaking." He heard Commissar Piri's unmistakable hoarse voice.

"Of course, go ahead." He bit his lip nervously as he listened. "No. Impossible... impossible," he repeated, clutching the telephone tensely, his face ashen. "When did this happen?" There was a pause, and then he said, "I'll see you before I leave for Istanbul. Thanks. You can send it to me as soon as you have it."

Replacing the receiver, he felt a sudden deadly fatigue. The air in the library was heavy with silence. Everyone waited for him to say something.

"It was the commissar... Metin Bey shot himself an hour ago."

All were stupefied.

"That's just what we needed," Touran said. "You and your fucking bright ideas."

"I've had enough of your insults, Touran. Shut up and listen to me."

Ramazan cut in, "Mind your own goddamned business, Nour. Besides..." His voice became harsher, "Besides..." He halted again.

Nour brought his fist crashing down on the desk. "Besides, besides, besides what?" He had always been pushed aside by these two. Each time he broached important family matters, they bluntly antagonized him. They bore a relentless grudge toward their younger brother, who had enjoyed a special place in their father's heart from the day he was born. "Spit it out, Brigadier-General, before you choke on it."

No one spoke. Trying to contain himself, Nour went on. "Maybe you had reasons to be afraid of that son of a bitch. Maybe he knew too much about things I don't know. But tell me it's not a bright idea to nab a crook before he destroys our business. By the way, he left behind an envelope for me."

"Damn it, Nour, you're getting too big for your britches. The envelope belongs to the family." It was Ramazan again.

"It's apparently addressed to me. My name is on it. Are you afraid of what's in it? Is there something maybe I shouldn't know?"

"You're being unfair to Nour," Altan interrupted. "He tried to save our enterprise from an unsavory employee. Our company, our family business... That bastard is now dead, and I'm glad. Leave my brother alone. Otherwise I'm leaving, just like Shahané."

Ramazan got up, like a general conceding defeat. "I think Altan *is* the best choice," he said.

Touran was stunned. "You can't decide without our consent, Ramazan!"

"But I can. I'm still the oldest."

Touran glanced at his watch. "I've got a few things to do before Nourettin Bey arrives." As he left, he avoided having to look at Nour.

Nour wasn't one to harbor a grudge. He was prepared to overlook his two oldest brothers' offensive words. His rebellious conduct at today's family meeting, though, had done more to establish his reputation among his brothers and sisters than all his previous efforts to endear himself.

When everyone else had left, Altan said, "Thanks for your faith in me. I won't disappoint you."

"I know you won't," Nour said, and added, "To tell you the truth, Altan, I'd have loved to lock horns with the old man in court. Too bad he shot himself."

"It's better this way."

After a moment's hesitation, Nour asked, "Don't you think it's curious that my brothers always get upset when I voice my opinion about family matters?"

Nour's remark dismayed Altan. "Heavens, yes! But they're like that. Touran and Ramazan want to control everything related to the family... decisions, money, property...'

There had always been a kind of aversion, a hostility on the part of Touran and Ramazan toward Nour. No one could deny it. But, as for the reason, Altan couldn't begin to speculate.

# 6

$\mathcal{N}$ourettin Borahan, the old family lawyer, phoned to tell them he would be delayed because of a major collision between two trucks. The police had closed the narrow country highway between Antep and Karkamiş, and it would stay closed for at least another hour.

It was quarter to five in the afternoon when Nourettin Bey parked his Peugeot at the end of the tree-lined alley. He grabbed his briefcase and rushed to meet the family, sweat pouring down his face. The hellish temperature had remained unchanged since noon.

"A thousand apologies, *Büyük Hanim.* There was nothing I could do. Please forgive me."

"We understand, Nourettin Bey. You mustn't feel bad," Safiyé said in an attempt to stop him before he exhausted all the Turkish expressions of regret. "Please take a seat. Have a cold drink before we begin."

"Oh, you're very kind, *Büyük Hanim.* That'd be nice. Thank you."

She waved at one of the maids to bring Nourettin Bey a cold drink.

The family was waiting in the sitting room, known as the blue room because of the blue patterns of the Kütahya tiles covering the floor.

Anyone who didn't know Nourettin Borahan might assume he had been a wrestler, with his broad cheekbones, bushy eyebrows, square jaw, and deeply scarred face. Yet the middle-aged barrister was dressed in a conservative dark blue pinstriped suit, immaculate white shirt, burgundy silk tie, and old-fashioned black shoes, and he spoke softly, in an almost feminine pitch. He sipped his iced-fruit drink and chatted with Leila. Even without the usual sparkle in her eyes, she looked refined and comely. Nourettin Bey didn't make any attempt to hide his admiration.

Ramazan and Touran were in their military uniforms, pacing the room, sweating. Ramazan clicked his amber worry beads mechanically while keeping his eyes on Leila and the lawyer. "Shall we begin, Nourettin Bey?" he asked, as if losing patience.

"Of course, right away."

Like Leila, Safiyé and the daughters were wearing European-style dresses, with silk scarves covering their heads and part of their faces. They stood up, looking for better seats, and chose a couch that was uncomfortable but close to the lawyer.

Nourettin Borahan took a pile of thick files out of his briefcase and sorted through them until he found a large envelope, sealed with red wax. Suspense hung over the room. Nour didn't think the will would be a complicated one, but Rıza Bey had always been full of surprises.

After pointing out that it was the last Will and Testament of Rıza Kardam, Nourettin Bey began to read in a monotone:

> I, Rıza Kardam of the City of Gaziantep and the County of Karkamiş, therein residing and domiciled in my domain and on my property, being of sound mind, memory and understanding, do hereby make and declare this to be my Last Will and Testament.

Nourettin Bey sped through the first seven articles, designating by name the wives and children as the heirs, then stopped.

"Now for the important part of the will," he warned, and began to read:

> I do hereby make the following particular bequests: I bequeath to my wives Safiyé, Makboulé, and Leila in equal shares my life insurance policies and the two family mansions in Gaziantep and Yeniköy, Istanbul. As my second wife Makboulé is already deceased, her share is to be divided in equal parts among her children, on the condition that the two said properties cannot be disposed of before the year 2000.

The two women, setting aside their old sexual rivalry, looked at each other approvingly.

Nourettin Bey raised his eyes from time to time to gauge reactions. On each of these occasions they came to rest on Leila's face, each time a bit longer than before.

> I divide all my moveable and immoveable properties, including my plantations and the buildings thereon, business enterprises, shares, bank accounts

in Turkey and abroad, and precious objects equally among my two surviving wives (Safiyé and Leila) and my six sons (Ramazan, Touran, Altan, Kenan, Erol and Nour) and my three daughters (Shahané, Emel and Zehra).

Nourettin Bey again checked each face in the room. Everyone seemed overwhelmed with the fairness of the distribution. There were even a few mutterings of approval.

I leave it to my children to decide and to modify when necessary, to their own best interests, the administrative structure of Kardam Tobacco International and ask them to change its name to Kardam & Sons International Exports and Imports Ltd. I further appoint my youngest son, Nour, Chairman of the Board, as his expertise in corporate and international law is a great asset to the solid growth of the family business and company.

Grumbles were heard.

"Please be so kind as to be silent," the solicitor said coldly.

Nour's eyes met Leila's. Leila was obviously exhilarated that Rıza Bey had esteemed her son so highly, but Nour was worried that this would add insult to injury, making him a broader target for his brothers' attack.

Nourettin Bey read a few minor bequests to servants, loyal staff members, needy relatives, and charities, and then stopped once more. "Now I'm about to read the final statement made by your beloved husband and father, Rıza Bey." He read without a pause:

I truly believe that I have been right, proper and fair in the disposal of all my worldly goods and possessions. I would, however, like to make one last bequest to a very old friend. I bequeath the entire content of my account at Societé de la Banque Suisse in Geneva, Switzerland, to Maro Balian of New York City. I make this special bequest to a very special person who has, over the years, helped me to understand the secret of life and has left me her own precious legacy. I ask my son, Nour, to get in touch with Fred Goldwater & Associates, a law firm in New York City, to process the transfer of the funds to Maro Balian without undue delay. If the said Maro Balian is deceased, the funds should be left to the Faculty of Medicine of the University of Istanbul for research in cardiology.

Should any member of my family contemplate contesting my last bequest, I must caution them most strongly not to do so. I must also point out that this will is irreversible, irrevocable, and absolutely watertight. It cannot be contested in a court of law. I appoint my son, Nour Kardam, the only expert in legal matters in the family, as executor of my estate.

The room was as silent as a tomb. Taking his final inventory, Rıza Bey had dared reveal the genesis of his solitude. Even Nourettin Bey felt overwhelmed by the silence, unable to read the remaining words of the will. Finally, Leila asked what everybody wanted to know.

"*Beyefendi*, how much is in the account?"

The lawyer hesitated and then, in a barely audibly voice, said, "One million, two hundred thousand dollars." Nourettin Bey's halting and slow articulation made the large figure seem even larger. There were loud protests and exclamations.

Up until that very moment Leila had never contemplated that Maro's name would ever be mentioned under Rıza's roof. Now the sound of it struck her forcibly. She was up in a flash. "I always said she was an expensive whore." She made her way to the door. As she passed Nour, she hid her face so he wouldn't see how troubled she was.

Meanwhile, Nourettin Bey had finished reading the will.

Safiyé stood up too. "*Ilâhi*, Rıza Bey," she sighed. "He was full of surprises when he lived, and he's full of surprises even after he's gone. May Allah bless his soul!"

Touran's temper flared. "Father must have been out of his mind to leave money to that slut."

"It's unbelievable," blasted Ramazan. "I remember the bitch."

"And her bastard," Touran added, glaring directly at Nour. "I'll have her killed before I give up any of our fortune to her." He stubbed out his cigarette furiously.

Touran's words "and her bastard" echoed in Nour's head. He felt sick with anger and uncertainty. He remembered a group picture taken years before, forgotten until now. He could still see clearly the face of a woman standing next to a fragile-looking boy. He was told that they were houseguests. The woman's scarf partially hid her face, but she had such beautiful eyes...

He drifted off. In the distance, he could hear his brothers and sisters arguing fiercely, but a few moments later he heard Altan say: "It's what our father wished, Touran, so knock it off." Objections resumed, so impassioned and loud that nobody noticed Nour slip silently away.

Safiyé's trembling voice put an end to the rowdy exchange. "I want to remind you that Nourettin Bey is still with us." She turned to the old lawyer. "We're most grateful to you, *Beyefendi*. Thank you so much. We'll be in touch with you for the remaining formalities."

"It's an honor to be at your service, *Büyük Hanim*. Please, let me know if I can be of any further assistance. And please convey my respects to your charming sister-in-law, Leila Hanim." He bowed, collected his briefcase, and left.

When Nourettin Bey was gone, Safiyé suddenly felt faint. She managed a dignified exit by leaning on Kenan's arm.

Upstairs, Leila, as soon as she shut her bedroom door, broke down and abandoned herself to sobbing. She felt betrayed. For the first time in her life she was angry at her husband. His romantic fantasies had sunk the family into a quagmire. Safiyé had been right when she said, "Stormy funerals always bring bad luck."

Altan looked frantically for Nour—the only person to whom he was attached by the bonds of affection, admiration, and blood. He dashed upstairs to his aunt Leila's room and knocked at the door, but she did not answer. He asked everybody, but no one had seen him leave.

Altan was beside himself with unimaginable speculations. He ran out into the courtyard. The family Mercedes wasn't there. He rushed back into the house. "Nour's gone," he said. "The car isn't there."

"Yes, *Beyefendi*," the little *evlâtlik* said with an automatic curtsy. "He left right after the older *efendi* who was here this afternoon."

"Thank you, dear. Thank you." Altan was relieved. "Would you please make me a cup of coffee with no sugar?"

"Right away, *Beyefendi*."

Altan sat alone in the dining room. The siblings were still arguing so fiercely in the sitting room that he could hear every word they said.

# 7

Nour drove slowly along the road following the cotton fields as if inspecting the immensity of his father's property, deliberately dawdling, irresolutely emptying his mind. He could still hear Nourettin Bey's voice: "I bequeath the entire content of my account... " His head ached as if it was shrinking and there was no more room for further thoughts—only the old sepia photograph—its yellowish-brown color, and two very distinct faces, that of a beautiful woman, hidden partly by a veil, and the sad, emaciated young boy beside her. Now once again they were gazing at him in fading sepia colors, evoking his childhood.

He reached the main highway and, before turning right, he took one last look at the undulating fields without really seeing them. The car almost came to a standstill. Then suddenly he changed gear and began to travel at a steadier pace.

He was driving north. It was past seven. The car swung onto Highway 85 to Maraş, the ancient capital of the Hittite Kingdom. The open steppe spread out into the distance, covered with soft green whirling thistles that gave life to the arid landscape. Highway 85, in spite of its name, was no more than a paved country road. It wove through a landscape studded with ruins, caves, goats, cows, and mud-brick beehive houses.

Nour had been driving for about forty minutes and had another forty left before he reached the village of Pazarcik. He was tired. He was practiced at hiding his emotions, but the events of the past few days had been almost too tragic to bear. And, to top it all, his father's bequest to Maro Balian. He hoped his doubts were just tricks of an overactive mind. But there was more to Touran and Ramazan's remarks than simple jealousy.

Nour was on his way to see Deniz Abla, his mother's former chambermaid, the kindest by far among Leila's maids. Deniz was slim and had eyes as black as charcoal, with equally dark hair. She had gone to live in Pazarcik fifteen years before, after marrying a local blacksmith.

Deniz had been his confidante since he was a young boy. She was like an older sister, who never denied him a warm smile or a loving word. When she talked to Nour she looked directly into his eyes, and he could almost see his reflection in those big dark eyes of hers. She had been twenty-nine, old for a woman, when she married the hard-working blacksmith, who was a widower with no children, and he had missed her desperately.

Nour wished he had never looked at the family albums. It was his grandmother who had gotten him interested. She had an inexplicable passion for photographs. "They are precious moments of life rendered visible, to be cherished forever," she used to say. Now, dimly, Nour was making connections: Touran and Ramazan, their insults, the secrecy surrounding the identity of the woman in the picture...

Nour had memorized the photograph. His grandmother looked dignified, perhaps a little uncomfortable; his father was almost expressionless; the woman beside him had a magical half-covered face. Why did his mother and aunts refuse to talk about that picture? Only Deniz had spoken to him about it, explaining to him that the woman was a houseguest. She hadn't been able to remember the woman's name.

Nour drove by the open-air café in the village square. There were only a few people in the street. A yogurt vendor on his donkey, with a pair of copper urns hanging on each side of the saddle, was on his way home. Nour stopped and called out to him:

"*Hemsherim*, how do I get to Deniz Abla's house?"

The bearded man approached the car with his donkey. He touched his colorless skullcap with his right hand in greeting, examining the sedan, so out of place next to the donkey. The animal lunged forward to touch the shiny chunk of steel with its head, but its master tightened the reins.

"Who are you?"

"A friend."

"You're not a friend. You have a car."

"Believe me, I'm her friend. She took care of me when I was young."

"Oh, so that's who you are."

"Now will you tell me where she lives?"

"Yes, I will tell you. Do you see the big chestnut tree over there? Just turn there and stop the car. It's the first house. Anyway, there's no other house on that street."

"Thank you, *hemsherim.*"

Nour drove slowly to avoid stirring up the thick dust blanketing the dirt road. When he arrived at Deniz's door he cleared his throat and called out: "Deniz Abla, please open the door. It's me, Nour."

Deniz and her husband, Mourtaza, in his sleeveless undervest and striped pajama bottoms, came to the door, surprised.

"Nour! Come in, please, come in. What wind has blown you here to honor our humble home so late?" Deniz asked, feeling a little discomfited by this unexpected call.

Nour entered the house and spoke without preliminary. "There are some things I need to ask you, Deniz Abla."

"All is well, I hope."

"No, Abla. Unfortunately, we lost our father two days ago."

"I'm so sorry. The last I heard, he was well and strong." Deniz wiped her eyes and nose on the white muslin draped over her hair.

"Old age, Deniz Abla. His heart failed."

"Oh, how terrible! We didn't know, or we would have been at the funeral. "

The blacksmith interjected, "We must go down for the memorial service."

The three of them lapsed into a brooding silence. Deniz was thinking: I guess I know what he wants from me now. Nour was reflecting: I wonder if I'll be able to ferret the truth out of her. Blacksmith Mourtaza was wondering: if his wife was going to make some coffee for the guest and for himself.

"I had a strange dream last night," she said. "I knew I was going to receive bad news. I dreamt that I fell into a ditch filled with sharp black rocks and broke my teeth. Losing teeth is a bad sign. It means losing a loved one." She sighed. "Let me make some coffee for you."

"No, Abla. I have no time, I must drive back tonight."

"You're not going back tonight, *Beyefendi*. The road is dangerous. Deniz will make us coffee, and then she'll make up a bed for you," Mourtaza insisted. "You're very welcome here, if you don't mind our modest home."

"Of course I don't mind. Thank you." Then he told them about the funeral and the unexpected thunderstorm.

"Allah, Allah!... Allah, Allah!" both husband and wife exclaimed after every sentence.

"It's the evil eye, my poor *efendi*. I always told Leila Hanim to use a blue bead to avert the evil eye."

"It must be that," her husband agreed.

Then they looked at him expectantly. Nour didn't have to delay the actual reason for his unexpected visit. He was sure that husband and wife were waiting for him to come right to the point.

"Tell me, Abla, have you ever heard of a woman named Maro Balian?"

No answer.

"Who is she? Tell me, is she the woman with beautiful eyes in that picture I asked you about many years ago?"

"She was a houseguest."

"What else?"

"Just a guest, I told you." Deniz burst into tears. "Please, please don't ask me such questions. I know nothing about it."

She was sitting on a wooden stool. Nour got up from the *sedir* and moved closer to her. He held her by the shoulders and looked beseechingly into her eyes.

"There's nothing to be afraid of, Abla. It's no longer a secret. Ramazan and Touran seem to know everything. I'd be grateful if you told me the truth before I hear it from them. I want to know who she is. You mustn't be afraid of anybody. My father is dead, and my mother... I couldn't give a damn how she feels about it."

"Please, Deniz, my sweet *Hanim*, tell the *beyefendi* everything you told me," urged her husband.

Deniz seemed lost and helpless. She stared at Nour, as if beseeching him not to insist.

"Please, Deniz Abla, I tell you there's nothing to worry about."

First she looked at her husband and then at Nour, and finally, gathering her courage, she mumbled, "I'm sorry. So sorry for hiding it from you for so long." Then she began crying so loudly that Nour had a hard time following her words. "I met Maro Hanim when I came to Rıza Bey's house as a foster child. I was thirteen years old. And... '

"I know the story, *Beyefendi*. I'm going out for a walk." With that, the soft-spoken blacksmith put on his white skullcap and walked out into the night.

"I was an *evlâtlik* in Rıza Bey's home," said Deniz. "He bought me from a dealer who banked on selling young Armenian refugee girls to the court. I was so happy to find a comfortable home after seeing my parents, brothers, and sisters slaughtered by the gendarmes. I was among the few who escaped."

Nour hadn't paid much attention to the rumors circulating in the house that Deniz was an Armenian. His sadness deepened.

"My name was Vartouhi, which means rose in Armenian. At first Rıza Bey called me Ayla, but after I had been there a while he changed it to Deniz. 'I'll call you Deniz, the sea, because your eyes are deeper than the oceans,' he told me. I lived with them until my wedding day." She stopped, then continued with a subdued voice. "One fine day your father showed up with the most beautiful woman I've ever seen in my life. She was a young Armenian deportee."

In his mind Nour saw Maro standing before him in her expensive Turkish dress. Just like in the picture, as if in the flesh. He wanted to stretch out his hand and tell her he had known her all his life. She was the only living image among all those "precious moments of life." And for the first time he grasped what his grandmother had meant by that expression.

"She was educated and came from a good family. She taught me how to read. Her little boy, Tomas, was five or six years old at the time. He and Kenan were the same age, and they played together for hours every day."

Nour couldn't imagine his brother Kenan playing and sharing his toys with another child, let alone with a poor refugee boy who must have seemed completely alien to him.

"And?"

"Some years later she left."

"Please, Abla, not so fast. Where did she go?"

"She went back to Istanbul. Rıza Bey let her go, but..."

"But what, Deniz Abla? When I was a little boy you used to play with me, take me to the movies. My mother loved you. She let me stay with you whenever she was not there, and I loved it. I'm grateful for all that. I'm asking you one last favor. Please don't hide the rest from me."

Nour had sat down on a stool next to hers. Deniz put her hand on his head and sighed, "God bless you a thousand times. I was very fond of you, *beyefendi.*"

The word *beyefendi* irritated him, but it was no time to tell her that.

"Your father was forced to let her go. You know how it is in a large, illustrious family like yours. The servants talk. You can't stop their tongues." She waited for him to say something, but Nour was silent. She went on, "For about two years, Maro Hanım wasn't allowed to leave the house alone. She went out only with the other wives. Your father kept her with him against her will." She paused again, then, with difficulty, continued. "He was in love with her, *beyefendi.* I've never known a man to love a woman that much. He worshipped her. There isn't any other word for it. He wanted her to marry him but she refused."

"Why?"

"She didn't trust anyone else, but she used to confide in me. She said she had a husband in Istanbul. I forget his name. He must have been looking for her, I'm sure. Any man would travel to the four corners of the earth for a woman like her. One day she told me she could never get used to the idea that a man might have more than one wife. Besides, she was a Christian, and she didn't want to marry a Muslim."

"Deniz Abla, did she love my father?"

"Not if you asked her. But one day she said, 'Vartouhi'—she always called me by my Armenian name—'do you believe a woman can share her heart with two men?'" Deniz paused. "Then one good day, Maro and her son, Tomas, suddenly disappeared for about six months. She had gone to see her parents in Sivas, they said, but that wasn't it. She had gone away to have her baby in secret, her baby boy."

Nour's face darkened. Everything was falling into place. He imagined the scandal at the time: for the governor of the province to have an illegitimate son with a Christian refugee.

"Your father was jubilant, crazy about his baby son."

Unable to wait, Nour exploded, "And the baby boy was me!"

"Yes, Nour, my darling Nour." She put her arms around Nour Kardam, the corporate lawyer and the new Chairman of the Board of the Kardam Empire, and pulled him closer to kiss him. "Yes, it was you, my handsome *efendi*!"

Nour held her tightly. "That's what I suspected, since my brother's remark." His voice was trembling. Then he added as an afterthought, "Why didn't Maro take me with her?"

"Because she wasn't allowed to. Your father wouldn't let her, no matter how much she wept and begged. I can still hear her shrieks as she left. He had lost the woman he loved, but he wouldn't lose her child."

"And her other son?"

"Oh, Tomas! The poor boy! One afternoon he rode his horse into the nearby woods and never returned. They said he had been kidnapped, but no one knew it for sure. Months of searching didn't bring Tomas back."

Nour didn't know what to say before such cruel providence. The sudden emotion of discovering his real identity dampened his rage. His father and Leila must have tried so hard to hide the truth from him. He understood the suffering and the cruel destiny of this woman, his biological mother, to be deprived of her sons and her husband.

Nour looked at Deniz gratefully and with affection. His mind was still rife with conflict: a father who saves Deniz from the slave merchants, the same father who keeps a Christian mistress against her will, then finally lets her go and keeps her son. Then years later he leaves her the entire contents of one of his Swiss bank accounts.

How hard they must have tried to keep Maro's pregnancy a secret. Deniz told him that, with the help of lovable Eminé, Rıza's old nurse, Maro had been moved to a small apartment above the stables for a few months before and after Nour's birth. Upon strict orders from Rıza Bey, the wives kept it to themselves. There were rumors, but they were squashed, and no major incident had blown their secret—until today.

After Maro's departure, Rıza Bey had asked his third wife, Leila, to become Nour's mother. Leila was ecstatic. Her daughter had died, and she had no other children. She took it as a wonderful affirmation of his love and faith in her. She couldn't have been more pleased if Nour had grown in her own womb, cell by cell.

Telling him all this, Deniz seemed relieved. How could she have lived with such a secret bottled up inside her for thirty-two years?

"Your mother told me many things," she said. "I loved to listen to her stories. When she left, Rıza Bey changed your name to Nour. Your mother had named you Nourhan, after her father.* One day she called me to her room and asked me if I would like to be your godmother. I didn't understand what she meant. She said, 'Considering the situation I'm in, I can never have my son baptized by a priest. But the Church says that I can baptize him myself if there is no priest available.' Then I understood, of course. I held you in my arms, your mother put you in the basin filled with water and immersed you in it three times, in the name of the Father, the Son, and the Holy Spirit. Then we prayed together in Armenian. I'm ashamed I've forgotten my mother tongue, but I can still say my prayers. I say them to myself, even when I'm in the mosque."

"So you're my godmother?" Nour asked awkwardly, not really understanding what a godmother was. But he was happy to be related in some way to such a kindly soul.

"Yes, I am, and you are my godson," she repeated, smiling proudly, wiping away her tears. "When your mother left, I cried for months. It was like losing an older sister. I know she wrote to me, but her letters never reached me. Your father had security guards everywhere, to protect you from being kidnapped. He acted wisely, because there had been a couple of attempts to kidnap you while you were playing in the front courtyard. Leila Hanim loved you so much. Everybody believed you were her flesh and blood." Her eyes took on a distant look. "I wonder if Maro ever received my letters. I'd like to see her again someday. She should be fifty-nine or sixty by now. Is she still in Istanbul?"

"They say she lives in America."

America was the other end of the world to Deniz.

---

*Nourhan is an Armenian name. Nourhan; a compound noun, also means radiant and sovereign in Turkish.

"Thank you, Deniz Abla, for telling me this," Nour said. "Thank you very much." Then he corrected himself. "Thank you, Godmother!" And he smiled for the first time since Altan's call to tell him that Father had died. "You've always been kind to me."

Blacksmith Mourtaza was at the door, looking at his wife. "Did you tell him you were his godmother?" He turned to Nour. "I don't know what it means, but she told me it's something good, a big honor." Then he said to his wife, "Deniz, prepare something for your godson to eat."

"It's getting late. I must leave early in the morning. I can sleep right here on the *sedir*."

They insisted on feeding him. Husband and wife were proud to have him as their houseguest, and excited to have gotten a huge secret off their chests. When they did finally go to bed they didn't sleep for hours. The three of them jabbered away like little children put to bed in the same room.

Nour had a multitude of mixed emotions, but mostly he was relieved. The uncertainty that had harassed him had now disappeared. He felt like crying at the deliverance. At the same time he felt cheated, for everyone who had loved him so dearly all these years had deprived him of his birthright: to know his mother and to grow up in the warmth of her presence... What a deception, to discover that Leila, whom he adored so much, wasn't his real mother! And what was he to think of a father who had acted like a demigod among his people? The thought of it infuriated him. To think that he had been denied his identity: a half-breed, a baptized Christian, the offshoot of tragic circumstances and violent passion!

Nour didn't sleep. The *sedir* was too small for a man of his size, and he was unable to check his mind, which was racing faster than his thoughts, which were trying to recover all at once the misplaced stretch of time between the day he was born and the day his father died. He wanted to find out everything about his past. The changes in his identity had taken years. As Leila would say, he couldn't turn the clock back. His name, his religion, his mother, even his half-Armenian complexion had been altered by the searing sun of southern Anatolia.

When he pushed the curtain aside, it was dawn. The sun lay behind a thin cover of cloud. He got up quietly, trying not to awaken Deniz and Mourtaza, whose snoring made the little hut shake. He lit a cigarette. Leftover food remained on the table from the modest banquet Deniz had prepared for him before going to bed: bits of stuffed green peppers and tomatoes and salted lamb.

How neatly she had arranged her modest home! There were two rooms, a bedroom screened off by a pair of colorful print curtains and a combined sitting room and kitchen with an open hearth. A lantern hung from a roof beam. Beyond the kitchen was the stable, and through the door came the warm, damp smell of fresh cow dung and straw. Apart from a wooden table, a few stools, a chest of drawers, and the *sedir*, there was no other furniture. A small framed picture of a young woman stood on the chest, and Nour went to look at it.

"That's my mother," Deniz said suddenly. Nour hadn't heard her slip through the curtains into the room. She was wearing a long purple-and-orange cotton nightgown.

Nour looked more closely at the photograph of the young woman in Armenian costume seated on a carved bench, holding a violin. "You look like her."

Deniz ran a self-conscious hand through her hair. "Everybody says that. That's the only thing I have left from my family."

Her husband had also gotten up, still in his pajamas. "Did you sleep well?" he asked.

"Like a log," Nour said, but they both knew it wasn't true.

It was almost six o'clock. The sun had just risen and the mountain-tops were rosy in the morning light. The villagers were driving their cattle out to pasture. It was a pleasant sight. Mourtaza was late opening his shop; peasants arrived as early as five in the morning to have their horses shod. Deniz always got up early too. She had to do the washing, milk their two cows, warm the milk to make yogurt, help her husband, and, if she had time, churn butter. She was a happy woman, and even happier today.

"I must be on my way," Nour said. "My family must be in a panic. They don't know I'm here."

He gave Deniz a warm hug and shook her husband's hand, holding it in both of his while he gave them his good news: "I forgot to tell you, my father left both of you a little something in his will. I'll see that you get it soon. Spend it in good health."

Husband and wife were ecstatic that Deniz's old master had remembered them.

# 8

*R*ıza Bey had abducted Maro during one of his routine inspections of Armenian refugee camps in 1915. Her husband, Vartan, had been arrested by the Ottoman police a few days before the deportation orders. Her mother, Azniv, exhausted after walking for days in the scorching heat of the southern wilderness, had died in Maro's arms.

The refugees were being herded toward an unknown destination in the Syrian Desert. Great numbers of them died at the hands of brutal gendarmes. Others succumbed to the harsh conditions of their insufferable odyssey. When Rıza Bey found Maro, her dress was torn, and the convoy guards, aroused by her nakedness, were preparing to rape her before the eyes of her seven-year old son, Tomas.

Governor Rıza raced up to stop the soldiers. Maro's beauty, along with the cruel treatment by the guards, had kindled his passion beyond imagination. He talked to Maro calmly, as if nothing unusual had taken place. Maro, pulling up the pieces of her torn dress to cover her bare breasts, briefly told him her story. Rıza Bey discovered that, besides being exceptionally attractive, Maro was also refined. She sounded like she had been educated in the West. He explained to her the perilous conditions of the ongoing war; bombs were spreading like lava from a volcanic eruption. In the end he persuaded her to return with him to Aïntab, bringing Tomas. From there they should be able to board a French war vessel and rejoin her family in Constantinople.

Maro had no choice but to agree to follow him. Once in Aïntab, however, Rıza Bey forgot his promise. The prospect of losing Maro was too painful. He experienced an unfamiliar sense of well-being whenever she was with him. As the days went by, he realized, much to his consternation, that he had fallen hopelessly in love. The fact that Maro was an Armenian Christian excited him all the more. Never before had he had any sexual relations with a partner of a different origin. He was reminded of the harem of the Grand Seraglio, where the odalisques had all been non-Muslims of extraordinary beauty, plucked from the slave markets.

Despite his romantic fantasies and noble intentions, Maro was Rıza Bey's hostage. Every time she asked him about the horrendous treatment of the Armenians by the Ottoman government, he repeated the same explanation: "We still have plenty of Armenian friends, Maro. The two communities have happily coexisted for centuries. You know that these atrocities have been partly the result of Kurdish tribes."

Maro stayed in Rıza Bey's mansion for four years. She surrendered herself to the air of the southern desert and the monotony of life in Rıza Bey's household. She lived mostly through her dreams and her son, and then her baby boy, Nourhan, a present from the governor. She put up with Rıza's half-camouflaged and divisive accounts until her husband managed to kidnap the governor during an official trip to Constantinople and forced him to release Maro in return for his freedom. It had meant absolute humiliation for a man like Rıza. Ever since that unfortunate event, Maro's name had become taboo in his house.

# 9

Nour ran into his niece on his return from Pazarcik. "Uncle Nour's here! Uncle Nour's back!" Oljay dashed into the sitting room to be first with the good news.

Nour was greeted with cries of alarm and anger. "Where have you been? What happened? Are you all right?" Zehra and Emel scurried around him like a pair of little girls reunited with a lost little brother.

A policeman showed up in the doorway, a small man dressed in a white summer uniform. A second policeman, much taller and older, peered out warily from behind him.

"Where have you been, *Beyefendi*?" asked the first policeman.

"What's it to you where I've been?" Nour snapped at him.

"Don't be like that, *Beyefendi*. Everybody thought you'd had an accident. We came to help."

The second policeman stared at Nour open-mouthed, with the telephone receiver poised in mid-air. He was trying to call the police station for the umpteenth time for some news.

"Damn it all! Leave me alone and mind your own business." Nour walked to the stairs.

"Oh, you're back! You might have called us," Altan cried, grabbing his arm. He was on his way down to talk to the policemen.

"So? I didn't. Call the police, call the prime minister, send out a search team!"

Altan looked affectionately at his brother. He was happy to see him back safe and sound. He turned to the policemen. "Thank you, officers. Please excuse our over-excitement. Everything seems to be all right."

"But we still have to report that Nour Bey was missing," the short policeman explained.

"He's not missing anymore," Altan said. "Thank you."

The policemen nodded, not totally convinced that they didn't have to file a report.

"Your mother has been worried to death," Altan said to Nour.

This was supposed to make him feel guilty, but it didn't. "She can worry herself to death."

Altan comprehended immediately that it wasn't the right moment to call on Nour's compassion. "The commissar sent you this," he said, and handed him the brown envelope. The handwriting was Metin Bey's.

"Must be a love letter." Nour pushed it into his pocket and went up to his room.

Not a minute had passed when Leila opened the door. She rushed over and hugged him. "Nour, my love, where have you been? Couldn't you have called?" Her eyes were swollen and red, but her face was glowing with relief at the sight of her son.

"Drop it, Mother. I'm sure you were worried."

"Then you have no excuse at all for not calling."

Nour ignored the remark. This wasn't the most favorable moment to appeal to his reason. "Damn it, Mother, you weren't worried because I had disappeared. You were worried because you held back the truth from me all these years."

Nour's head-on assault disarmed her. She had planned on telling him the truth gradually and tactfully. "It wasn't my idea, Nour." She was close to tears. "Your father insisted. I was sworn to secrecy."

"I know everything, no need to tell me. I know who Maro is, I know who—"

"Who told you?"

"That's not important. I don't feel like discussing it now. Please just leave me alone."

It wasn't the first time Nour had had a clash with his mother, but it was the first time that he had spoken to her so harshly. Leila was crushed. She had never dreamed that one day she would be faced with such a reality. She was unable to assess the extent of Nour's resentment. It was no use arguing with him. She knew that her son could be very stubborn. And the bitterness on his face saddened her even more.

"Nour, I love you so much! I couldn't face the idea of losing you. You have to understand."

No response.

"I knew it would come out one day. It was impossible to hide. I am truly sorry."

Still no response.

Leila shuddered. Was this the end of her relationship with her only child? She had lost a three-year-old daughter to meningitis years ago, and she still felt the pain whenever she remembered her. But this was much worse. It hurt so badly that her pain hindered her from crying. She'd rather die than let Maro take Nour away from her. Never, never!

She remembered it all: Nour as a two-year-old, then as a handsome little boy, an adolescent, a college student in Istanbul, his years in America... How she had worried that he would come back with an American wife and a couple of spoiled brats. But she would love him, no matter what, even if his mother had been her rival.

Leila tried again desperately. "Night after night I'd lie awake worrying that you'd eventually work out that I wasn't your mother." She gazed at him imploringly. "I wanted to tell you the truth about Maro right from the start, but your father convinced me to wait until you were old enough to understand all the implications."

"And what happened when I was old enough? Nothing."

"I told you... It was your father. He forbade me to say anything. 'There's no point in burdening him with the past,' he said."

"But he thought it would be okay as soon as he was dead? Naturally he knew that I'd discover everything while executing his will. How do you expect me to make any sense out of all this?"

Leila wished her son would show just the merest sign of understanding. Why had Rıza put her in such an awkward situation? She was convinced that Nour was far more hers than Maro's. Nour had blossomed under Leila's caresses. Maro was distant, half-forgotten, a memory.

"I'm tired," he said. "I haven't slept all night. I want you to go now. I'm leaving in the morning."

Leila would have preferred Nour's anger and insults to these unaffected, factual statements. As for Nour, there was nothing he wanted more than to meet the lucky heiress, talk to her, get to know her, and even tell her that he already had a mother whom he had grown to love all these years. It was funny, in a way. He had inherited not only a sizeable fortune and the chairmanship of the Board of Directors of the company but also a brand-new mother. Did his father think of rewarding him, or of letting him know at last that he was different from the rest? Didn't he ever think this could turn out to be a punishment for both Nour and Leila? But it was no secret that there were two sides to Rıza Bey's character. Everybody knew it: the gentle, thoughtful father and husband, and the authoritative despot whose actions could surprise anyone.

Mother and son took one last disappointed look at each other before Leila opened the door and left quietly.

Nour checked the envelope warily. He held it against the light pouring through the window, but couldn't see a thing. The paper was thick. He opened it unwillingly. Yes, it was Metin's child-like handwriting.

Dear Nour Kardam:

Your lack of judgement has obliged me to take drastic measures clear the air. Under the circumstances I have no choice but to inform you of the following painful details concerning your father.

Rıza Bey and I were close collaborators during the 1915 Armenian massacres. Documents in my possession would provide valuable proof to the War Crimes Commission in the United States and to the international press. Even after my death, they would incriminate Rıza and drag the Kardam empire into an embarrassing scandal.

As for your family's legendary fortune, it's mostly laundered money. Your father amassed it while he was in Geneva, through major questionable deals with European and Anatolian drug cartels.

I'm leaving all the names and incriminating details against your father and the company with a close friend. In order to ensure absolute silence you are advised to bestow upon my widow, Münevver Hanim, and my two sons a generous settlement, in recognition of my long years of service to the company. I'm sure you wouldn't like this scandal to endanger your financial empire. Life has treated me generously, and I'm thankful to Allah and to your father for that.

Signed Metin Haydar

Halfway through the letter, Nour was clenching the paper so tightly he almost tore it. He read it over three times, without skipping a punctuation mark. Its contents came to life. They answered many of the questions he had never dared to ask his father. He tossed the letter onto his bed, flaring up in another blaze of anger. Events were occurring so quickly he was unable to keep up. His father's ostentatious bequest to his favorite mistress couldn't conceal the old man's guilt and reckless conduct.

But Nour preferred to doubt the letter, to see it as one of Metin Bey's reckless scams.

There was a light tap on the door. "It's me, Altan."

"Please leave me alone."

"I have to talk to you."

"Later."

"Right now."

Nour sighed. "The door's open."

Altan walked in, looking exhausted. "And?"

"And what?"

"The letter."

"Just a private matter."

"Don't bullshit me, Nour."

"That's all it is."

"I know you're mad at me. Believe it or not, I didn't know anything. Don't you know that those two assholes never trusted me?"

"I'm leaving in the morning," Nour said. "You won't have to call in the police again."

"Stop it, Nour. You know, I am on your side. Let me see the letter."

"It's on the bed."

Altan picked it up and read out the opening sentences in a bitter tone. His throat froze up. "Shit."

"I guess your mother was right," Nour said with a touch of sarcasm. "The way Father was buried was a bad omen. Metin put a jinx on the family."

This wasn't the time for jokes, and Altan didn't appreciate it. "We must think carefully before doing anything."

"We won't do a thing, Altan," Nour snorted. "We don't even know if Metin's bluffing. I'm going to assume he is. This must remain a secret between you and me, guarded every bit as carefully as Maro's identity."

Altan ignored the barb in the last part of Nour's remark. "By the way, Nourettin Bey called. He says he tried to get in touch with the law firm in New York. Apparently it doesn't exist anymore."

"Nonsense. He's either misinformed or lying. I've decided what I'm going to do. First I'll see if I can arrange things from Istanbul as soon as I get back tomorrow. Then, of course, I'll fly to New York. Isn't it fabulous to have a superfluity of mothers?" Nour's smile couldn't conceal his bitterness. "Keep a close eye on Ramazan and Touran while I'm gone. And let me know what's in that mystery desk."

# 10

When Nour entered his office on Friday morning there was a letter waiting for him on his desk. He opened it. It was from Esin, offering her condolences in a few polite lines.

A smile lit up his face. He had arrived the night before and had tossed and turned all night in his bed, a thousand concerns on his mind. The lawsuit against Kardam Tobacco International: Metin was liable for the fraudulent shipments whether dead or alive but his suicide complicated the case. Then the American law firm, Fred Goldwater & Associates: it was the key element in settling the legacy. How would he be able to find his biological mother if the firm didn't exist anymore? Would Maro still remember him, or had decades of separation severed her from the son she had left behind?

He pressed the intercom: "Alev, can I see you for a minute?"

His secretary came in instantly. Her round face always wore a permanent smile, but today she was subdued. "My heartfelt condolences, sir."

"Thank you, Alev."

"You got hundreds of phone calls," she said. "Mostly condolences. They're all on the pad."

"Thanks. I'll get to them eventually." He handed her a slip of paper, the Goldwater & Associates telephone number. "Would you please ask the operator to connect me to this number in New York?"

As the morning went by, the thought of the various ordeals that lay ahead disheartened him. "Think about pleasant things," he kept telling himself. "Think about Esin," which always brought a smile.

Alev's voice on the intercom took his mind off the young doctor. "May I see you for a second?"

When she came in, she said, "There are two guys outside, Sabri and Özkoul Haydar." She looked nervous. "They insist on seeing you. They say it's urgent."

"Metin's sons!" Nour frowned. "Tell them I'm busy."

"I did, but they keep insisting."

Nour had no time to tell her what to do, for just then the door opened and two well-dressed men in their thirties burst through it.

"I'm Sabri, Metin Bey's son."

"And I'm Özkoul, Sabri's brother."

Sabri was enormous, six feet four or even taller, at least three hundred pounds, with a barrel chest and close-cropped hair. His brother was the reverse, shorter than average, slim, squinting through granny glasses, and completely bald.

Nour stared at them in irritation. The deep hatred he harbored against their father was suddenly revived. He took a cigarette from his silver case and lit it, struggling to keep his voice calm.

"Would you please leave my office as quietly as you entered, before I call the police?" He rose to show them the door.

Alev was alarmed.

Nour raised his voice a notch or two. "Did you hear what I said?"

Sabri said, with barely concealed anger, "Sorry to interrupt," he said.

Özkoul also sounded contrite. "Yes, I'm sorry, too. You must understand that we buried our father only yesterday."

"We'll take only a few minutes of your time," Sabri said. "We'd like to discuss the charges against him."

"That would be a breach of legal ethics. I can't discuss anything related to the case before the hearings."

Özkoul gave a sudden raucous laugh. "Don't fuck around with us, Kardam."

Nour turned to his secretary. "Please leave us alone, Alev. It's okay."

She complied uneasily, closing the door behind her. Sabri and Özkoul sat down in the leather wing chairs facing Nour's desk. Nour broke the silence. "May I know the reason for your intrusion? What's so urgent?"

Özkoul had calmed down. His voice was polite. "The hearings are coming up next week. Now that our father is dead we thought we might come to an agreement with you."

Nour knew that behind this feigned docility there lurked a well-calculated plot. "What kind of agreement did you have in mind?"

Sabri crossed his legs and leaned back in the chair. "Money's no problem."

"I see."

"I'm sure we can settle things much more agreeably out of court."

"I don't understand your concern," said Nour. "Kardam Tobacco faces a civil action for damages, and your father was responsible for it. He sent the wrong shipments to the wrong customers, degrading the quality of our service and our product. Unfortunately, as we were depleting our high-grade tobacco stocks, he had to make a choice, and he chose to send the best stock to a new client. And in return he received a large payoff, if I may call it that."

"Commercial gratuities," Sabri interjected.

"Commercial horseshit!" Nour corrected. "This isn't the first felony charge against him. Metin Bey also bribed his clients to place bigger orders. His commissions reached astronomical proportions."

"So did your company's profits," Sabri reminded Nour.

"It's not exactly the same."

"Two sides of the same equation."

Sabri was right. Nour chose not to dwell on it. He said only, "You realize, of course, that you're not implicated. You're not even subpoenaed."

"Yes, but you don't seem to understand. Our father was part of this company almost his whole life. The fact that you fired him so suddenly upset him to such an extent that he took his own life. In fact, we should be the ones suing you—for your cruel, unwarranted decision." Sabri was getting impatient. "But that's another matter. In the meantime, we wouldn't want our father's reputation stained with groundless charges."

"You're most welcome to sue us, if that's what you intend to do. As for your second point, only the court can decide that."

"And if the court finds him guilty?"

"Then he'll suffer the consequences."

"How can a dead man suffer consequences?"

"Not him, may he rest in peace, but his estate." Nour could see in the brothers' faces that their primary concern was the enormous fine the court could impose on Metin Bey's estate. He shrugged. "I'm sure he has good attorneys. He can be tried posthumously, if you're familiar with the expression."

Özkoul looked at Nour with hatred. "You'll have a hell of a time proving him guilty."

"We won't take much more of your precious time, Mr. Kardam," Özkoul continued. He glanced at his brother. Nour saw him nod. Then Özkoul went on, "We would like to offer three hundred thousand cash. Just drop the charges and the money is yours. A fair deal."

The brothers watched Nour expectantly. The figure Özkoul mentioned was itself incriminating. Nour doubted if they were really bothered about their father's reputation, offering such a pay-off. They were there to prevent an investigation into their family's business concerns. This boosted Nour's morale. After a long silence he said, "Is that your final offer?"

"We could raise it to four hundred," Özkoul suggested. Then, seeing that Nour was still dissatisfied, he said, "Half a million. Our final offer."

Another long silence. Nour cherished every second of it, then said, "Sorry, gentlemen. It's very tempting but I cannot accept it."

Their faces dropped. "I hope you read our father's letter carefully," Sabri said.

Nour didn't reply. His silence was more intimidating than words. The brothers looked at each other in frustration.

Sabri hauled his gigantic frame out of the leather wing chair. "I'm sorry, Mr. Kardam," he said. "We thought we could make a sensible deal with an intelligent attorney like you, and save you and your company a lot of trouble."

Nour also got to his feet. "If I were you, I wouldn't attach too much importance to that letter." He ground out his cigarette in the ashtray on the desk.

Sabri and Özkoul opened their mouths at exactly the same time:

"Don't—" Then Sabri continued alone. "Don't say we didn't warn you. This will be the end of the Kardam dynasty."

Nour reached for the door and opened it. "Good day, gentlemen," he said with a smile. "I'll see you in court."

After they left he went back to his desk, pulled open the center drawer, and played back the conversation he had just recorded.

Saturday evening. Nour and Esin were having dinner at Façyo's, a fashionable fish restaurant only a twenty-minute drive from the Yeniköy residence. The *beau monde* of Istanbul packed the place. The restaurant overlooked the straits, the lights of the Asiatic shore in the distance. The balmy weather was more typical of summer than of early September.

They were finishing their grilled swordfish, sliced finely and layered with tomato wedges between each slice. Esin's cheerful presence across the table from him had calmed Nour's troubled mind. He had even been able to recount some of the events of the past turbulent week. Esin's face shone with happiness at being with him, until he broke the news about his upcoming trip to New York.

"When?"

"In two weeks."

"For how long?"

"Not very long, I hope."

A shadow crossed her face. "A week, two weeks, two months, three?"

"Two years, three years!" Nour took her hand in his. "No longer than I can help. I have no choice. I have an inheritance case to settle in America."

"I thought you were a corporate lawyer."

"I am, but this is an extraordinary case. I happen to be the executor of a rather unusual will."

"And the deceased is in America?"

"No, the inheritor. She lives in New York City."

Esin was curious but kept herself from questioning. Nour declined to give more details and quickly changed the subject.

"Last time I was in the States was almost two years ago," he said.

"Visiting friends."

"You like it there, don't you?"

"Yes and no. But there are times I miss it."

"I'd love to go there one day."

"I'm sure you will."

"So am I," she said with a laugh.

He liked looking at her. There was something incredibly young and vital about this woman. She was only twenty-seven, was finishing her internship, and would probably open a private practice before long if she could raise the money. She came from a modest family, her father an accountant in a clothing company and her mother an English teacher in a public high school.

Nour took out a packet of Lucky Strikes and offered her a cigarette before taking one for himself.

"No, thank you."

"Oh, I forgot I'm with a doctor." They laughed. "I don't care whether I live that long," he said. "But when I die I don't want to leave any enemies, and the only way I can make sure of that is to outlive them all. So I suppose that's a reason to give up smoking."

"Someday, right?"

"Yes, someday."

She smiled, shaking her head, then took the lighter from beside his plate and lit his cigarette for him.

The Greek waiter came over to take their orders for dessert and coffee.

"Not for me," Esin said.

"And you, sir?"

"Thanks, no dessert tonight."

When the waiter left Esin smiled. "I have a feeling you have a sweet tooth."

"I can't eat when my calorie intake is under supervision."

"The fish wasn't fattening, you can have your dessert tonight." She patted his hand as if to console a child.

"Let's have the dessert at the *yalı*. It's not even midnight."

"Let's," she replied without the slightest hesitation. In fact, she was dying to see the house.

As for Nour, he questioned his spur-of-the-moment suggestion. He was afraid she'd think he was showing off. He knew she lived in a modest apartment in a middle-class neighborhood in the city.

Outside the restaurant the cars were double-parked all along the asphalt road. Nour caught the eye of the valet in charge of parking. In a minute his Jaguar—a silver-gray sports model—pulled up beside the pavement, and they got in.

Before Nour turned the key in the ignition, their eyes met. He pulled her gently toward him and they kissed: no words necessary.

A pleasant breeze was blowing from the Asiatic side as they drove along the shore road. Esin nestled her head comfortably on Nour's shoulder. The steamers and ferries looked like great crystal liners with their bright lights, crossing the straits between Asia and Europe. Turkish music from the outdoor restaurants floated through the night.

"If it's too windy, I can put the top up, *shekerim*."

"It's just fine."

Nour was very sparing of endearments, unlike most Turks. This was the first time he had addressed Esin using the popular endearment *my sugar*.

When they arrived at the *yalı*, Nour got out to open the wrought-iron gate. It was late, and Kerim and Aysha were asleep; otherwise, the old servant would have come hobbling out to the car to find out if his young master needed anything before going to bed.

Nour used the side door. Esin paused in the main hall, spellbound by the splendor of gold and crystal. She hadn't realized that she had been invited to an ancient Ottoman palace. Chandeliers and candelabra sparkled with a thousand glittering drops. The grand staircase, covered with Persian runners, climbed gently to the mezzanine floor and the reception hall. Portraits of Ottoman sultans, viziers, and Kardam ancestors decorated the walls.

"Nour, you didn't tell me you lived in a castle." She went from one painting to another, stopping in front of each and enjoying it like a child set free in a gigantic toy store. Paintings always fascinated her. She stood in front of some portraits much longer than others, marvelling at their beauty.

Nour was so used to the house and its interior he hardly noticed any of these things. "It's nice, but I'm more at home at my apartment," he said. "Too bad it doesn't have the same view." Then, not to sound too full of himself, he added, "My father loved this place. He was proud of the Ottoman past, with all the traditions. It was his decision to buy the *yalı* from Kibrisli Mehmet Pasha."

"The grand vizier."

"Yes. But then he decorated the house to his taste."

"Good taste."

He took her up to the main sitting room and then the grand salon. "The house incorporates elements from both the traditional Turkish *konak* and the wooden *yalı*," he told her, then stopped suddenly. "I sound like a tour guide, I'd better shut up."

"No! Give me the dollar tour. I love it."

"First things first," he said, smiling. "Don't think I've forgotten the dessert. I'll be right back."

Esin examined the grand salon. Until today her knowledge of places like this had come entirely from glossy art books. Chinese rugs covered the parquet floor. A wide divan ran all around the wall, as in the harem of the Grand Seraglio. The walls were covered with fine paintings. Their beauty had intoxicated Rıza Bey to such an extent that he had allowed these representations of the human form to adorn his walls without thinking twice about the restrictions imposed on him by Islam.

Nour came back with a silver tray of assorted pastries and a bottle of Taittinger.

"Are you still going to refuse my dessert?" he asked? He picked up a piece of baklava with his fingers, "Open your mouth, but don't bite!" He chuckled. "When I was a child my mother used to do this to me. I had fun biting her fingers every time. Ouch!"

Esin giggled. Then, pointing to a painting of an odalisque, she said, "You must have had a broad-minded father to let his children savor such delectable nudes."

"They were all kept in his bedroom until we had all come of age.

Before that we used to sneak into his bedroom to drool over them. There was this servant who used to recite verses from the Koran, no doubt to ward off the evil spirits he felt were emanating from my father's collection."

Nour offered her a glass of champagne and took one for himself.

"To your health and success, Esin."

"And to yours, Nour."

He wished he could open up his heart to her, but that wasn't possible. They drank, then set their glasses down on the inlaid table.

"I wish I didn't have to go to the States," Nour said with a sigh. "I called New York twice yesterday. The attorney who's supposed to help me is dead, and the old firm has changed hands. I guess I'll have to play Sherlock Holmes for a while."

She smiled. "Like tracking down an unknown virus."

He drew her closer, his hands on her bare shoulders, and they kissed for a long time. The light from the crystal chandelier poured down too harshly; Nour switched it off, leaving only the two electric candelabra on the mantelpiece to illuminate the room.

He helped her out of her dress. Underneath, except for a bra and flimsy panties, there was only her gorgeous white skin and graceful body.

The weak glimmer of the candelabra spread like impalpable dust over the divan. Nour finished undressing, and then they were lying on the divan in each other's arms. Nour caressed her as she lay under the weight of his body. He touched, he kissed, and she kissed back. She removed her bra, exposing her breasts. Nour felt the warmth of her flesh overwhelm his entire being. The only sounds were those of their frenzied love-making.

The next morning, Nour and Esin lay sound asleep in each other's arms as the sun rose high in the sky over the Bosporus.

*Part* **two**

# 11

$\mathcal{T}$he first two weeks of September turned out to be New York's hottest that summer. The rattling buzz of air conditioning units in store and office building windows added to the din of Manhattan traffic—the ceaseless rumble of the flowing yellow cabs, lumbering trucks and pushcarts, and an endless stream of humanity that seemed to be getting longer and louder every day.

Ever since its foundation in 1926, the *Armenian Free Press* had occupied offices over a corner hardware store on the Third Avenue elevated subway line. Every time a train came into the 27th Street station, the brick structure shook.

As editor of the *Free Press*, Maro Armen Balian had considered moving the paper to Flushing Meadows, where there were new offices available, with all the modern conveniences. But since her husband, Vartan, was mostly away on lecture tours, she had given up the idea of moving.

It was twenty-six years since Vartan and Maro had started the paper, at a point when neither of them really had time for such a demanding venture. Maro was busy raising children. Vartan and his brother Noubar ran a modest Oriental grocery store to earn their daily bread. he *Armenian Free Press*, however, was an ideological outlet for them: a way to preserve their national identity.

Two years after their arrival in America, they had been advised to change their name from Balian to Armen for security reasons. Vartan was still a wanted man in Turkey. Those were difficult years. As soon as Turkey declared itself a republic in 1923, the new government monopolized the opium plantations that were in private hands. Under the circumstances, the brothers had no choice but to shut down the decades-old family opium business—hail the days of hardship!

It was six o'clock. Maro was listless at the end of a long, sweltering workday. Despite her advancing years she hadn't slowed down. Like her husband, Vartan, nine years her senior, she worked from eight to six every day. Maro didn't look her age, though. She had retained her slim figure and youthful appearance. If it wasn't for a bit of gray in her hair, no one would guess she had just turned sixty.

Today, as usual after the staff were gone, she turned back to her desk to check the galleys for the next day's issue. She still had the American news highlights to condense.

Her office looked as if a desk had somehow been squeezed into a phone booth. It was cluttered with files, documents, books. Maro made herself a cup of coffee and picked up a copy of *Time* magazine. The first thing she always checked was the "Milestones" column—part of her late-afternoon coffee routine.

"Find anyone you know?" Vartan used to ask with a grin.

Maro would shake her head and say, "Not this time."

Today her eyes instantly fixed on an announcement. She set her coffee cup down abruptly on the desk and read it:

DIED. RIZA FAROUK KARDAM, 75, billionaire tobacco king and renowned philanthropist, of a heart attack, in Gaziantep, Turkey. Over the past two decades, the one-time governor and founding member of the Young Turks Party turned his tobacco and cotton plantations into an industrial empire. After retiring from politics he began a career of good works, raising millions for the Turkish Red Crescent Society and many other national and international charity organizations. He is survived by his two wives, Safiyé and Leila; his sons, Touran, Ramazan, Altan, Kenan, Erol, and Nour; and his daughters, Shahané, Emel, and Zehra.

Maro read it a few times before the words began to sink in. She closed her eyes, her heart pounding. "Nour... Nourhan, my son." Thirty-two long years! She could still visualize him at play under the magnolia trees in the harem gardens. Nourhan had grown into a handsome young man in Maro's imagination. She pictured him with dark, strong features, taller than Rıza and even better looking. She thought of Rıza, the "billionaire tobacco king and renowned philanthropist"! How money glossed over the grotesque! Along with her anger, she also felt a passionate hunger, and then shame. She had been helpless when Rıza made love to her. Not weak—that was not what she felt. She was overwhelmed by his emotional intensity and his physical power, torn between her desire to remain faithful to a long-missing husband, who could be dead or alive, and her response to a passionate lover who had saved her and her son from death under the sizzling sun of the Syrian Desert.

She cut out the obituary and put it in her pocket.

Later, on the way home on the F train, Maro reread the clipping until she had memorized it. She wondered if, now that Rıza Bey was dead, it would at last be possible for her to see Nourhan. But there was Vartan's narrow-minded anger regarding her illegitimate son! She was convinced it wasn't her son who brought Vartan's bitterness to the surface. Nourhan was only a medium, reminding him of Maro's relations with Rıza, sparking his never-fading jealousy and hatred toward the ex-governor. Maro didn't wish to rekindle the old quarrels. They had caused the two of them too much unhappiness already. She had finally decided never to utter Nourhan's name in her husband's presence. But she wondered if Vartan really believed that Maro could have forgotten her son, her very flesh and blood.

After she left Turkey, Maro tried to find a way to get the boy back. She wrote to Diran, Vartan's cousin, for help. Diran, as an experienced activist involved in clandestine political actions, tried to convince her to give up the idea. "It's too dangerous, Maro," he insisted. "Vartan is a wanted man in Turkey. He's still being accused of Halit Pasha's murder." The pasha, who had been Vartan's dear friend, had also saved him from the gallows, but the new government still blamed Vartan for a murder he had never committed.

She got off the subway at 71st Avenue in Queens, feeling strangled in the heat as she followed the flow of the mob up the stairs and then down a narrow corridor, trailing the human stream until they emerged from the Continental Avenue exit.

On the street, there was a breeze, and it wasn't dark yet—Maro's favorite time of day. She walked in the direction of the Forest Hills tennis courts, still thinking about the obituary, reliving her life with Rıza, alternately evoking her two images of him: the benevolent father and tender lover, and the political despot who insisted on keeping Maro for himself. And now he was gone, he had ceased to exist; he had become a memory, like the war itself.

Despite the long years of separation from Nourhan, the child had always been on her mind. Every year, on 27 October, she celebrated his birthday in absentia, in her own quiet fashion. She repeated the prayer she had said when she baptized him, then she went to sit in the deep stillness of the dingy living room, a glass of wine in her hand, bringing the past to life, like paper flowers blooming in slow motion, bit by bit, one by one: her futile and dangerous attempt to abort Nourhan, not wanting to carry Rıza's child... Nourhan's birth... her quarrels with Rıza over her son's name. Then her unexpected departure to Constantinople and her agonizing pleas to Rıza's mother: "Please, great lady, please let me take my child with me!" The conditions of Rıza Bey's release had specified only Maro's freedom. "Please, then let me stay here with my son... you cannot do this to me... I've already lost Tomas... " But she'd had to go back alone to her husband in Constantinople.

As she walked, she looked absent-mindedly at the large stucco houses on both sides of the street, the few fading flowerbeds in the front yards. In spite of the heat, summer had been left behind.

Maro and Vartan lived in one of those ordinary three-storey semi-detached houses with brick facades. They all looked alike, the only distinguishing mark the number stuck on the front door. Rows of rhododendrons separated the lawn from the pavement and the two adjoining properties. As she neared the house, Maro spotted her daughter Nayiri's old jeep backing out of the driveway. She waved, and Nayiri stopped the vehicle and jumped out, her face beaming.

"Hello, *Mayrig*. I couldn't wait for you any longer." She hugged and kissed Maro noisily on both cheeks.

"Come in for two minutes."

"Sorry, Mom, I've got to go."

"How are the exams going?"

"Just fine."

"Wonderful, my sugar. I called you last night, but you weren't home," Maro said in Armenian.

"You've been checking up on me, Mom," Nayiri shot back in English.

"Don't be silly, dearest. I only wanted to know how you were doing."

"I know, I know. I'm just teasing you, Mom." Nayiri chuckled. "I've got another exam on Monday, and then I'll be free as a bird." Changing her cheerful tone, she added: "Except that I've got to pay the rent so I'll have to sweat all summer at Macy's, selling underwear!"

It broke Maro's heart. Why should such a bright, attractive girl slave eight hours a day selling ladies' lingerie in a department store? Nayiri was the prettiest of the three daughters, a carbon copy of her mother, both physically and in character. Magda, at thirty-one, was the oldest, and was married to Robert, an Italian-American and a pharmacist by profession. With her slim figure, dark brown hair, plain-rimmed glasses, and sober navy blue skirts, Magda looked like a plain schoolgirl. Her sister Araxi was two years younger and still unmarried. She taught high school in a middle-class neighborhood in Ozone Park, Queens. Despite her very average looks, Araxi had a warmth and gentleness, like her father's, that drew people to her. The two sisters had a philosophical attitude to Nayiri's undisputable beauty: "We let Nayiri inherit Mother's looks, and saved her intelligence for ourselves."

Nayiri was the rebel of the family. She had been a handful as a child, an agitator as a teenager, and full of surprises as an adult. It was mostly her wild imagination that got her into trouble. While all her friends drove ordinary cars, she had chosen a fourth-hand army jeep. If anyone asked why, she replied, "Because it's cheaper, and it's a World War Two relic." The car was her little toy. It sucked oil by the case and periodically refused to start. While all the girls in her class ran after the members of varsity teams, Nayiri fell in love with her math teacher, seventeen years her senior. As the years went by, she didn't seem to lose her keen interest in doing things differently—certainly not for the sake of attracting attention. She was a little taller than her mother, not quite as slim, with light brown hair that was usually undone and reached halfway down her back in frenzied ripples. Her brown eyes, long eyelashes, and gently tilted nose betrayed her Middle Eastern blood. Whether in Turkey, Armenia, or Israel she would fit in perfectly. Every man in town had been after her, but when she met Greg Selian, a young Armenian lawyer, things changed; she calmed down. And before they were engaged she moved into her own apartment near Columbia University, where she was finishing her master's in psychology. As traditional Armenian parents, Vartan and Maro objected to her decision to move out, but there was no way they could stop her.

"Forget your old-country habits," Nayiri told them. "You're in America now."

Her remark hurt them deeply, but, knowing her fiery temperament, they agreed, to avoid squabbles. They knew that after each mutiny she would charm them with her tenderness and a tact not seen even in the sophisticated circles of foreign diplomacy. Vartan thought Nayiri had missed her vocation; instead of psychology, she should have studied labor arbitration or international relations!

It was getting dark. Mother and daughter were still chatting on the pavement in front of the house.

"What do you think my house is? A laundromat? Stay and eat with me, Nayiri."

"I've really got to go. I've already eaten, Mom. I can't eat too much: I'm busting out of my jeans." Patting her hips, she added, with another loud chuckle, "I'll soon be modeling for the fat girls' league."

Like her brother Jake, Nayiri was always in good spirits. "What's the use of moping?" she would ask her sisters when anything went wrong. "It doesn't help." She was optimistic and lucky—lucky, indeed, Maro thought, to be engaged to Greg. He came from a good family and had a bright future ahead of him. The fact that he was Armenian was a bonus. Maro still couldn't solve the mystery, however: what made Nayiri choose Greg over so many other suitors? An ordinary-looking guy with a conventional profession and a secure future. She hoped that the passing of years had had its effect on her daughter, and that she had begun to see things from a new perspective.

"Bye for now, Mom. I'll see you at the weekend."

"It'd be nice if you stayed."

Such insistence was unusual. Nayiri noticed a hint of sadness on her mother's face. She took her hands. "What's wrong, Mom?"

"Nothing's wrong, sugar."

"I'll stay if you want me to."

"No, no, I'm just fine. I know you have to study." Maro swallowed hard, trying to compose herself.

They embraced. Nayiri hopped into her jeep. Before pulling out of the driveway she blew a couple of kisses.

As Nayiri pulled away, Maro seemed to see in her daughter a reflection of herself, and wondered why this disturbed her.

Maro unlocked the door and entered. In the kitchen, the sight of the unwashed dishes and cluttered counter depressed her. She took the magazine clipping from her pocket and read it again by the failing light of the window. The shock, which had first attacked her stomach, was now attacking her nerves. She put the clipping back into her pocket and went up to her bedroom.

When she turned the light on she felt better already. The bedroom was her sanctuary. After a hard day's work she would undress, take a bath, exchange her work clothes for something more comfortable, and rest quietly on her bed with the newspaper before going down to prepare supper. Maro had always wanted to furnish her room according to her taste, but she never had the time or the money. She still couldn't figure out what had made her choose the existing bedroom suite. She jokingly referred to it as "Bronx Renaissance."

She went into the bathroom and turned on the taps to fill the tub. She would have just enough energy left to lower herself gently into the warm water and read the paper... But just then the telephone rang, and she turned off the taps to answer it.

"Hello, *anoushes*." It was Vartan, calling from Albany.

"I just got in."

"A lot of work?"

"The usual."

"I'm bogged down with the seminar. I didn't have time to write the editorial."

"So you want me to write it, I suppose."

"You read my mind. But if you don't want to, we can skip it this week."

"I'll see what I can do."

The paper had appeared daily, with no interruption, even during the war, with an editorial once a week, usually written by her husband. Vartan was still an idealist, concerned with the tragic destiny of his people. It was unthinkable for Maro that they should skip the editorial.

"How are the children?"

"They're fine. Nayiri was here. She left a while ago."

"How are her exams going?"

"Apparently very well."

Maro made a real effort to concentrate on the conversation. She was staring at the little clipping, which she had placed on her night table, wondering whether to mention it or not. She decided it had to remain private for the time being. That part of her past had remained her very own world, always hidden but always present in her mind, like a classic overplayed black-and-white silent movie.

"I'll be back tomorrow," Vartan said. "I'll come straight to the paper so we can have lunch together. Then I'll go see Noubar."

"That'll be nice."

"Maybe the *Free Press* should do an editorial on McCarthy this week," he said.

"You'd better do it. You're much better at that sort of thing than I am, Vartan."

"We'll talk about it."

As soon as they hung up, Maro was back in an imaginary world. Her exotic past clashing against her mundane life and the political realities of today. All sound became muffled, even the humming of the air conditioner, as the memories flooded her again.

# 12

The Cilicia on East 2nd Street was one of the few Armenian restaurants in New York City. Eating there was like going to a private club; everyone knew everyone else. Gevorg Kerobian, better known as Georgie, owned the place. While his wife and mother managed the kitchen, he looked after the clientele, talking to them, explaining the specials of the day, and even sitting down with them for an occasional drink.

Maro and Vartan strode down the street, unmindful of the cars and pushcarts threading through the steel columns of the subway line. Maro, in her beige cotton suit and black blouse, looked out of place among the merchants of the Lower East Side. At one point, startled by the hellish noise of the train rushing by overhead, they stumbled and almost upset a basket of apples outside a fruit and vegetable store.

The restaurant was full. Georgie was excited by their visit. "Oh, the journalists are here! Nice to see you, my friends," he said as took them to their usual corner near the front window. Heads turned, and a high-pitched voice cried, "Welcome, my children," in Armenian. It was Mama Martha, Georgie's eighty-year-old mother, coming out to greet them. Since the death of her husband years before, she dressed entirely in black, even, in spite of the heat, covering her head with a black scarf.

"How are you, my children? Long time no see. God bless you, I read your paper every day."

"Thank you, Mama Martha, we're just fine," said Vartan, his hand still on her shoulder. "You look just great—tell me your secret."

"It must be work," Maro said, before Mama Martha answered him. "You never stop, do you?"

The old woman's face lit up. "Thank God, I feel fine." Then she switched to her favorite subject: "You must try my artichokes today.

Stuffed with fresh peas and dill, and cooked in olive oil. The aubergine is also excellent."

"Fried or stuffed?" Maro asked.

"Fried, with garlic yogurt on the side."

"Sounds delicious! I'll have that."

Georgie was waiting politely for his mother to finish. "*Mayrig*, let me take the orders."

"Enjoy your meal, my children. I'll come and see you later." With that, she hobbled off to the kitchen.

The restaurant was below street level. Customers sitting along the front window could see only the legs and feet of people passing by. It was as hot inside as out: the air conditioning unit was out of order. Maro took off her suit jacket and hung it on the back of her chair. Vartan looked at her admiringly—her pale skin glowed against the black blouse.

Maro ordered without checking the menu: fried aubergines, some lamb patties with cumin, and cracked-wheat pilav.

Vartan peered over the half-glasses perched near the end of his nose, still checking the menu. "No appetizers, Georgie, just a few meat balls in yogurt sauce and an artichoke."

Vartan hadn't even opened the wine list when Diego, the young Puerto Rican waiter, appeared with two glasses of ouzo.

"From the *dueña*," he said.

A delighted smile crossed Georgie's face. "It's from my mother."

"Spoiling us, for a change," Vartan said.

Maro, noticing Mama Martha at the kitchen door, raised her glass. "Thank you, *Mayrig*. To your health."

Vartan turned to Maro and covered her hand. "I'm glad to be back. The older I get the more I miss you when I'm away."

Maro smiled. When he wanted to he had the ability to make a woman feel her best—attractive, feminine, desirable. Although in his seventies, he was still a good-looking man, tall and well-built, though slightly on the heavy side. Vartan Armen-Balian: the staunch liberal, the avid human rights advocate, and the loyal Armenian nationalist. This latter attribute was sometimes so exaggerated that it exasperated his wife.

Maro had a hard time overcoming her urge to break the news of Rıza Bey's death. She had lain restless most of the night, turning over in her mind what and how to tell her husband. She wanted to tell him. But sitting across from him in the restaurant, she lost her nerve. Instead she said, "Vartan, you said you were going to see Noubar later. I hope nothing's wrong?"

He shook his head. "He said he wanted to see me. Nothing important, I'm sure. He probably wants to discuss business."

"With you?"

"Yes, with me. After all, I'm his brother, aren't I?"

"I didn't mean that. I just wondered if he's going to want you to go into business with him, like before."

Vartan smiled. "I'm too old for that. Our son is with him now. I'm sure he'll give him enough new ideas to revitalize the Oriental grocery business. Poor Noubar! He's been slaving for peanuts."

"We aren't doing much better," Maro said, then regretted the remark. "No, no, we mustn't complain. We've worked hard, and we've brought up five lovely children."

Vartan nodded. "Yes. And we survived the deportations, the depression... We've done what we wanted."

At that moment Maro was ready to add: "And we've forgotten about a son, who, nevertheless, survived in my memory!" But she dared not spoil the lunch.

"Jake is a real whiz at business," Vartan said. "I hope he can turn his uncle's business around."

Noubar was Vartan's older brother. He was a cheerful, good-hearted family man, and loyal to his origins. After closing down the family grocery store, he had gone into the wholesale Oriental grocery business. Despite the modest turnover of the company, Jake went to work for his uncle after graduating from college with a bachelor's degree in commerce. It was a real challenge for an enterprising young man of twenty-five, but he seemed perfectly integrated into the business. He had come up with a plan to import many of the foods they sold directly instead of buying from the few importers who had monopolized the market.

Maro made sounds of approval as she sampled the aubergine and lamb patties with garlic yogurt. But Vartan hadn't yet touched his lunch. He furrowed his brow. "I've decided I'm not going to accept any more seminar invitations. The years are going by, and it's time I spent more of my time at the paper and concentrated on my writing."

He'd thought the news would surprise Maro, but she said, simply, "It's a wise decision. I'm sure your books and articles will make up for whatever you earn as a guest lecturer."

"I think so too." He pursed his lips, looking thoughtful. "And, with more time, I can even be more helpful to our community."

Maro put down her fork. "Vartan, you've done more than enough for the community—you've written so much about them. The U.S. government knows much more about the Armenians, their culture, their religion, their past than it has ever known before, and all because of your efforts."

He sighed. "I hope you're right, but I'm not so convinced. There's always more to be done."

"It's ironic," Maro said. "You're retiring from lecturing, and yet the colleges are full of old, incompetent people who are desperately clinging to their positions. They should've been put out to pasture eons ago."

He shrugged, but what she said pleased him. She smiled and added, "I won't mind having you next to me more often."

Vartan touched her hand. "Let's drink to the future."

Maro wasn't terribly sure what the future had in store for them. Since yesterday she had refused to imagine a future without Nourhan's presence in her life, somehow. But would Nourhan accept a mother who now, suddenly, showed up after severing herself from him for three decades?

"The future! Yes! Let's," she said.

Swiveling in his chair, Vartan caught the Puerto Rican waiter's eye for two more glasses of ouzo, and when they came he held up his glass: "To us." Then he said, softly, "You're so precious to me, Maro."

She raised her glass and sipped, but remained silent. She was wondering if it was the right time to broach the subject. "May I have a cigarette?" she asked.

Vartan reached into his pocket. It was unusual for an occasional smoker like Maro to want a cigarette before the end of the meal.

She smiled nervously as he lit it for her, but the smile soon faded. "Vartan," she said. "I've been wanting to talk to you about something." Her courage surprised her. Perhaps it was the second drink.

Vartan didn't know what to expect. First the cigarette, then the seriousness on her face, and now such a loaded opening! "Why did you hesitate?" he asked

"Considering your past reaction, I preferred to keep my mouth shut."

Vartan stared at her uneasily. "What's troubling you, Maro?"

She didn't reply.

"What is it?" he insisted.

She said, in a voice so low it was almost a whisper, "It's about my son, Nourhan."

"What about him?"

"I'd like to know where he is; what he's doing, what he looks like. I know you don't like me to mention his name."

"You're exaggerating." Vartan tried a smile, but it wouldn't come.

"I'd like to see him at least once before I die."

Suddenly Vartan saw Rıza as vividly as if he was standing before him. And in his shadow was Nourhan, Rıza's spitting image. "I don't think that's a good idea."

"Damn it, Vartan! Always the same dumb reply! It wasn't Nourhan who persecuted our people. It wasn't Nourhan who sent you to the gallows. Nourhan is not responsible for what his father did. When will you be man enough to accept the truth?" She had raised her voice to such a pitch that heads turned to see what was going on. "I'm warning you, Vartan. I'm going over there, and I intend to find my son!"

Maro crushed out her cigarette, leapt to her feet, and headed toward the door.

Vartan closed his eyes. Rıza and Nour Kardam: both were caught and held in his mind, along with all the pain they had caused him. He couldn't move. He couldn't even call after his wife to tell her to wait for him.

Like any New Yorker, Vartan was accustomed to the city's crowded streets and shabby pavements. In a haze of mid-afternoon heat, the walk from the restaurant to his brother's store on Lower Broadway felt longer than he had anticipated. He was still in shock over Maro's unexpected explosion. Her words clamored in his head: "I'm warning you, Vartan: I intend to find my son!" He had a sudden urge to fight someone. He would explode if he didn't find some outlet for the tension inside him.

Vartan tried to convince himself that he was being ridiculous. He had always been a pig-headed, jealous husband when it came to Governor Rıza. He knew he should show some understanding. After all, Nourhan was Maro's son, regardless of who the father was. That, though, was where the entire problem began.

The heady scent of spices drifted through the open door of Noubar's store. Inside sacks of lentils, dried beans, shell beans, bulgur, rice, and couscous were piled up along the wall; dried okra, large, long, and small, hung like necklaces from the ceiling beams. Cans of olive oil and olives were stacked together in the back of the store. Next to them were the pickle barrels and Oriental spices and herbs. The smell of *bastırma*, pressed meat treated with garlic and cumin, dominated all others. The ground floor of the store, although not terribly spacious, served as a warehouse. The upper floor was used for offices: a kind of hallway, a tiny room for the secretary, a larger one for Noubar, and a cubicle where Jake had his desk and a filing cabinet.

No one was around. Vartan climbed the stairs. Hearing his footsteps in the hallway, Noubar's longtime secretary came out to meet him.

"Good to see you, sir. How are you today?"

"Just fine, thank you, Irene."

"Your brother is on the phone—he won't be long."

Before Irene had finished complaining about the uncommon heat and telling Vartan how much Jake's presence was appreciated by all the clients, Noubar walked out of his office.

"I was expecting you earlier, so we could have lunch together."

"I had lunch with Maro," Vartan said, thinking: *More or less...*

The brothers hugged, clapping each other on the back and kissing each other on both cheeks. Had Irene not known them, she would have thought that they hadn't seen each other for decades.

Noubar walked with Vartan to his office. The humid air had inflamed his chronic arthritis, and he moved slowly. Once inside the office, he said, "What's the matter, Vartan?"

"Nothing—why?"

"You look tired. Subdued."

"It must be the trip."

Noubar looked skeptical. "Come on, Vartan. What is it?"

"I told you, absolutely nothing. You tell me what's going on. It was you who wanted to speak to me."

"I called because I want to show you something."

Noubar took his pipe out of his pocket and lit it. Then he reached for the latest issue of *Time*, which was lying on his desk. He opened to the "Milestones" page and showed it to Vartan.

As Vartan read, his face furrowed into a scowl. "The son of a bitch himself! Have you told Maro about this?"

"Of course not."

"She must've seen it," Vartan said.

"What makes you say that?"

"Because she doesn't let a week go by without reading the 'Milestones' section." He threw down the magazine. "That's exactly it. And she didn't want to tell me."

Vartan saw clearly, as if thrown upon some inner screen, the face of Rıza in many guises. The elegant governor of Aïntab, kidnapped in Vartan's custody. The governor inspecting the Armenian refugee convoys heading to the Syrian Desert. The wealthy tobacco king. The grotesque, obedient bureaucrat, carrying out the horrendous instructions of the Ottoman administration. Then that unbearable image... as Maro's handsome lover. Nourhan's father.

He said, "She and I had a little argument at the restaurant."

"Oh, so that's it."

"I couldn't let her get her hopes up in vain."

"What hopes are you talking about?"

"Hopes of getting in touch with her son."

Noubar gave Vartan an odd look. "That wouldn't be a good idea."

"That's exactly what I told her. But she says she's going to Turkey to look for him."

"What!"

"And you know she's capable of doing it."

Noubar, ever compassionate, said, "In a way, you can't blame her, Vartan. Put yourself in her place. He *is* her son."

Vartan ignored Noubar's observation. He said, "I'll expose him as a war criminal. Now that he's dead I no longer have an obligation to hide his past. Our pact has expired."

Noubar regretted having shown him the obituary. "Vartan, don't waste your time on that bastard. Think of your wife, think of your family. Mind your own business."

"This *is* my business," Vartan snapped. "This is precisely what my business is all about." He smiled grimly. "We've been sizing each other up all these years, and now, too bad, the son of a bitch won't be around for our final showdown."

"You haven't got an iota of evidence."

"I have more than you think, Noubar."

"Times have changed. The evidence you have doesn't mean a thing. The empire doesn't exist anymore."

Noubar knew that following the Second World War Turkey had become a serious player in Middle Eastern politics. The Americans considered it an important ally in their open aggression against Communism and were forced to woo it with favors. Consequently, they were reluctant to take actions that might open up an old can of worms. Vartan was also aware of all that, but to admit it was equivalent to surrendering.

Vartan got up and walked over to the window overlooking the city: hundreds of buildings, hundreds of streets... But he was back in his own world: years ago, in an Anatolian town flanked by Ottoman military guards, walking toward the gallows that had been erected in the public square. Military drums beat monotonously in the background. Then the vision of a southern Anatolian mansion, a group of women wrapped in *charshafs*, and among them, the prettiest of them all, his wife Maro, with the baby son she had borne to Vartan's arch enemy, Governor Rıza Kardam.

All he was aware of was a powerful urge for revenge.

# 13

At nine-thirty p.m. the taxi stopped in front of the Waldorf Astoria. A corpulent doorman in uniform appeared, opened the door, and summoned a porter to carry the two suitcases.

Nour filled out the registration card and gave it to the petite, neatly coiffed clerk. She checked a complicated chart. "It's one of our best suites, sir," she said with a smile, and handed him the key, along with a sheaf of messages.

"Thank you."

One message was from Altan, saying to call him. The others were from Leila, who had been calling him almost hourly. Nour felt sorry for her: her ancient worries were now suddenly renewed. She was being threatened by the woman who had once usurped her husband, and that woman would now claim Nour as her own flesh and blood.

The suite was regal: a huge bedroom off a sitting room with heavy, plum-colored brocade curtains. A bowl of fruit awaited him on the Sheraton coffee table. Nour didn't care for such elegant accommodation. The Kardam Exports travel clerk had made the booking. He was hungry, but not for fruit. Before jet lag caught up with him, he wanted to go down to the restaurant and order a jumbo hamburger, with French fries and a Coke. Even in Istanbul he had frequent cravings for American junk food.

The phone rang as he was leaving. It was Altan. "The police found your witness strangled," he said.

Nour sank down on the bed. "That's really bad. He knew too much."

"They found his body in the city dump. It must have been a hired killer."

"I'm sure the Haydars are mixed up in it."

Altan agreed. "I'm worried about you. Drop the charges."

"You must be out of your mind!"

"I'm not. Be reasonable, Nour."

"I *am* reasonable. The whole thing stinks. The only problem is that the deeper I delve the more I discover things I don't want to know."

"Ramazan and Touran are getting impatient. They expect you to transfer the money in the Swiss account to the Faculty of Medicine."

"How interesting! What makes them think that Maro Balian doesn't exist? I'm the executor. According to the terms of the will, I have three months to settle it."

There was a moment's silence, then Altan's voice came back. "Listen, Nour. You wanted to know what was in the mystery drawer."

"Yes."

"I got the key from Aunt Safiyé. It's Father's memoirs: a thick leather-bound diary."

"And?"

"You won't like it. It's his war journal. It's bad."

"Has anybody else seen it?"

"No."

"I wouldn't know what to do without you, Altan. Let's talk about this another time."

"Before I forget, my wife sends her love. She says you should be careful with those blondes."

"Tell her I'm very choosy."

Altan laughed. Then he added, as an afterthought, "By the way, Aunt Leila still feels miserable. If I were you I'd treat her more gently."

"I will."

"Will you call her?"

"Eventually," Nour said, but when he hung up he said to himself: "I wish you'd leave me alone, Mother."

A strange idea crossed his mind: had it been his father's plan to send Maro not one but two presents? Not only a considerable fortune, but a son along with it, as proof of his undying love for her and, incidentally, a demonstration of how well he had brought the son up without her?

He considered ringing Esin. From the start Nour had thought of her as a pleasant interlude; yet now he found himself wondering if he really loved her... if he was ready to make a long-term commitment.

Suppose he did pursue the relationship: the family would insist that he was marrying beneath him. But it would make no difference; he would only marry the woman he loved.

He decided to call her tomorrow. Right now he really needed a hamburger.

# 14

Nour stepped aside to avoid walking over a man curled up asleep on the pavement. Despite the heat, the young man was dressed in a filthy, tattered army coat, his chest covered with layers of newspaper. Endless lines of people hurried in every direction, paying no attention. This was Manhattan.

Nour was on his way to find the law firm of Fred Goldwater & Associates. He refused to ask for directions and kept on walking, absorbing the extraordinary atmosphere.

Canal Street, the nerve center of Chinatown. There was a teeming mass of Chinese people everywhere. The windows of hundreds of tiny store fronts displayed vases, figurines, flagons of pink and green homeopathic liquids, jars stuffed with herbal remedies, roasted ducks hanging from hooks next to rows of strange-looking dried fish, toys, watches, and pens beside obscene-shaped vegetables. Cabs, trucks, and vans honked and advanced inch by inch through the constant flow of people.

Another four blocks and, crossing Little Italy, Nour was at the Bowery. The building he was looking for was a two-story warehouse, with loading bays on one side and a huge block-lettered sign on the building's façade: MARITIME CUSTOMS BROKERS AND SHIPPING. It was the right address, but there was no indication of Goldwater & Associates anywhere.

The building was drab, with an entrance next to the loading bays—an odd location and structure for a law firm, Nour thought. He climbed a narrow flight of dirty wooden steps to the top floor. He was confounded to find a cheery, open reception area with an equally pleasant woman receptionist with Hispanic features.

"May I help you, sir?"

"I'm looking for the law firm Goldwater & Associates."

"I'm sorry. There's no law firm in this building. We're customs brokers."

"This is 435 Bowery, isn't it?"

"Yes, but... '

"Would you know if there were lawyers here before?"

"It's possible," replied the woman. "I'll ask Mr. Garcia."

"Thank you."

While waiting, Nour scanned the modern open layout of the office. It must have gone through several transformations. With its concrete columns, exposed brick walls, colorful pipes, stripped supporting beams, and giant metal-framed windows, it looked more like an avant-garde art gallery than a customs brokerage.

A man in his fifties emerged from one of the offices. "How can I help you, sir? I'm Chris Garcia."

"My name is Nour Kardam. I'm looking for a law firm: Goldwater & Associates."

"The firm doesn't exist any more. They moved to the Upper East Side after we bought the building."

"When was that?"

"A long time ago, at least fifteen years. The firm disbanded after Mr. Goldwater's death. Until then they handled most of our business."

"What happened to Mr. Goldwater's associates?"

"He had two: Frank Harding and Max Sherman, nice people. Poor Frank was killed in a car accident a couple of years ago."

"And Mr. Sherman?"

"He's semi-retired, but still has an office. I don't know the address, though."

"Thanks for your help, Mr. Garcia."

"Most welcome." Garcia walked back to his office.

Nour turned to the receptionist. "Thank you for your help, miss."

"No trouble at all, sir."

Nour would look up Max Sherman and see if he knew anything about the will. He was about to hail a cab when he decided to take the subway instead.

He descended the stone stairs to the subway station. Cool, stale, earth-smelling air blew briskly along the stairwell. He waited on the dimly lit, crowded platform for the train. He spotted a telephone booth and looked through the phone book for Max Sherman: there he was, still in business, an attorney with an office on Madison Avenue.

He found a dime in his pocket and dialed the number.

Nour made his way to Madison Avenue, found the building, and took the elevator to the fourth floor. Max Sherman had agreed to squeeze Nour in between two other appointments.

Nour stepped out of the elevator onto a thickly carpeted floor. At the far end of the corridor was Sherman's office. The receptionist quickly concluded her phone conversation when she saw him enter. Nour gave her his name. "Yes, Mr. Sherman is expecting you. This way, please."

Sherman was peering at some papers through thick, black-framed glasses. He looked up as Nour entered and came quickly around the desk.

"Mr. Kardam."

"Nice of you to see me right away, Mr. Sherman."

"Please take a seat."

Fixing his cool, searching eyes on Nour, Mr. Sherman said, "I'm sorry, but I'm not really familiar with the case. But I inherited all the files of my defunct associates, and I've asked my assistant, Nicole, to see if we had anything on your father."

"Rıza Kardam. He died about a month ago."

"I'm sorry to hear that." Sherman pressed the button on the intercom. "Nicole, would you please bring me the Kardam file."

In a moment the door opened and the young woman walked in with a yellow folder.

"Mr. Kardam, this is Nicole Ripert."

"How do you do, Nicole." They shook hands.

"Nicole, can you explain to Mr. Kardam what you've been able to dig out?"

"Certainly." The young woman sat across from their client. "Apparently, Mr. Goldwater himself was Mr. Rıza Kardam's attorney," she said. "And when Goldwater died, the file was given to his associate,

Frank Harding. As Mr. Harding also passed away a couple of years ago, the file has remained, inactive, in the archives ever since." Her voice was low. "By the way, correspondence between Mr. Goldwater and Mr. Rıza Kardam was handled by another gentleman." She opened the file to verify the name, "Mr. Nurti... '

"It must be Mr. Nourettin, my father's attorney."

"That's the name."

Mr. Sherman opened the file that Nicole had just put back on his desk. "Yes, here it is: your father's last will and testament."

"May I see it, please?" Nour glanced at it briefly. "Yes, this is it. I've full responsibility for executing my father's bequest to Maro Balian. I'm a lawyer myself." He handed the document back to Mr. Sherman. "Would you please read article thirty-seven, section six, sir?"

The lawyer took it, scrutinized it, and read article thirty-seven carefully, then took out another document: a single typewritten sheet. "At the request of your father's attorney, my ex-associate checked with the Registry Office of the New York City Department of Health and found out that Mrs. Balian died six years ago."

"There's also the death certificate, in triplicate," Nicole added.

Mr. Sherman looked for them in the slender file, took one out and read it. There was a handwritten note at the bottom of the page: "Rıza Kardam insists that this is a mistake, that the certificate doesn't belong to Maro Balian."

"It's strange," said Mr. Sherman, and passed the certificate to Nour.

"Yes, my father is right; this isn't the person I'm looking for. I'm trying to locate a certain Maro Balian, whose maiden name was Artinian, not Tevonian. And she was born in Istanbul, not Izmir. Besides, this certificate doesn't even indicate her date of birth, only when she died, 12 February 1951." Nour breathed a sigh of relief.

"It's quite common not to have any date of birth for people from that part of the world," Mr. Sherman explained. "As for the rest of the mistakes, the missing information, I'm sure it's a question of oversight or even incompetence on the part of legal assistants, who often rush through files." He smiled. "They haven't all been like Nicole."

"I'll go check it myself," Nour said.

"If there's anything we can do to help you, let us know," Mr. Sherman said, giving Nour the impression that there was nothing they could possibly do for him.

"Yes, as a matter of fact there is one thing. Just a little favor."

"Of course."

"I realize you're not in a position to do anything at the moment. But please leave the mistake as it is. Don't show the file to anyone else, as I'm the official executor. I'll take care of the rest."

Sherman and his assistant both looked surprised.

Nour added, "After graduating from Harvard Law School, I practised in Chicago for some time. I'm familiar with the American legal system and procedures, but if I need any help, I'll certainly get back to you."

He knew he had impressed them with his legal background. Before leaving, he asked for a copy of the death certificate. The lawyer handed him one of the three copies from the yellow folder.

Nicole accompanied him to the door. "I'm also a graduate of Harvard Law," she said, with a spark of mischief in her eyes.

A haze of brown dust and gasoline fumes hung over the traffic. Nour walked along Madison, but it was so hot he hailed a taxi to take him the few blocks back to the hotel.

While the driver fought the traffic, Nour relaxed in the back of the cab, reflecting. All in all, it had been a successful day: at least he'd been able to confirm that the Goldwater firm didn't exist any more and had invalidated the existing death certificate. Now, with the copy in his pocket, he would be able to verify things himself. He felt a surge of energy at the thought of actually finding Maro. A picture of her was beginning to emerge, like the one in the Moroccan-bound album. He wished suddenly that he had brought that photograph with him.

The fortune he was going to pass on to her was huge. Perhaps she had no need of it. That wouldn't change anything. It was his father's wish that the money go to her, and she certainly had every right to it. Was she still as attractive as she had been in the photograph?

Did she have other children? If she did, Nour had brothers or sisters he knew nothing about. Half-brothers or half-sisters, he corrected himself, and smiled. What a thought.

# 15

While Nour was on the phone talking to Irving Leonard, a good friend and classmate from Harvard Law School, Maro and Vartan were having a heated dispute at their Exeter Street home.

"I had no idea about the announcement in *Time*." Vartan looked at Maro, whose face was crimson.

They were in the kitchen. Maro poured herself another cup of coffee from the aluminum percolator.

"For heaven's sake, say something, Maro."

"Now that you know, what does it change, Vartan? I have no words for a hard-headed fanatic like you." She had experienced the same awkward feeling toward Vartan when she returned to him after four years of captivity at Rıza Bey's mansion. Alienation; it had been a long time before she was able to touch him, let alone sleep with him. It had taken her even longer to open her heart and confess to him that she had had a baby boy by the governor and had left him behind.

"How would you feel if you were separated from your children for years? From Tomas, from Jake, from Nayiri." She had the impression she was fighting a custody battle in front of a judge.

"That's different. They're *our* children and—'

"And this one is a bastard. Is that it?" Her voice rose in pitch. "Just shut up, Vartan. Sometimes I doubt your intelligence. What do you mean, they're *our* children? Nourhan is also my child. No, not by you, but he had a loving father, regardless of his notoriety."

Vartan exploded. "A loving father! A charming, polygamous lover! A hideous criminal! A bloodthirsty Ottoman who relished the opportunity to eliminate our people. Do you want me to list more of his admirable qualities?"

She felt the rush of blood to her face. "Tell me, how would you feel if you had a child by your beloved Aroussiag, whose bed you shared, whose love you cherished, whose breasts you caressed in the middle of Anatolia during the years of our separation? And how would you feel if *you* were not allowed to see your flesh and blood?"

Vartan lapsed into dour silence, thinking about what Maro had just said. He often dreamed about the woman he had loved so dearly, about her humble cottage, her dedication, her warmth, her smile, her courage, her gruesome death at the hands of Rıza's henchman. If he hadn't been able to find Maro, he would have gone back to her. He had been able, though, to justify his relationship with her by telling himself that Aroussiag was a widow, and like Vartan she had dedicated herself to helping her people, to saving their orphans... Vartan had neither forced her into his arms nor kept her against her will. He also remembered how dreadfully painful it had been for Maro and him when they searched so desperately for their son, Tomas. He had been kidnapped and sold by Arab highwaymen to a farmer in Baghdad. Much later Tomas was saved by Swiss missionaries and sent to an orphanage in Geneva.

Vartan broke his silence. "She was an Armenian, and we had no child to complicate things."

She was an Armenian! Maro couldn't believe what she was hearing. "Whether Nour's father was Turkish or Chinese should never have kept me from seeing my own child. I'm not going to see Rıza. He's six feet under. Vartan, don't try to hide it: you don't want me to see Nourhan because you've always been jealous of Rıza. You've never been able to accept that I slept with a Turk who carried out orders to massacre our people. You wouldn't allow yourself to accept Nourhan as my son because the boy was brought up as a Muslim... as a Turk. Tell me the truth. Confess it, Vartan. Swallow your pride for a change, for your wife's sake, and say it! For Maro's sake, for whom you put your life in danger, combing Anatolia from east to west as an *oud* player in a group of fanatic dervishes. You abducted Rıza in order to liberate her from his clutches. You demonstrated Job-like patience while she overcame her guilt, her shame... I *am* that woman, Vartan! Have you forgotten your wife, Maro Balian? Have you stopped loving her? Do you call this affection? Do you see any difference between yourself and the bigots who don't even try to put aside their centuries-old hatred?"

Noubar had been right about his brother: Vartan hadn't yet been able to avenge his former enemies the way he had planned. Politics had changed; nations refused to take sides as they had done during the aftermath of the Great War. And this was consuming Vartan.

Vartan's mind was in turmoil. "A mistake once planted cannot be eradicated," he retorted. This was a quote from Aramaic, from the Talmud. "And hatred sown forcefully in a person cannot be reduced without pain."

Maro stared at him in disgust. "What bullshit you're talking! Spare me your erudite garbage." She was trembling with indignation, the grooves in the corners of her mouth and the lines on her pale face visible. Suddenly she looked all her years. She carried all the weight of her age and memory.

She looked at Vartan and suddenly imagined Rıza sitting there on the kitchen chair, grinning, smoking his cigar, and looking at her with affection.

The telephone rang, and Vartan answered.

"It's Perg—for you."

They were having problems with the printing press, Maro's assistant told her. Maro replied, "I'm feeling a little under the weather this morning. Please call the technician. I'll be there soon." She hung up and said calmly, "I'd better get ready. I have to hurry."

"We'll talk it over later, when you feel less emotional."

"I'll always feel emotional about this subject. No matter what you say or how you feel, I *am* going to see my son."

Repugnant and unthinkable as it seemed, Vartan realized that his wife was determined, and no one would be able to stop her. To his utter dismay, he also realized that he was wrong. But it was hard to get rid of his prejudices. He was on the verge of losing his wife, and the rock that had supported him and formed the one immutable element in his life might give way beneath him. Until today this thought had never occurred to him. Nourhan had remained their secret. How many times had Maro pleaded with Vartan to be brave and explain all their wrenching ventures to the children, without hiding a thing. But the children knew nothing about that part of their parents' past, except for Tomas, in whose mind Nourhan was a vague memory, faded like the colors of a garden at the end of summer. He had promised his parents not to say anything to his sisters and Jake about a brother he had been told to forget, along with the harrowing experiences of his childhood.

Nour was in a dingy basement of the New York City Health Department Archives, checking the thick, neatly bound registers that were spread out on a long table. He had already gone through the records of everyone who had died since 1947. Fortunately, the names were in alphabetical order. He had been there since nine in the morning; now it was mid-afternoon. He was glad he had called Irving Leonard, his class-mate, and asked for a quick rundown on Goldwater & Associates, Mr. Sherman, and, as a matter of curiosity, Garcia, the customs broker.

So far the records had turned up no Maro Balian. He wanted to check a bit more, to put his mind at ease. What he was doing was really a shot in the dark. If Maro was dead, she could have died anywhere. What a mess his father had landed everybody in. He lapsed briefly into reverie: what was it about love that moved people to extraordinary things? Then a wild thought crossed his mind: was it possible that Rıza had left Maro the fortune as a punishment for her jealous husband? His father was certainly capable of such twisted schemes. Nour shook off his thoughts and went to ask the archivist for more records.

The archivist was an awkward, gangly woman, close to retirement age. She seemed to have committed the registers to memory, and could rattle off so many names and dates by heart that Nour wondered if he might not indeed be in the presence of a true case of second sight.

"What can I do for you now?"

"1944 to 1947," Nour said, exhausted by the heat and the stuffiness of the room.

"Haven't you had enough yet?"

"If you want to know the truth, I've had more than enough. But I haven't yet found what I'm looking for." He loosened his tie and unbuttoned his collar.

"Hmm!" She disappeared for a minute or two and came back with another tall, thick register.

"How do you know she died in Manhattan?"

"I don't."

She looked puzzled. "This is really strange, if you'll excuse my saying so. You're looking for somebody, and you don't know if she's dead, and if she is, you don't know if she died in New York City, and if she did, you don't know what year, and even if you knew the year, you don't know where. Now that's what I call a super-duper wild-goose chase!"

"It's quite complicated," Nour said, a smile curling the corners of his lips. "I'm trying to find my mother."

That threw the woman off completely. "That's quite something. You don't even know if your own mother's dead."

"Until recently, I didn't even know I had a mother."

"That's the best one I've heard yet. Even Jesus had a mother. Lord forgive me!"

Nour chuckled all the way back to his chair.

He worked for another two and a half hours. The only Maro Balian he found was the one mentioned in the death certificate, maiden name Tevonian, born in Izmir. At least he had now eliminated the possibility of a mistake or an oversight. He checked his watch: three o'clock. It would be a waste of time to continue searching.

Five minutes later Nour walked to the requisition desk, his attaché case in one hand and his jacket in the other. The woman was still at the desk, expecting him to ask for another register.

Nour smiled. "My mother isn't dead after all. Thanks for your help."

There was a sealed envelope waiting for Nour when he got back to the hotel. It was from Irving Leonard. He opened it as he walked to the elevators.

Dear Nour,

Ronny Malewski dropped in unexpectedly and we decided to surprise you, but you weren't in. He's in town until Thursday. How about dinner tomorrow night at Chez Vidal on 57th?

As for your Goldwater & Associates, they closed offices sixteen years ago. Max Sherman, one of the partners and a good, respected attorney, is still practising, but not full-time. As for Chris Garcia, he isn't a customs broker by profession; he is, in fact, a lawyer, still under a five-year suspension. The grounds given by the judges of the New York State Appellate Division were that he had engaged in activities "not conducive to the practice of law" by offering a bribe to the DA during the Privacy Act scandal of the Department of Health, Education, and Welfare in 1951.

Irving

# 16

The clock of the church on Park Avenue struck three times. Nour's last call had been to an Oriental carpet dealer named Haïg Balian, who was out for lunch and would be back after three. Nour was tired and hungry. He lit another cigarette to dull his hunger and picked up the telephone to try the number again.

"May I speak to Mr. Balian, please?"

"Senior or junior?"

"Senior."

In a moment, a friendly voice came over the line: "Hello, Haïg Balian speaking."

"Hello, sir, my name is Nour Kardam. I've come from Istanbul, trying to locate a woman named Maro Balian, a relative of mine... " Nour knew his lines by heart after unsuccessfully repeating them a thousand times during the past forty-eight hours. He explained the reason for his call.

"The name sounds familiar. Did you say she's from Turkey?"

"Yes, originally from Istanbul." Nour's heart accelerated, hoping the rug merchant would be able to come up with the clue he had been seeking.

The man let out a long sigh. "I remember a Maro Balian from Istanbul. I met her years ago, at an AGBU dinner."

"An AGBU dinner?"

"Yes, the annual ball of the Armenian General Benevolent Union."

Nour repeated the initials, and wrote the full name down on his note pad.

"The reason I remember her," the friendly voice went on, "is that she was so beautiful roses would pale with envy if they saw her. I've never seen anyone so lovely in my whole life. Could she be the woman you're looking for?"

Sounds about right, Nour thought. He liked the man's metaphor. He dragged deeply on his cigarette. "I think she is, very likely, sir. Would you happen to know where she lives?"

"I haven't the slightest idea what happened to her."

"Would you be able to remember the year and the place of the dinner?"

"The place I remember; it was at the L.A. Hilton, but the date... Hmm, it was at least twenty years ago."

"Do you think I could find out from the AGBU?"

"Maybe. Their head office is in New York. They're in the Manhattan telephone book."

Nour was surprised that the rug dealer, after all these years, could still remember the name of a woman he had met only once.

"I commend your memory, sir," he said.

"You wouldn't say that if you'd seen her. She was an astounding beauty, and I was an eligible bachelor," he chuckled. "But much to my dismay I found out she was already married."

"I'm sure that it wasn't long before you found another beautiful woman and married her."

The man roared with laughter. "How did you guess?"

"Because you don't sound like the sort of man who's able to remain idle for very long. Many thanks, sir. You've been more than helpful."

After joking a minute longer, they both hung up. It was still a desperate chase. Nour was now more than impatient to meet Maro. The rug merchant's words explained his father's obsession with her.

Suddenly he thought of Nicole, Mr. Sherman's assistant. Nour was spending endless hours on the phone and running from one address to another in his effort to trace Maro. Time was getting short. He had prepared a list of all the Armenian churches, associations, and newspapers in New York so he could contact them, check their membership records and subscription lists, and place ads in the newspapers. He could shorten the search by asking Nicole to give him a hand. He picked up Sherman's card and dialed the number.

"Mr. Sherman's office." It was Nicole's voice.

"It's Nour Kardam."

"Yes, Mr. Kardam."

"I'm calling about your offer."

Nicole wondered a bit before grasping what Nour meant. "You mean—'

"I'd like to know if you could help me."

"I'd be happy to, Mr. Kardam."

"Thank you, I'm staying at the Waldorf. Could you meet me there? In the lobby?"

The lobby was crowded with a Pan American aircrew checking in. Nour glanced casually at the daily bulletin board. His attention was drawn at once to the word *Armenian*. Curious, he approached to read it: SATURDAY, SEPTEMBER 19: THE ARMENIAN ASSEMBLY ANNUAL DINNER DANCE. That could be the perfect occasion to see if he could find a lead. It was at that moment that he noticed a young man in a white jacket watching him.

"Mr. Kardam!" It was Nicole's voice. "I called to tell you I'd be a little late, but you weren't in your room."

Nour greeted her with a smile. "You're not late, Nicole."

She was wearing a yellow organza dress with short puffed sleeves. She looked like someone on her way to a reception. Instead they walked to the bar, where only a few lunchtime stragglers remained at that hour.

Nour came straight to the point: "I'd like you to do some investigative work for me." After a pause he added, "I'll pay you, of course."

It was the last thing on Nicole's mind. "It's not necessary. We're from the same alma mater."

"I appreciate that, but business is business." Nour preferred a professional relationship to a friendly arrangement that had the potential to develop into a complicated liaison.

"I've made a long list of Armenian associations, churches, and newspapers that I'd like you to contact. See if you can locate Maro Balian or anyone who knows anything about her. I'll take half the list and you take the other half. At the end of the day we can meet and compare notes."

"You don't waste a second, do you?"

"Not when I'm working to a deadline."

There was something innocent about her manners. She had big brown eyes and a sweet smile. Nour could hardly fail to find her likable.

"You look worried about something, Mr. Kardam."

He didn't reply, only shifted in his chair and stared off sideways. She followed his gaze to where two women sat at a table near the bar. He said, in a whisper. "I want you to take a look at the tall, skinny man sitting behind you at the bar, next to those two women. He's wearing a white jacket. Do it discreetly."

Nicole dropped her pack of cigarettes onto the floor beside her and bent down to pick it up, carefully examining the man with the thin moustache.

"He's watching you."

"He must be a reporter."

Nicole couldn't understand why a reporter would be following Nour Kardam.

At that moment Nour heard his name. He was being paged.

"Excuse me for a second." He got up and headed for the front desk.

"There's an overseas call for you, Mr. Kardam. You can take it in the second booth."

It was Leila. "You don't even answer your mother's messages any more." She put special emphasis on the words "your mother."

Nour sighed heavily. "I beg you to leave me alone, Mother. I'm in no mind to speak to you, do you understand?"

Leila wasn't listening. "Did you find your mother?" she asked in a helpless voice.

He gritted his teeth. "I'll let you know when I do."

Leila could no longer stand his terse remarks. "Nour, if that woman ever takes you away from me, I'll take her to court," she said grimly. "She has no right over you. Let a judge decide who your mother is."

She must be losing her mind, Nour thought. "Listen to me, Mother. This is not a custody case. No one's taking me away from you. Your imagination is running wild."

Nour's words gave her enough reason for new tears.

"I promise I'll call you as soon as I find Maro Balian. Then we'll talk things over."

"I hope you never find her," she said vengefully. "I hope she's dead and stays dead."

Nour hung up. He walked back to the bar, deeply upset.

Nicole noticed the agonized expression on his face, but she didn't dare to ask him about it. Instead she said, "I've never been to Istanbul."

Nour was aware that she was trying to divert his attention from his problems. "It's like New York without the skyscrapers—as dirty and noisy as Manhattan, two thousand years older than all the cities in the United States. It's an exotic, open-air museum filled with riches and poverty."

"And the sultanas, the harems... "

"They're imprisoned in history." Nour grinned briefly. "Your name's French, isn't it?"

"I *am* French. I was born in Grenoble. My parents came to the United States when I was eight years old."

"Do you speak French?"

"Of course. I'm a U.S. citizen, but deep down I'm very French."

Nour approved with a nod. "Stay that way. I love France. I love the language. My father was a great Francophile and studied in Paris."

"Then you must speak French."

"Would you like to test me?" he asked in French. Then, assuming a serious air, he went on in English: "Tell me, Nicole, the file I saw in the office—was it the only file on the Kardams or are there others?"

Nicole's eyes narrowed slightly. It was evident that she hadn't anticipated such a question. "Is that what you wanted to know?" She sounded upset.

It wasn't Nour's habit to beat around the bush. "Since that's what I asked, the answer is yes. But that's not why I called you. Never mind. Just forget it."

Nicole's cheeks flushed. "Did you really want me to help you find Mrs. Balian, or did you want me for more complicated tasks?"

"Sorry for giving the wrong impression, but it's the lawyer in me, and I'm stuck with a complex case. Please forgive me."

Nicole flushed even redder. She was like Nour: she liked things to be out in the open. If she hadn't been attracted to him from the moment she laid eyes on him, she would have walked away right then and there. "Before I begin working for you," she said, "we should sort out our differences. You forget that I work for somebody else, and my position obliges me to respect privacy."

Nour realized that he had been rash; lowering his voice, he said, "I'm sorry. Rest assured, I didn't call you to stick my nose into confidential files, if that's what you're thinking."

Nicole wasn't entirely convinced, but she acknowledged the apology with a nod. Nour kept looking at her. She would do a good job, he thought. She was articulate, professional, and probably sincere, and she wouldn't accept being bullied by anyone. Nicole, on the other hand, was busy persuading herself not to be upset. Nour seemed to be powerful and competitive, and was probably materially successful. Working with him could be a feather in her cap.

Suddenly Nour said, "He's leaving." He excused himself and walked over to talk to the bartender. "I think I met the guy who just left at a journalists' convention some years ago. You don't happen to know his name, do you?"

"I know he's a reporter, but I'm afraid I don't know his name."

Nour returned to the table. "I was right, the guy's a reporter."

Nicole smiled. "Are you a celebrity or something?"

"Fat chance."

# 17

*A*fter his quarrel with Maro in the kitchen on that Tuesday morning, Vartan had a feeling of doom, a feeling that nothing would ever be the same again.

They had tried to iron out their differences about Maro's relentless determination to find Nour. In spite of Vartan's surprising concession—to write first to friends in Turkey to find out more about Rıza's youngest son—Maro categorically rejected the idea. Vartan was trying to buy time to dissuade her gradually, she thought. Their children had noticed a sudden change in their parents, who had become aloof, cheerless, and seemingly unable to communicate with each other. When they phoned their parents, the conversations didn't last long: the usual "how are you" followed by a condensed version of small talk. How unusual for Maro and Vartan not to talk about the upcoming Armenian Assembly dinner dance. When Nayiri asked her mother about it, Maro said, "I guess we'll have to go, but to tell you the truth I don't really feel like seeing those same faces again, year in year out."

"But Mother, I have to know so I can get ready."

"If I know you, Nayiri, you can get ready at the drop of a hat."

This was a very odd reply, coming from her mother. She would usually begin preparations for such important social functions a month in advance. Who was going to wear what? Who would escort her daughters? Who was Jake taking to the dance? It was even stranger for Maro to show such apathy when her husband was to be honored at this year's annual dinner, in recognition of his long years of service to the community and to his people.

"What's wrong?" Araxi asked her mother on the phone.

"What's the matter with you two?" Magda asked when she dropped in at the newspaper.

"They're behaving like teenagers. I can't believe it," Jake said to Nayiri.
"It's happened before."
"This time it's different."

Vartan was thoughtful when he returned home that evening. Maro
was there already. They talked to each other sparingly. He had stayed
away from the *Free Press* in order to avoid embarrassing clashes with his
wife in front of the staff.

Now that Maro had made up her mind to search for her son, she
showed no sign of hostility toward Vartan. She was neither warm nor
cold. She mostly ignored him and insisted on being left alone. Deep
down, however, she was badly hurt.

She was in the living room watching the rain fall on the front lawn
when Vartan came in. His expression was a touching mixture of regret
and hope: to overcome his uncontrollable hatred for the Kardams and
make up for his harsh remarks. How could he win back Maro's heart
when she was plagued so deeply?

Vartan knew silence wasn't a solution. He remembered that, as a
child, whenever something happened that he didn't want to hear or see
he would rush to his bedroom and hide under the blanket. Now, just
as in the old days, muteness had become his shelter, his eiderdown. He
hesitated, wondering whether he should say exactly what was on his
mind. Finally, he said, "It's ridiculous, Maro, that we can't talk like two
adults who have loved each other all these years." He wasn't expecting
much of a response. "Do what you want," he said. "Handle it the way
you think is right. I won't interfere. I've said everything I had to say."

"Thanks for permitting me do what I want." She couldn't conceal
the sarcasm in her voice.

Vartan frowned. "You misunderstand me."

"Maybe I don't want to understand you any more."

The remark stabbed him in the heart. "It's up to you, Maro. I want
to assure you that I still care for you."

Maro doubted she could say the same about him. "If you're worried
about Saturday evening, I'll be at the dinner. I don't want the children
to think their parents are incapable of overcoming their conflicts.

"All right," Vartan muttered. He didn't have to lie to himself. He was well aware that the cause of the friction between them was a personal issue—a large fragment of an old principle—just as when he had accepted being led to the gallows instead of agreeing to praise the Ottoman deportation scheme, write against his own people, and, in return, save both his family and his own life. Years hadn't changed Vartan, apart from his physical strength.

And Maro was well aware of that.

After leaving Nour, Nicole visited the offices of the three Armenian political parties that were still active in the diaspora. Their offices weren't terribly impressive. They had no permanent staff. Their premises consisted of one or two rooms in the back of a store or a community hall, and the staff was mainly volunteer workers. They suggested that Nicole place an ad in the party news bulletins, but unfortunately the majority of these papers appeared only once a month.

One of the young volunteers at one headquarters asked her to have lunch with him. He was a skinny, bespectacled law student called Vrezh. Nicole agreed: why have lunch alone?

They headed off to a pizzeria, an unpretentious little place, with half a dozen booths ranged along one wall. As they were about to enter, Nicole spotted the reporter from the Waldorf bar.

She and Vrezh grabbed the first available booth. The reporter, she noted, took the last booth, which had just been vacated, and sat facing them. Nicole leaned across the table and said to Vrezh, "I want to ask you a favor. The man in the last booth is a reporter. After we leave this place I'd like you to keep an eye on him and tell me what he does."

"Great! A clandestine mission. What's going on?"

"I need the information for an upcoming trial." Vrezh raised his eyebrows, but that was all she said. "Of course, I'll pay you for your time. Call me and let me know everything you find out." Nicole wrote her telephone number on a scrap of paper.

Vrezh shrugged his shoulders. "Whatever you say."

# 18

*A*s it neared eight o'clock, cars were beginning to clutter the hotel entrance on Park Avenue. Extra doormen ran back and forth between the automobiles and the onlookers crowding the pavement. Maro stepped from one of the taxis, followed by Vartan, and they progressed across the lower hall. The president of the organizing committee, Dr. Archie Gregory, and his wife, Nancy, were waiting for them at the foot of the double staircase leading to the ballroom. In spite of her misgivings about attending the dinner, Maro had done her utmost to look more stylish than ever—perhaps a deliberate attempt to raise her husband's jealousy to its peak.

On entering the ballroom, Maro paused to examine the place. It was impressive with its crystal chandeliers, plaster sconces, tall mirrors, and tables elegantly set with English bone china and classic silverware. Before being asked to step into the receiving line, Vartan took Archie aside and asked him if it would be possible to spare them the agony of greeting everyone individually.

"Don't be silly, Vartan. It's your night."

Unable to convince him, Vartan got in line with Maro: in the middle stood the Armenian Primate of the Eastern Diocese of America; on his right was the guest of honor of the evening, the mayor of New York City, with his wife; on his left was Maro, then the president of the Armenian Assembly, his wife and, at the end of the line, Dr. and Mrs. Gregory.

Although the doors to the ballroom were wide open, the receiving line slowed down the flow of the crowd at the entrance. The guests didn't consider this a delay. On the contrary, it was part of the ritual. It gave the women the opportunity to exhibit their expensive gowns and jewelry while exchanging the latest news with friends.

Vartan and Maro's children mingled with the crowd. This was the one and only Armenian event that they attended, and they saluted people and joked cheerfully. Her sisters were more subdued, but Nayiri was completely caught up in the excitement. Suddenly she noticed a commotion, and nudged her fiancé, Greg, who was standing next to her. "Look! Something's going on. Do you see the tall guy in the gray suit? The security stopped him. There's some kind of problem." She stepped away from Greg. "I'll go see what it's all about."

Greg took her arm and said, "Stay where you are, Nayiri. Don't ask for trouble." She shook it off.

The presence of government people among the invited guests had necessitated a few additional security men, both inside and outside the ballroom. Nayiri tried to listen in on the loud conversation between the guard and the young man, but the buzz in the hall made it difficult. She heard the security guard say, "Hold on, there. You can't go in. You don't have an invitation. Besides, it's a black-tie affair."

"My name is Nour Kardam. I'm a guest at the hotel. I need to talk with a few people here."

"This is a testimonial dinner, sir."

"I know that, and I don't give a damn. This will only take a moment."

Nayiri missed the rest of the argument when a nearby group broke into loud laughter, but the man in the gray suit turned angrily on his heel and left. What was his name? Nour Kar-something. His face, his authoritative manner, even his anger, which had a kind of fervor about it, fascinated her. She couldn't take her eyes off him.

On his way back to the lobby, Nour noticed her staring at him. He stopped and stared back. Nayiri blushed and turned her head. When she looked again, he was gone.

Greg came up beside her. "I'll be back in a second," she said.

"Where are you going?"

"The ladies. Do you mind?"

She walked toward the lobby to see if she could spot him again. There he was, waiting for the elevators. She accelerated her steps and then stopped. She had no reason to follow this stranger, yet she felt like talking to him. She wanted to know what the problem was, to see if she could help. This wouldn't be the first time she'd meddled in other people's affairs. But she stayed back and watched him from a distance. The grandeur of the crowded lobby disappeared, and she was in an unfamiliar world of alien sensations. The feeling grew even stronger as she walked back to the ballroom. Nour... and his family name was Kar... Something. It couldn't be Armenian, or English. "Whatever... I don't care," she muttered, loud enough for the man standing nearby to hear her words.

Greg was waiting for her, worried. "I was beginning to wonder what had happened to you."

It was just the reaction Nayiri had expected. "I fell into the toilet bowl," she said irritably, and returned with him to the ballroom.

It was a moving experience for Vartan and Maro as their children came along the receiving line. As she kissed her mother, Nayiri whispered, "Careful, Mom, His Eminence seems more interested in your boobs than in the guests." Maro frowned disapprovingly, and Nayiri burst into a giggle.

The dinner, with its elaborate menu and impeccable service, went as planned. Vartan and Maro were seated at the head table, chatting with their hosts. The archbishop was talking to Vartan, but the latter wasn't really following his words. Scanning the people in the room, Vartan saw his past flicker before his eyes like a silent movie. Many years had gone by since they had walked down the gangplank of *The Star of the Peloponnesus* at Ellis Island, with Tomas in knee breeches. Now, years later, right before Vartan's eyes, here was that wide-eyed little boy, a well-respected surgeon, sitting beside his wife, Anna, with the rest of Vartan's children, his brother Noubar, and his sister-in-law.

"I hope you agree with our decision, Vartan?" asked the archbishop.

"Certainly, Your Eminence," Vartan replied, forcing himself to remember what the priest had been talking about.

As the reception reached its climax, the band stopped playing. The master of ceremonies, a young disc jockey from WQXR, called upon the archbishop to speak first. The old clergyman began in English with an impressive introduction in praise of Vartan's commitment to public life, then switched to Armenian, and finished in English again, emphasizing how much he agreed with the Assembly's choice to honor Vartan, who had devoted body and soul to his people and his nation.

The next speaker was the mayor, a seasoned politician. He began with the standard opening phrases: "It is a great honor for me to have been invited here tonight to give my impressions of one of the Armenian-American community's most distinguished members. He's known as the guru of political science in academic circles. The person we're honoring tonight is a scholar, an indefatigable social advocate, and the Armenian bard. Outside our circles he is also known for equally superlative qualities, including his ethnic activism..."

The mayor's last two words raised immediate cheers. Vartan looked at Maro and saw that her eyes were proudly fixed on the speaker in order to avoid looking at her husband. The mayor kept his speech short, to everyone's delight, and before closing he wished Vartan Armen Godspeed in the future.

At last, the MC announced cheerfully, "Ladies and gentlemen, our man of the evening, Vartan Armen."

Everybody in the great hall burst into spontaneous applause. Vartan rose from his seat and walked to the podium. A dozen or so flashbulbs went off like a wall of strobe lights, momentarily blinding him. He was nervous, not so much on account of the large crowd and the occasion, but because the past week with Maro had been so difficult.

"*Srpazan Hayr*, Your Eminence, Your worship O'Donnell, distinguished guests, and very dear friends." His throat went drier. He reached for the glass on the lectern and took a gulp of water. For a second he heard his wife saying, "No one can deny me the right to see my son." He took another gulp. "I stand before you now" —he cleared his throat— "more nervous than when I made my first speech, decades ago, in the Turkish National Assembly during the last days of the Ottoman Empire. At that time, my friend and savior, Halit Pasha, noticing my anxiety, dropped his files on the floor to distract attention from me. He said loudly, 'How clumsy of me to interrupt the maiden speech of our newly elected MP. Excuse me, honorable colleague, please carry on.'"

The brief burst of laughter and applause calmed Vartan's nerves.

"More than thirty years ago," he continued, "I came to this country, accompanied by my wife and son. We had fled persecution and injustice. America received us not as wealthy immigrants capable of creating jobs for the population, but as individuals hungry for a just society."

The applause continued for several seconds.

Vartan had no notes in front of him. He gazed at his audience. "We tried to make a success of our lives," he continued, explaining America's unique place among the global community of nations. Finally, he embarked on his pet subject: politics. "It is unfortunate that there is a growing tendency among the American population to think of politics as a less than honorable, even unworthy profession. On the contrary, it should remain a high calling. Nowadays politics is reduced to a witch-hunt, denying tolerance or the acceptance of differences." In the audience, some cheered and some remained silent. "I don't blame our youth," Vartan went on, "who consider politics a career for power-starved people who haven't been successful in their own professions. How can I alter this view when they speak the truth? I realize that my articles have often been criticized because I don't agree with the policies of our present administration. But all the same, I intend to continue pursuing the same line of thought with my pen and with my voice."

Nobody had expected a political speech from Vartan aimed at Washington, but many in the audience, especially Maro and Nayiri, appreciated what they heard, especially his caustic remarks about McCarthyism, which he said had spread like a plague, victimizing the American elite and intellectuals with preposterous accusations.

The speech he gave wasn't exactly the one he had prepared. He changed it on the spur of the moment, when he began talking about the horrendous events of the past. Had they not been the result of rotten, prejudiced politics?

He brought his speech to an end, saying, "I thank each one of you sincerely, from the bottom of my heart, for having bestowed on me this great honor and giving me the opportunity to express my opinion on a current problem so close to my heart." He turned to the archbishop: "Please, Father, pray for us, pray for humanity, that we may learn tolerance and greater understanding for one another."

Vartan stepped back from the lectern, and the entire room rose to its feet. Those at the head table joined the others in the ballroom in a standing ovation.

When Vartan returned to the table, Maro leaned over. "You were brilliant," she said, and couldn't resist adding, "I wish you were like that all the time!"

# 19

ater that evening, Nour and Nicole had supper at Da Marcello, a small place in the heart of Little Italy. Like Nour, Nicole was downcast. All her contacts with the Armenian associations had been unsuccessful, except for her little adventure with Vrezh, the young law student. She told Nour about her chance encounter with the reporter at the pizza parlor.

"Vrezh called me back. He followed the reporter. His name is Howard Lehman, and he works for the *New York Times*."

"I knew it." Nour said grimly. He said nothing more, and she bombarded him with questions. Why was he so obsessed with finding Maro? Who was she?

All he would say was that it was about an inheritance, and that she should continue her efforts, then quickly changed the subject. They had a pleasant dinner, talking mostly about their law school backgrounds. Nour didn't mention the case again.

When Nour woke up the next morning, the sheets were damp with sweat, and the clock on his night table read nine-thirty. He had had a night of bad dreams —dreams that, if he told Leila about them, she would say augured a threat. For her, dreams were messages from Allah— portents of things to come.

Lying in bed, Nour remembered the frustration of his argument with the security man, and then he recalled Nayiri's face, the strange familiarity of her bewitching eyes. Among the hundreds of faces gathered outside the ballroom hers was the only one that he recalled distinctly.

He opened the *New York Times* and checked the classified section first. His announcement was there. Then he looked at the headlines.

The markets were quiet. The last contingent of Turkish troops was now returning home from Korea. Senator Joseph McCarthy was still making news with his rabid hallucinations that Communists were wrecking American democracy. Then he spotted the name Howard Lehman, at the head of a gossip column: scandalous relationships of celebrities, a bit of rumor, and then a small headline: "Turkish millionaire visiting New York," followed by a titillating tidbit:

> The millionaire playboy Nour Kardam does not bother to hide his frequent rendezvous with Nicole Ripert, a young lawyer who works at Max Sherman's Madison Avenue law firm. Mr. Sherman has denied speculations that the two are romantically involved.

"Son of a bitch!" Nour threw down the paper in disgust. If the Turkish press ever caught a whiff of this, the newspapers would be ablaze with front-page headlines. He picked up the phone and dialed Nicole's number.

"I don't understand. You're the millionaire?"

"I guess you could say that."

"A playboy too?"

"Well—sort of. Whatever that means."

"I can't believe it. Why did you hide all this from me?"

"What did you expect me to do, hoist my family crest?"

"I don't know, I'm confused." Most of all, the slim hope she had entertained of seducing Nour had now disappeared. The man was a major-league player.

"You should sue Lehman," she said.

"I'd be playing straight into his hands."

"What, then?"

What indeed? There was nothing he could do. "I'd tell him to go screw himself," Nour said angrily, and then immediately apologized for his language.

# 20

The success of his speech at the Waldorf, its echoes in the Armenian press, the congratulatory telegrams, letters, and cards—none of this improved their relationship. Maro and Vartan lived like strangers under the same roof. At the office their conversation was reduced to professional exchanges about editorials, news items, and galley proofs. Vartan's efforts to make Maro feel better didn't mollify her. After years of silence in the face of Vartan's refusal to acknowledge Nour's existence, Maro was now in total revolt. She had tried for so long to jolt her husband out of his prejudices about that part of her past. She had appealed to his reason, but her attempts had only driven him further into his shell.

It was a week later, 9:30 in the evening. Vartan wasn't home yet. The table she had set for two remained untouched. She was going up to her bedroom to watch the evening news when she heard the front door open and Vartan walked in.

"I stayed late to finish the weekend editorial," he said.

"Have you eaten?"

"No, but I'm not hungry. Wait," he said, as she turned back to the stairs. "I wanted to talk to you this afternoon, but you left early."

"I had a few things to do." Maro continued upstairs, but suddenly stood motionless. She had decided before Vartan came home to break their silence. At dinner she would talk to him; she would once more do her best to convince him. His late homecoming had changed her strategy, and she had felt relieved, but now she knew she had to speak.

"I phoned Gaziantep," she said

"You *what?*"

"Gaziantep. The Kardams."

He ran his hand nervously through his hair. "And?"

"I had Safiyé on the phone, but she hung up on me."

He smothered the temptation to say it was what she deserved. "How did you get their number?"

"Through cousin Lucie in Istanbul. She managed to get it through the tobacco company."

"I can't believe you've done this, Maro."

"But I have."

Vartan sighed, resigned. "I understand that you have to know. But please—give me some time," he said. "I'll see if I can trace where your son is, what he's doing, whether he's married or has any children."

"It's too late, Vartan," she said. "I'm going to Istanbul. I bought my ticket today."

This jolted him. "Have you told the children?"

"I didn't tell them the reason for the trip. They aren't blind. They see what's going on. But I just told them that I need a change."

"A change!" Vartan raised his voice.

"I'll tell them the truth when I get back. I've asked Nayiri to give you a hand at the paper until then. Perg will take care of the administration work. The editorials are your responsibility—that is, if you want the paper to continue as before."

"For heavens sake, Maro! If I want the paper to continue—if I want our years of sweat and sacrifice to go on—if I want our ideals to carry on, to pass the flame to the next generation! What's happened to you, Maro? Have you gone mad?" Vartan said all this in a long single string of words, rising in a crescendo.

"Nayiri understands the situation. She thought it would be a good thing for you and me to be separated for a while."

"Nayiri, Nayiri. Like mother, like daughter!"

"Don't tell me you're against her because she agrees with me!"

"I'd better shut my mouth, Maro. Everything I say will be misunderstood."

"I'm leaving in a week."

Vartan knew she didn't have the money for the airfare. As if guessing what was in his mind, she said, "I pawned my pearl necklace to pay for the ticket. I'll redeem it when I get back, as soon as I save up the money."

She had the talent to handle all sorts of difficulties. She had worked miracles to keep the newspaper going; she had pulled the family out of many hardships, especially on the frequent occasions when Nayiri had become involved in rash affairs. But she couldn't believe that she was able to lie so naturally.

As expected, the principal Istanbul dailies were full of gossipy speculation about Nour's rendezvous with Nicole. Although Altan was displeased, he blamed the scoop-hungry reporters. Esin was another story. When he called her with an explanation, she refused to believe it. She kept asking, "But who is she?"

"She's a legal assistant who is familiar with Maro's file. She's helping me find her. If you don't want to believe me, it's your choice, Esin."

Jealousy stabbed her; the mere idea of breaking up brought a rush of misery. She didn't want to end their conversation on a sour note, but she had her pride. His absence had given her enough time to think about their relationship. She knew that she loved Nour—truly loved him. Would she be able to turn a deaf ear to all the gossip circling around a man who would always be in the public eye?

Her last words to him were, "I'm glad you're in New York. It'll give us both time to think."

A brief storm during the night had cleared the air. The wind blew gently through the towering skyscrapers. After two weeks of intensive probing, Nour was on his way to the *Armenian Free Press*. It was Nicole who had brought it to his attention that he had placed an ad in a minor monthly but had overlooked the Armenian daily with a respectable circulation.

As the cab reached the Third Avenue El line, the crowd got thicker and the potholes in the street larger. If it was not for the train running overhead and the English signs on the stores, Nour could imagine himself in a busy commercial section of Istanbul. Merchants bellowed out jingles to attract customers, some of them even going so far as to stop passers-by on the street. Porters carried cardboard cases and fruit crates, trucks dropped off bundles of magazines and newspapers. A couple of winos harassed onlookers for nickels and dimes.

"Are you sure this is the place?" Nour asked when the driver stopped the car.

"Yes siree, that's exactly it!" He pointed to the narrow entrance next to the pharmacy.

There were no signs, not even a building number, except for the one on the drug store. Nour paid the cabby generously.

"Thank you, thank you very much, sir. Have a good day."

Nour went up a flight of warped stairs and opened the door reluctantly. He had a sudden feeling that Maro might be dead and all his efforts futile. He was confronted by huge piles of newspapers stacked to the ceiling. Behind two oak desks sat a young man and an older woman. Both were busy typing. A large map of historic Armenia was stuck on the wall. A door on the left gave access to the printing shop, and he could hear the constant clicking of the press. The door on the right was half-open.

The woman whose desk was closest to where Nour was standing raised her head, took off her glasses, and asked if she could be of any help.

"I'd like to place an ad. It's in English. I'd appreciate it if you'd be kind enough to translate it for me."

"Of course. May I see the text?"

Nour took out a folded sheet of Waldorf Astoria stationery and handed it to her. She put on her glasses, read it slowly, and pursed her lips. She cast a questioning glance at Nour, and reread the text:

Maro Balian (née Tevonian), born in Istanbul on 14 September 1895, is urgently sought in connection with the settlement of a legacy. Anyone who knows the whereabouts of or has any information concerning the above-mentioned person, please get in touch with Nour Kardam at the Waldorf Astoria, New York City. Tel. CO3-4592. Collect calls will be accepted.

"Excuse me for a minute," she said and headed for the half-open door.

"May I ask what's wrong, ma'am?"

"Nothing. I'll be right back."

Nour lost patience. He was remembering some of his recent experiences with Armenian zealots. They refused to talk to him as soon as they discovered he was a Turk. His annoyance apparent, he said,

"Listen, miss, I'm trying to place an ad for the umpteenth time to help one of your compatriots. Yes, I *am* a Turk: a respectable, educated Turk, a lawyer, not a criminal."

Just then, Nayiri came to the door. She said, "Please, come in. Perhaps I can help you."

It was the mysterious woman he had been unable to erase from his mind. "I'm Nour Kardam," he said, and, after a brief hesitation, added, "We met at the Waldorf, if I'm not mistaken."

Nour took the announcement from Perg. Her eyes held a mischievous glint. "Indeed we did!" Yes: Kardam, she thought. That was the name she hadn't been able to catch. "My name is Nayiri Armen," she said. "I'm replacing my mother while she's away. She's the editor of the paper. "

"I'm a lawyer from Istanbul. I'm supposed to find the person in question."

Nayiri looked at the ad and read it, puzzled. "You're a lawyer from Turkey?"

"You make it sound like a disease."

She blushed. "Of course not. I just—"

He broke in. "If I don't get any results before my departure, my legal assistant will place another ad with an Istanbul address and telephone number."

Nayiri struggled with the situation. A lawyer from Turkey looking for her mother... and a pending legacy!

Unable to suppress her curiosity she asked, "Can you tell me any more about this?"

"I'm sorry, but I'm not at liberty to discuss any details."

"I understand," Nayiri said, not sure that she did.

Nayiri was both intrigued and worried. Wasn't it strange that after so many years her mother had suddenly decided to leave for Istanbul— and now this ad? She would not tell her father about it. She knew his prejudices regarding the Turks. She said: "I'll take care of the announcement myself. It'll appear in tomorrow's paper."

"Thank you, Nayiri." He pronounced her name better than all the Americans around her.

Nayiri thought for a moment. She needed to know where he was staying. "Sometimes people call us instead of calling the number in the announcement," she said. "If anyone does, can we reach you at the Waldorf?"

"Yes, of course."

"And how much longer will you be in New York?"

"I wish I knew, probably not much longer."

There was a silence between them. Nayiri knew exactly what she would like to do, but inviting a total stranger to lunch wasn't like choosing a cake in a pastry shop. Then he surprised her: "Could we have dinner tonight? Maybe you could give me a few ideas to speed up my search for Mrs. Balian."

# 21

*A*fter Nour left, Nayiri charted her strategy. Her primary goal was to bring her mother and Nour Kardam together. She told Perg not to mention the ad to her father for the time being. As for her mother, Nayiri would tell her eventually, but not right away. She preferred to find out more first. She knew that, if her father knew she was having dinner with a Turkish lawyer, it would turn his agony into torment, but at that moment nothing mattered but her chance to be with the mysterious green-eyed stranger.

Suddenly she remembered the dinner party she and Greg were invited to that evening. She reflected for a second, then picked up the phone and dialed Greg's number.

"Yes, Nayiri? What's up?"

"I have a terrible headache, Greg. I'd rather stay home tonight, if you don't mind."

"You might feel better later."

She knew it had been a poor excuse, but his reply still irritated her. She reached for a cigarette. "I don't think I will," she said calmly. "It's better if you call your friends and tell them we'll make it some other time. I'm really not feeling well at all."

When Nayiri's jeep came to a halt in front of the Waldorf, the doorman didn't exactly know what to do: he could hardly walk up and open the door because there was none. It wasn't every day that a young, well-dressed woman hopped out of an army jeep with the top down and tossed him the keys so he could have her World War Two relic parked.

Nayiri chuckled at the expression on his face. "I'd appreciate it if you could have it washed, too."

By the time the doorman reacted to her remark, she was already at the hotel entrance. Heads turned to look at her as she swept up the marble stairs. Something odd was happening to her. She didn't bother to try to understand it, but she liked it. She felt like a married woman who was about to cheat on her husband. Greg was a distant figure on the far periphery of her conscience.

"Good evening, Nayiri."

Nour's voice brought her back to reality. She had carefully worked out a sophisticated opening remark, but when she saw him she forgot what it was. "Hi, Nour! I'm so glad to see you again!"

He took her hand. "I'm glad to see you too."

"I don't think the doorman has ever seen an army jeep before. He looked at me as if I was a martian."

Nour laughed. "You drive an army jeep?"

"Is it a crime?"

"Not at all, I love it."

"And what do you drive?"

"A GMC truck," he said, and they laughed. "I thought we could eat here at the hotel, if it's okay with you."

"That's fine."

Nayiri was glad she had dressed up. She wore a tight-fitting light-blue dress, and she had pinned her favorite green glass brooch onto one of the lapels, a gift from her parents on her eighteenth birthday. The only makeup she wore was a touch of coral lipstick, but she had swept her hair up and caught it with a gold barrette. Nour was struck by her radiance and, again, the nagging familiarity that he couldn't place.

On the way to their table Nayiri said, "Your ad will appear tomorrow." How easy it was, once you told one lie, to tell another. "Any further luck today with your search?"

Nour regaled her with stories of his afternoon adventures at the Armenian Diocese of America. He transformed his experience with them into amusing anecdotes. "The moment I said I was from Turkey, they wanted to see my *yataghan*."

"That doesn't really surprise me. They're a bunch of fanatics!"

"But nothing came of it. I'm really hoping the ad will help."

When he asked about her family, Nayiri told him they had come to America in 1922, started the paper, and added four more children to the one they already had. She left out a few details in order not to raise suspicion. Nour wanted to know more about how they had left the old country, under what kind of circumstances, and whether they had been deported.

"I don't have a big family, no grandmothers, no grandfathers, no aunts—" And suddenly she stopped. She hesitated to say that many of them had disappeared during the Turkish massacres.

Nour, noticing her discomfort, changed the subject to a more personal topic: Nayiri herself.

"I'm an ordinary American girl with Armenian parents, a lot of joy and a lot of trouble to my family—or so they say." She chuckled. "I'm finishing an M.A. in clinical psychology at Columbia. And I'm engaged to an Armenian-American lawyer..."

"Oh?" Nour tried not to sound as interested as in fact he was. "I hope I didn't take you away from him this evening."

"As a matter of fact, you did," she said, blushing, then quickly asked about his own family. All she knew about him was that he was a bachelor and a prosperous lawyer.

"I have a battalion of sisters and brothers," he said. "But all of them half."

"How come?"

"Because my father had three wives." Three wives and an Armenian mistress, he thought, and the unusual fate of having a heart attack while screwing one of his wives.

"And did the wives have many husbands?" Nayiri asked with a smile.

He answered with another smile, and the case was closed.

In spite of his evasive reply to her question that morning, Nayiri repeated it in a different version. "Is this a simple case you're working on or a complicated inheritance battle?"

"If you ask me, I'd say it's as simple as one two three. But certain people related to the case are making it as complicated as a hydrogen bomb."

She kept her expression bland. "How can it be complicated if this woman is the rightful heir?"

Nour shrugged. "You know, Nayiri, if people could only feel as powerful from making others happy as they do from keeping them continuously miserable, it would be a much better world."

She didn't know exactly what he was alluding to, but she persisted. "And if the woman involved is not miserable?"

"So much the better, but—that's not really what I mean. I don't think I can explain it."

"Can you tell me where the money comes from?"

He looked at her curiously. "I'm sorry, I'm not in a position to discuss such details. I hope you don't mind."

She blushed again, and said, "Well, I have a couple of ideas about how you might find the woman. If I were you I'd place the same ad in the two Armenian dailies in Istanbul: *Jamanak* and *Marmara*, with your address and telephone number in Istanbul. There's a large Armenian community there. They might know her whereabouts. After all, she's originally from that city. She might even have relatives or friends there. Just an idea." The real reason for her suggestion was to obtain Nour's Istanbul address and telephone number. "I'll send telexes to the two newspapers right away if you think it's worth trying."

"I think it's a very good idea."

Nayiri was pleased. She stared at him, trying to understand her fascination. It wasn't just that he was a handsome man. Although he was quiet, she sensed that he was someone with an unquenchable spirit—a joyous soul. She warned herself not to exaggerate, not to assume too much, as she tended to do on meeting people for the first time, immediately labeling them with extreme qualities, features, and peculiarities. But something drew her to him, and she couldn't deny it.

Nour too was attracted to Nayiri. Since their meeting at the *Free Press* office, he had been comparing her with Esin, asking himself how much Esin meant to him, how committed he felt. Conclusion: he liked her, he found her beautiful and intelligent, and he felt good when she was with him. But now here he was, absolutely magnetized by a young American-Armenian woman he'd only just met, but had the feeling he'd seen her many times before. "I'm glad you were taking your mother's place," Nour said. "Otherwise I wouldn't have met you."

"Call it coincidence. It's not often that I work in the office. Call it fate."

What else could she call it to justify her wilful acceptance of his sudden invitation without thinking twice, her lie to her fiancé, just for the sake of going out with a total stranger—and a Turk? To waylay her guilt, she reminded herself that Nour wasn't responsible for his people's past, regardless of what her father had preached all these years. As for going out with a stranger while she was engaged to Greg, maybe she needed a break from being with someone so conventional. Besides, she wasn't jumping into bed with the guy. Was she?

When they left, Nayiri's jeep was brought to the hotel entrance.

"You shouldn't be driving alone at this hour of the evening," Nour said.

"Why not? I'm used to it. Besides, who else would want to drive this old jalopy?"

"I would, if you let me."

She chuckled, then suddenly put her arms around him. She meant it to be just a hug, but he embraced her tightly, and kissed her.

She pushed him away, whispering, "I don't know what's happening to me." Then she got into the jeep and drove off.

*Part* three

# 22

Gaziantep. It was noon. Altan mounted his Arabian thoroughbred and started down the dirt road that ran through the network of embankments. He was heading home. The sun was high in the sky and shining directly on the vast cotton fields. This was the ancient caravan route between Aïntab and Aleppo. It passed through the ruins of the old caravanserai, which stood like blasted ramparts in the middle of the plateau. Red irises, running rampant, stood in striking contrast to its black walls and shattered lines. The plantation plots were always deserted during these hours of scalding heat. Altan, big and squarely built, in a white cotton shirt, a pair of beige riding pants, brown boots, and a wide-brimmed straw hat, looked even bigger and taller than usual.

As he rode along the dusty pathway, the irises blurred his vision into a sea of red. Everywhere he looked was red; even the mansion at the far end of the fields gleamed in brilliant scarlet and crimson. The tents of a small Kurdish nomad tribe were pitched beside the road. Despite the scorching sun, fires burned in front of them. The flames made the women, in their elaborate headgear, sweat profusely. They were cooking and boiling milk for yogurt, preparing lunch in time for their men's return from the fields.

In the distance Altan spotted Memo, his servant, galloping toward him. As he approached his master, Memo brought the horse first to a trot and then to a complete halt.

"*Efendi*, your brother Nour Bey called. He wants you to call him back immediately."

"Thank you, Memo."

The urgency of the message upset Altan. Nour would never have asked Memo to travel at this hour of the day, under the smoldering sun, if he didn't have something urgent to say. Altan tucked his head down and rode back to the plantation building he had just passed, where there was a phone.

Nour's words confirmed Altan's concerns. "There's something fishy going on here. Do you remember Nicole, the assistant I hired?"

"How could I forget? The whole of Istanbul is talking about her."

"This is no time for jokes, Altan."

"I'm not joking."

"Okay, listen to me. Nicole told me about this guy, Jonathan Ebenezer. He had a meeting with that fucking reporter, Lehman. He owns a company called Independent Tobacco Limited, a fairly new outfit. It has taken over Import Tobacco Limited. Do you remember that the son of a bitch Metin shipped high-grade tobacco to a new client?"

"Of course."

"According to my lawyer friend, Irving Leonard, Import Tobacco ran a drug trafficking network some years ago. A lot of people were arrested after a year-long investigation. When the business was shut down, Ebenezer bought it. It means that whatever we exported, tobacco or any shit, went to them. Maybe Haydar and Özkoul were right when they accused Father of drug trafficking."

"Take it easy, Nour! Stop it! Don't say this until you make sure what you're saying is right."

"I will, believe me. Touran and Ramazan must have been part of the whole scheme. You remember how passionately they defended Metin."

"Nour, before you go further with this, think of the family's reputation. Think of the press."

"Altan, I—"

But just then the line was cut, and their conversation abruptly ended.

On Irving Leonard's recommendation, Nour put Charles Burto on Ebenezer's trail. Leonard said Burto was a real professional when it came to digging out tough inside information, with private channels to the highest levels of the police force and the lowest criminals of the city. "Which, in New York, often amount to the same thing," Irving commented.

For the moment, nobody seemed to know anything about Ebenezer: he was a total mystery. When Nour called him and told him the situation, Burto said, "Don't worry, he won't be a mystery for long."

A few days later, Nour met the detective in his office, and Burto was less confident. "No one knows this guy's real nationality," he told him. "He has dealt with Jews, Levantines, Greeks, Chinese... all in the so-called import-export business. All phantom companies set up to sell, to liquidate, today under one name, tomorrow under another, all of them legitimate but all of them borderline. The more you investigate them, the deeper you drown."

Nour was disheartened. "I must know who this man is, where he comes from, what he did before he bought the company."

Burto spread his hands. "It's frustrating. One address takes you to another. You go through all the docks and warehouses and you end up where you started. You can call them, write to them, but you can never meet any of them in the flesh to pry out information. In this goddam city, you need a lot of weird contacts, and I've got them. But it's not easy to trap a man who doesn't want to be found and who's got plenty of money to prevent it. But I promise I'll find him."

# 23

$\mathcal{E}$ ver since her dinner with Nour, Nayiri had been unable to get him off her mind. When she ate her solitary breakfast in her tiny apartment in the West 90s, she pretended he was sitting there opposite her. He was asking about her exams. She was pouring him a second cup of coffee as they traded sections of the daily paper. If she stopped to look at the clothes in a nearby boutique, where they were playing disco hits over the sound system, she imagined dancing with Nour at one of Manhattan's premier nightclubs. In bed at night she pretended he was there beside her, playing with the long strands of her hair spread out over the pillow, slowly unfastening the top buttons of her short nightgown, sliding the fabric over her knees, up around her hips, making love to her, slowly, in time to the music pouring out of the radio in the kitchen.

She was embarrassed by her own thoughts.

She hadn't called him since their dinner at the Waldorf, nor had Nour called her. As for Greg, she refused to see him, giving no excuses.

The fact that Nayiri hadn't told Nour about her mother and hadn't informed her parents about him put her in a quandary. She didn't want to shorten his stay in New York, either.

A few days later, on an impulse, she decided to go to the Waldorf and see him.

In the hotel lobby a film crew was assembling banks of spotlights, putting up a camera crane, embellishing the lobby with tropical flowers to create a lush and exotic setting. On his way to his room, Nour paused to watch them, then spotted Nayiri, standing just inside the door.

He went up to her. "What a surprise!"

"I just wanted to see you." Beneath her large-brimmed straw hat, her smile was hesitant.

"I wanted to see you too," he said. "I was going to call you."

"Don't bullshit me."

"I mean it, Nayiri, but unfortunately you can't always shove things aside and—. Let's sit down." They found a sofa and sat beside each other.

Nour took her hand. "How have you been?"

Nayiri shrugged. "All right. Working hard. There's still been no news about the Balian woman. How about you?"

"Nothing." Only three people had answered the ad Nour had placed in the *Times*: an older woman claiming she was a relative who said Maro had died a long time ago; then a second woman, exactly the same age as Maro, who wasn't even sure where Istanbul was; and finally a man who insisted that he was Maro Balian's husband and that she had died during the deportations. "And time is running short," he said. "There are pressing matters at home. I'm afraid I'll have to leave for Istanbul before I find her, possibly at the end of the week."

Nayiri was stricken. "A few more days might make all the difference," she said. "Sometimes people don't read the announcements; then a friend sees the ad and informs them. And that takes time."

He sighed. "It's very troubling."

"This case is more important to you than it seems."

He looked at her sharply. "Yes, it is."

"But you still don't want to talk about it—right?"

"Right."

Instead of disappointment, she felt only determination. "Then tell me more about yourself."

"I've told you everything you need to know."

"Tell me about your childhood, about your girlfriend."

"I had a happy childhood, I have a girlfriend."

She smiled. "That's all? What about your parents? What do they do?"

"Am I being interviewed?" Then, with another sigh, he said, "My father died a month ago and my mother lives in Gaziantep."

Nayiri shot an inquisitive glance at him. Antep sounded like Aïntab, where her mother had been sheltered during the deportation years.

"And those half-brothers and half-sisters? What about them?"

"I have a dozen brothers, a dozen sisters, a couple of mothers, and a bunch of wives, four to be exact—as many as my religion permits. Are you satisfied?"

She blushed. "I know. I'm too inquisitive. I'm just always so curious about people. I didn't mean to pester you."

The truth was, she hardly knew what she was saying. She was almost overwhelmed not only by insatiable curiosity but by sheer physical longing. She felt she had known him forever, yet there was so much about him that was a mystery to her. She felt she had fallen in love with him blindly, instantly, by the elevators in this same lobby, even before they had spoken to each other.

To her surprise, he took her hand. "Listen. I have an idea."

"What?"

He smiled. "Let's go up to my room."

She stood naked before him in the dimness while he undressed. Then he kissed her, his hands gliding over her body. They fell back together onto the bed. He moved his lips to her breasts, then to her mouth again, and she spread her legs, encircling him tightly. He looked into her eyes, his face taut with lust, and began to move slowly, gently at first, then with greater urgency. Nayiri forgot any traces of guilt she might have had.

When he was lying beside her, she looked into his eyes. "A confession," she said, smiling. "Of all the men I've known, you're the first to make me feel that way."

"Nayiri." He touched her cheek. "I think I'm falling in love with you."

# 24

Nayiri was troubled. Telling Nour that Maro was her mother would complicate things; telling Vartan about Nour was altogether another problem. She refused to try to imagine how her father would react.

Nayiri had become entirely obsessed with Nour. She had asked Greg to leave her alone for a while, saying she was going through a difficult period.

"Is it your exams, Nayiri?"

"No."

"What is it then?"

"Just some family problems."

"What kind of family problems?"

"Greg, please stop asking me," she said. "I'll tell you when I feel like it," and she hung up on him.

Nayiri opened the door so the young waiter could push the breakfast cart in. She called Nour to come out of the shower before the eggs were cold. She poured herself a cup of coffee and started skimming through the pages of the *New York Times*. She stopped dead at Lehman's gossip column. There was her photo: she was in her cotton dress, gazing into Nour's eyes! The picture had been taken in the Waldorf lobby. She was part of a brief round-up of social events and high society gossip.

Playboy-millionaire Nour Kardam has recently been spending a lot of time with Nayiri Armen, a graduate student in psychology at Columbia. Kardam, a lawyer and international business magnate, is one of the most eligible bachelors in town. This new woman in his life is bound to make some eyes turn very green...

She gulped her coffee as if it was some acerbic drug. A millionaire playboy? A business magnate? Not just a lawyer from Istanbul?

Nour stepped out of the bathroom and Nayiri pushed the page before him.

He took it and immediately threw it down. "That bastard again." Never before had he experienced such deliberate intrusions into his personal life. "Sorry, Nayiri, but it's not the first time."

She was unprepared for such a response. "What do you expect me to do? Rejoice because it isn't the first time?"

"Please, Nayiri. I'm angrier than you are. This will set the Turkish press ablaze within hours."

"Their eligible bachelor, Nour Kardam, a millionaire and a Muslim Turk, is going out with an Armenian-American, and—"

"Stop it, please," he interrupted her. "You're being melodramatic."

"Damn it, Nour, why didn't you tell me earlier that you were such a big shot?"

No reply.

"I must confess, in a way it pleases me. That reporter has made me a celebrity."

"Cut it out, Nayiri."

Nayiri thought back to Nour's words: "It's not the first time," and cursed the gnawing feeling of jealousy that followed.

Nayiri was at the *Free Press* by ten-thirty. Maro hadn't yet arrived. She was relieved. There were messages from her brother Jake and her sister Araxi. She was looking for Araxi's business phone number in Maro's daybook when the telephone rang.

"It's me, Nayiri."

"Hi, Mom. I was just going to call you." She pushed the door shut with her foot.

"Nayiri. You've become an overnight celebrity."

Nayiri said nothing.

"Has your father seen it?"

"I don't know. I haven't seen him for the last couple of days."

"Damn it, where is he? Can't he keep an eye on his daughter, who seems to have lost her mind?"

"I'm sorry, Mom. I was going to call you and tell you about Nour. He's a lawyer from Istanbul. He's looking for you to settle an inheritance."

"What kind of gibberish is that? Are you making up an excuse to cover up your disgraceful, lunatic behavior?"

Nayiri began to cry quietly.

"Stop blubbering like an imbecile and tell me what this is all about."

"I'm sorry, Mom." She lost control and let out several loud sobs, but she managed to say, "Somebody has left you a lot of money."

There was a pause, and then her mother said, "I'll be there right away; stay where you are."

Maro took off her coat, placed her papers on the desk, and sat down at her desk. She hadn't said a word yet. Nayiri sat in a chair, trying to appear nonchalant, but the jerking of her foot betrayed her nervousness.

"I'm sorry, Mom: I never thought there would be such complications. I was going to phone you. He's a lawyer, visiting here from Istanbul. He's looking for a Maro Balian to settle an inheritance."

"Do you take me for a fool?"

"It's the truth, Mom."

"And that's why you're in the newspaper?"

"Wait, let me finish before you get all worked up. The paper— Okay, this isn't good. This man is someone important where he comes from. That's why a reporter follows him around with a camera."

"Someone important," Maro repeated. "My God!"

"Someone has left a huge sum of money to a woman named Maro Balian, your original name. The inheritance has to be settled as soon as possible; otherwise the money will go to others. Mr. Kardam came to the press to place an ad in Armenian forsaking about Maro Balian. I didn't tell him it was you. I wanted to speak to you about it first. In the meantime, he invited me to dinner. We went to the Waldorf. And that's where the reporter took the picture." Nayiri spoke so fast that she was out of breath.

Maro felt shaky. Her son was in New York!

"What does he look like, this Mr. Kardam... Is this a good picture of him?"

"He looks even better than the picture. In his thirties, handsome, dark, slender, graceful. Green eyes. You should see his eyes! Never have I seen a man with such green eyes."

I have, thought Maro. Nourhan, with his father's eyes. She hid her face in her hands.

"Are you all right, Mom?"

Maro raised her head, biting her lip. Nayiri didn't quite understand. Something much more serious than seeing her picture in the newspaper was bothering her mother.

Maro said, "Listen to me carefully. This isn't easy to say..." After a moment of hesitation she confessed, "Nour Kardam is my son."

"Your *what*?"

"My son. It's true. It's a very long story. I don't really know how to tell it."

Nayiri shut her eyes. She heard her mother's voice from miles away. "You already know part of it. As for the rest, your father and I kept it secret. It all began on the road between Sivas and Aïntab." She went on telling her daughter of the past, decades old, centuries old. There were moments when she couldn't continue. She choked with emotion. She restarted. She relived the past with such intensity that she was incapable of shedding tears. She wasn't addressing Nayiri anymore. She was confessing her past to herself. Only the noise of the traffic on Third Avenue disturbed the quietness of her voice.

"He held my arms tightly and stretched me on the ground and I didn't fight. I didn't struggle; he didn't force me; I gave myself to him. Rıza Bey. I spent a horrible night wavering between shame and hope. I wanted to die. And when the sun hid behind the magnolias in the garden, I put on my most elegant dress and waited for him again, praying to the saints that he hadn't forgotten me."

Nayiri listened. She was terrified of interrupting. Then, when Maro stopped, Nayiri leaned over the desk, grabbed Maro's hands, and held them tightly.

Vartan pushed the door open without knocking, and entered, holding the *Times* away from his body with two fingers, as if to avoid contaminating his hands. He dropped it on the desk.

"I didn't expect to find the two of you together."

"I've told her," Maro said. "She knows everything."

Vartan blew up. All Armenians were betrayed, time after time, their ancestral lands looted, their graves desecrated, the diaspora humiliated, and the family honor defiled. How could he ever forgive such a disgraceful act? To date a Turk, and what's more a Turk who was the son of Rıza Kardam, the repugnant governor of Aïntab. His wife's ravisher, lover...

Her own brother!

Vartan began to stutter, consumed by the sudden tide of indignation and jealousy.

Maro said quietly, "That's enough."

Vartan pulled himself together and realized that he was in Maro's office, facing his wife and daughter. "You," he said, pointing at Nayiri. "You're not my daughter anymore."

Her eyes blazed. The awful knowledge of who Nour was made her reckless. What mattered now? "I'm not your daughter? So be it. I want you to know that you're not dignified enough to be my father!"

Nayiri's words hit him in the face. Vartan walked out of the office.

They were at Aldo's. The bar was always deserted during the day. They sat in a back booth. Nayiri sipped the whisky sour she had ordered. She had been crying all morning, and there were dark circles under her eyes.

"I found the woman," she said.

Nour laughed. "Are you serious?"

"I know who Maro Balian is, and I know where you can meet her."

Nour still wasn't able to believe her. "That was fast."

"Not really." Nayiri drained her glass. "I'd like another drink."

Nour signaled the waiter, and when Nayiri's drink was in front of her she said, "Maro Balian is my mother."

He stared at her, stunned. "Is that true?"

"Yes. I wasn't truthful with you before, but now I'm telling you the absolute truth. "

"I can't follow you, Nayiri. Are you after a share of the inheritance? Or are you just making fun of me?"

She held up her hand. "Don't say anything, and let me explain. And stop insulting me. When I'm finished you can judge me."

He lit a cigarette. "Go on."

"My family changed their name when they came to the States. At that time my father was on the wanted list of the Turkish government. He changed Balian to Armen. I fell in love with you at first sight when you came to the press—you must have seen that. The only thing that mattered was to delay your return to Turkey. That's why I didn't say a thing: to keep you looking for her. I couldn't give a shit about the money, legacy, bank accounts... All that mattered to me was you. I don't regret a thing. I spent the happiest hours of my life with you." Over-whelmed, Nayiri paused before continuing. "My story isn't finished. My mother learned of Rıza Bey's death from *Time* magazine. When she saw your name this morning in the *New York Times*, she realized that you were his son, and—"

Nour cut her off. "Who told you my father was called *Rıza Bey*?" His heart was pounding.

"That's how my mother referred to him."

Only Maro would have called him that. It was proof enough. He had at last found her, the legal heir, his true mother, Maro Balian. He was so moved, it still hadn't sunk in that the woman whose name was Maro was Nayiri's mother as well as his. Suddenly he froze. He looked at Nayiri and shook his head. "No. No. No. It's not true. You're my sister!"

"Half-sister," Nayiri corrected.

Nour shrank into himself like a wounded animal. "But why, Nayiri, why didn't you tell me?"

"I didn't know who you were. I didn't know you existed. My mother told me this morning."

They stared at each other. "Nour," Nayiri said in a small voice.

He touched her hand, then stood up quickly. "I'll see you later. I need to be alone for a while."

# 25

Nour picked up the phone almost before it rang. It was Nayiri. "Mother would like you to come down to the press this afternoon, at five-thirty. The staff will be gone by then."

"You're sure she wants to see me?"

"Christ, Nour! You've looked for her all these weeks and now you hesitate."

"I know. I'm just nervous."

"She's nervous too, even more shaken than you."

"What do you call her, you American children? Mama? Mother? Or what?"

"I call her Mom, the others Mama and sometimes *Mayrig*. I'm sure she doesn't give a damn what you call her."

"Who else will be there?"

"Just me."

Nour climbed the steps to the *Free Press* office. All he felt was panic. The harrowing events of the past few weeks had changed him from a confident, determined lawyer to a nervous, distrusting son. He pushed the door open.

Nayiri was waiting for him in the hallway.

"Where is she?" Nour asked.

"In her office. Nour, please try to understand..." Nayiri stopped. They heard somebody calling, "Young man! Is that you?" Maro, too agitated to call him "my son," stood outside the door of her office.

She wore a plain print dress, and her hair was drawn back in a chignon. She was older, she seemed smaller, but he recalled the sepia photo in the album and remembered her huge dark eyes, which hadn't changed. He stood motionless.

Maro recognized the slight dimple in his right cheek, his determined chin. In her mind his face grew younger and younger, until finally she beheld the terrified face of the baby snatched from her arms—crying and beseeching her not to leave him.

Nour managed to say one word: "Mother!"

Maro ran to him and covered her son's face with her tears and kisses. They remained in each other's arms for a good minute.

In tears, Nayiri looked on anxiously. It was horrible. Revolting. He was only a half-brother, but it was incest all the same. And how was she supposed to stop loving him?

Maro stepped back from Nour, put her arm around Nayiri, led her into the office. "Come. Both of you. We have to talk."

Nour felt both exhilarated and as wretched as Nayiri. A mother he had only seen in a photo. Maro had been internalized in his mind the moment he had seen the sepia image in his grandmother's Moroccan-bound album for the first time. Now she was standing in the flesh before him, as well as his half-sister, whom he had made love to the night before—the only woman he had ever fallen in love with so quickly, so unexpectedly, so profoundly.

Nayiri sat on the edge of a chair. "Mom, why didn't you tell us that you had another son?

"I told you, your father wouldn't let me."

"Father! A fanatic. A bigoted zealot."

"Stop it, Nayiri." Maro was embarrassed.

"He's responsible for this mess."

"So am I," Maro repeated sadly. She looked at Nour. "As soon as I read your father's obituary, I knew it was time to see my son."

"Who prevented you from seeing me?"

"In the beginning, it was your father. Then it was my husband—no, it was me. I thought it would be better not to cause you any pain. For years I prayed for a miracle and now, thank God, the miracle has happened," Maro said.

"We both owe it to my father."

With a murmur of disbelief she asked, "Why?"

"I came looking for you because he included you in his will. He left you a sizeable legacy. He appointed me his executor. When the will was read, my brothers Touran and Ramazan made quite a stink about it. Their remarks made me suspect that Leila wasn't my natural mother."

"Leila," Maro said softly. Her name roused a thousand bittersweet memories for Maro.

"After you left, Father asked Leila to become my mother. I found this out from your young chambermaid, Vartouhi."

"Dear sweet Vartouhi!"

"She had once told me about the photograph that was taken on the day of your arrival in Antep. She said you were a houseguest, but never revealed your name until recently."

"Your father had the photographer make a copy for me. I still have it." Maro took out her handkerchief and wiped away her tears.

"I arrived in the States a few weeks ago to find you. I was ready to go back, and then I met Nayiri. She put my ad in the paper."

Maro glanced at her daughter with forgiveness. "Your efforts were unsuccessful because my name isn't Balian any more, it's Armen. It was changed for stupid political reasons."

"I hope you still have the papers to prove that Balian was your original name."

Maro was amused. "Did you say you're a lawyer?"

"Yes, ma'am."

"I can see that." She was proud. "Yes, I still have the papers, but please don't call me ma'am. Why don't you just call me Maro and keep on calling Leila mother. I know she'd love that. She must be terribly upset by all this. Rıza's death, then me resurfacing in her life."

"Yes, she's very upset. You probably know how emotional she is."

"And Safiyé and Makboulé?" Maro remembered their names as if it had all happened only yesterday.

"Aunt Safiyé has gotten old..."

"She must still be as serene and wise as ever," Maro said.

"She is. Everyone loves her. And Aunt Makboulé died a few years ago."

"I'm so sorry. I remember I used to teach her French. She even wanted me to teach her how to play the piano."

Nour thought Maro must have suffered immensely, and yet she seemed to remember so much with fondness: the place where she had been held against her will, a long, harrowing period of exile from her loved ones. He wanted to tell her more of her inheritance, but he was reluctant to bring it up. It would be like talking shop at a wedding reception. Nevertheless, time was running short, and she deserved to know.

"Maro," he said, addressing her by her first name with a great deal of effort, "my father left you the contents of one of his Swiss bank accounts. It is a great deal of money."

Maro stared at him, speechless. How could she benefit from such extravagant generosity from a person who had carried out orders to annihilate her people? Who had tried to take her by force? Who had deprived her of her child? And yet this was also a man who had truly loved her—worshipped her.

Nour sat quietly, waiting for Maro's reaction. Finally, she said, "Your father, bless his soul, was a man of extremes: extremely passionate, extremely intelligent, extremely handsome, and extremely generous. You're the spitting image of him." Then, reminding Nour of what Leila had said, she qualified her statement with, "But even more handsome."

Nour grinned. "Thank you."

"As I was saying, there's no doubt that he was a man of excesses. He had an obsession with power and wealth. I hope, Nour, you won't be offended if I refuse his legacy."

"What? Why?" Nour was staggered. "It seems you're also a woman of extremes."

"Not at all; it's just a matter of principle."

"Any good reason?"

"Because, although I loved your father, I refused to express it. I refused even to let him know I cared for him, refused to marry him. I already had a husband. It was my duty to go back to him." She looked at him, her eyes very sad. "I can't take his money. I'd like *you* to have it."

"Thank you very much, but I don't *need* money."

"My dear son, God has given me a modest life. I don't think money could add more to what I've already found. I've rediscovered my Nourhan. By the way, may I call you by your Armenian name?"

"Call me anything that pleases you. After all I'm an Armenian-Turk-ish-Christian-Muslim." Even Nayiri was glad to have something to laugh at.

"If you refuse," Nour said, "the money will go to the Faculty of Medicine in Istanbul."

"So? An excellent charity."

Nour got to his feet. "I will never give my brothers Ramazan and Touran that satisfaction."

Maro grasped the situation and thought for a minute. "Then do this: transfer the money into a trust fund in my name. In due course, we'll think about what to do with it."

Nour was relieved. He kissed Maro on both cheeks. "Thank you!"

Neither Maro nor Nour had noticed the autumnal dusk that had darkened the room. Nayiri turned on the light.

"I'm through with the paper for today," Maro said. "I don't know about you two, but I'm getting hungry."

"Let's go out and eat," Nour said. "My treat."

# 26

*A*ltan had never heard his brother speak with such exuberance before.

"I found her. I talked with her. Can you imagine?"

"I know two people in particular who'll be delighted to hear the news. What's she like? Tell me!"

"A beautiful woman. Attractive. Likeable. Pleasant. The moment you see her you want to get to know her. I'm meeting the rest of the family tomorrow night. Maro is cooking dinner for us all."

"Well! That sounds very good. Congratulations."

"The incredible thing is that the girl in the picture is her daughter."

"You mean the lawyer?"

"No, no, the other one."

Altan raised his eyes to the sky. He could no longer follow his brother's escapades. "What other one?"

"Nayiri, Maro's daughter."

"You line up your damned conquests with such speed that we can't keep track of them." Then suddenly it dawned on him: "You slept with your sister?"

Nour's heart sank. "How could I know we were related?"

"Well, I suppose it's okay then."

"It's not okay. You don't understand." Nour was shouting, unable to control himself.

"Don't shout! I hear you," Altan shouted back.

"This will explode louder than a bomb when it hits the Turkish newspapers."

"You're right. It will." Altan was wondering whose palms he would have to grease to stifle the press. "Your thoughtless conduct ruin your reputation. Or else cost us a damn fortune. Or both."

"Stop it."

"And the legacy?"

"That's complicated too. I'll tell you next time," Nour said, and hung up.

Nour kept Maro company in the kitchen while they waited for the others to arrive. With a rare clumsiness, he tried to help her prepare dinner.

"It seems that a man can't be two things at the same time," Maro said jokingly. "Lawyer and cook, for example."

"My education kept boys out of the kitchen. This was always a place reserved for women. The real power that builds and conquers empires always inhabits territories forbidden to men."

Maro glanced at Nour to see if he was serious or joking. He wore a somber expression, but his eyes were twinkling.

"I didn't have the kind of power you're talking about over your father."

"But you remained in his heart until the end of his life."

Maro was quiet.

"And how about Vartan?" Nour asked. "Will I see him tonight?"

"I don't think so. Vartan is a wounded man. In Turkey he was a pharmacist, against his will, just to satisfy his father. He entered politics as if he was entering a religious order. To defend the oppressed and promote human rights, to live with dignity as the right of every human being—that's his credo. Vartan has suffered and still suffers from the unjust martyrdom of his people. I'm afraid he'll never change. He'll stay the same to the end of his days."

"But you love him very much."

Maro ignored the remark. "The children politely put up with their father's lectures, but not one of them will take over his mission. And that hurts him."

"And Tomas?"

"He rubbed shoulders with death during the expulsion. Then the Kardam brothers treated him as an alien, as a bastard, until he was kidnapped by Kurdish brigands. He spent his childhood first as the slave of an Iranian farmer and then in an orphanage in Geneva, with other uprooted children.

148

We found him in the end and brought him to another world. We're all proud of him. He's a good doctor. His wife is American, the daughter of a Protestant pastor. They have two very sweet children."

"Is he coming tonight?"

"I don't know. He's been going through some kind of crisis recently, a mid-life crisis, perhaps. He doesn't want to see his sisters and brother. He can't stand his father anymore. Occasionally he opens up to me. Tomas is like a bottle thrown into the sea with an outdated message inside that he wants to forget."

"I'm afraid I'll awaken bad memories."

"If he shows up tonight, it'll mean that he's ready to face his people again. Ah—I hear Nayiri's jeep. The first to arrive. Will you go open the door?"

He welcomed his sister with a chaste kiss on the cheek.

"You're here already?"

"I slept here last night." Nour grinned.

"And I slept at the Waldorf."

Jake's warm, welcoming words eased Nour's apprehension. Jake talked to him like an old friend, about the Manhattan climate, his latest acquisitions for his uncle's wholesale grocery business, an article they'd both read in the *Financial Times*. They might have been picking up a discussion they had begun the previous week.

Araxi signalled her arrival by crying, "Where is he? Where is he?" until she found Nour with Jake. She pushed her old brother aside to scrutinize her new one.

"God, he's good-looking!" She kissed him on both cheeks without letting go of his hands. "I'm Araxi, the wallflower of the family. Single by conviction but also from lack of opportunity. Welcome, brother! I see that they haven't even offered you a drink. They're useless. I'll leave you with poor Jake and join the women in the kitchen."

"Don't worry. She's always like that," Jake said. "She's good-natured. She wears her heart on her sleeve. She helps everybody, to compensate for her loneliness. She's right. I should have gotten you a drink."

"That's all right, I'll wait. Araxi reminds me of my sister Shahané.

She devotes all her time to women's causes, which isn't an easy task back home. Those two would make excellent friends."

"Our other sister, Magda, should be here soon. She's not a bad girl, but she takes herself too seriously and has fixed opinions about almost everything. She pretends to be an intellectual and tries to prolong her adolescence by dressing like a college girl."

Nour suddenly felt overwhelmed. "I feel like I'm disturbing your family."

"Which is now also yours, don't forget. The family has a new member, and we must make room for you at the table. In certain families they set an extra place for a last-minute guest. Those families have more foresight than we do." Jake put his hand on Nour's shoulder. "You're one of us."

"Thanks, Jake, I'd like to be. Maro already means a lot to me."

"Call her mother. It won't bother me."

"I still have a bit of trouble with that."

Magda matched Jake's description: a nervous, chubby schoolgirl with granny glasses, pleated blue skirt, and white blouse. Interested but prudent, kept her distance, scrutinizing Nour as if he were an exotic pet. She mumbled a few conventional greetings and, without saying another word, walked out to the kitchen to join her mother and sisters.

Jake came back carrying two glasses. "I think we could both use a drink. Our Magda isn't terribly warm tonight. Anything new or foreign troubles her. It's a pity that her husband wasn't invited. He's a funny guy. Roberto is Italian, a big guy; he runs a pharmacy. Besides pasta, his main obsession is clocks."

Maro and her daughters joined them in the living room while they waited for Tomas to arrive. Nayiri was quiet and had kept a certain distance from Nour since her arrival.

"It's high time you told us everything, Mother. Why have you concealed the existence of this handsome brother all this time?" asked Araxi.

"Half-brother," Magda corrected.

"What a silly thing to say," Araxi snapped. "What difference does it make? Please go on, Mother."

Maro began to explain her past as she had done in her office, keeping one eye on the clock. Was Tomas going to stay away again tonight?

"But why did you keep it a secret?"

The usual question and the usual reply: "Your father wanted me to."

"How did you manage to find us, Nour?" Jake asked, to distract everybody.

"A few days ago I tried to get in touch with some people who were attending a banquet at the Waldorf. If I'm not mistaken, it was a special occasion: for an Armenian writer, or historian or somebody."

"What a coincidence," blurted Magda. "It was Dad. The dinner was in his honor."

Nour was surprised. "What a strange coincidence! Well, the security people wouldn't let me get close. But I noticed a pair of eyes staring at me."

Nayiri let out a loud laugh.

"Don't tell me it was you, Nayiri?" Maro said. "You didn't tell me that."

"Yes, it was me. There's a lot I haven't told you yet."

"How come you never tried to get in touch with your mother before?" asked Araxi.

"I was completely unaware that I had a mother in the States. My father died recently and—"

"Nourhan," blared Maro, "let's save the rest until Tomas gets here."

"We may wait forever," said Nayiri.

"He'll be here," Maro said. "Let's wait a little longer."

When Tomas arrived he looked tired. He kissed his mother, brother, and sisters and extended his hand to Nour. "Sorry for being so late. Isn't Dad here?"

"Aren't we enough?" Araxi asked.

"We should all be together on an occasion like this," replied Tomas. "But I understand."

"Understand what?" asked Nayiri.

"His absence. It's not every day that a brother falls from the sky. A wife's long-lost son. I suppose Mother let you all in on the secrets." Tomas stopped. "Excuse me, Nour. That wasn't aimed at you, just at what you represent. One can't choose one's family. If we could, no doubt you wouldn't be among us today." He put his head in his hands, then looked up and tried to smile. "Forget my harsh words. I'm tactless. I'm just trying to explain my father's absence."

Nour didn't know what to say. Tomas's remarks troubled him, but he didn't reply. Of course, Tomas was right. Why should Tomas welcome him? Or Vartan?

Maro raised her hand to interrupt on behalf of all her children. "Tomas has said what's in his heart. We're not gathered for a debate. Nourhan is going to tell us what brought him to New York."

After a brief silence, "My father, Rıza Kardam, left a large sum of money to your mother," Nour said.

Unable to restrain her curiosity, Araxi asked what everybody was dying to find out: "A large sum? How much is a large sum?"

"One million two hundred thousand dollars."

Astonishment froze their faces. Magda clapped her hands until she noticed the disapproving glares of her sisters.

"Unbelievable," said Jake. "I didn't think you'd crossed the Atlantic for a few dollars, but such a huge sum!"

"You can use it to buy a new couch, Mom; the springs on this one are digging into our bums," Araxi joked.

"May I ask where this money comes from?" Tomas asked.

"My family is wealthy," Nour said simply. "My father had vast plantations of tea, cotton, and tobacco."

"I've heard that a lot of landowners had no hesitation about growing poppies for the opium trade. Does this money also come from trafficking?"

Anger shone in Nour's eyes. "Turkey is one of the biggest poppy producers in the world, but my family have never been drug traffickers," he replied.

Tomas's question had discomfited Maro. To cover her embarrassment, she clapped her hands and said, "So. Shall I accept the legacy or not?"

They all began to express their opinions at the same time.

Maro stopped them. "I don't want an answer today. Think about it, and talk it over with your spouses."

"This money is a huge responsibility," Jake said. "No doubt you've talked about it with Dad."

"His reply was short," Maro said. "'If you accept it, I'll leave you.'"

There was another stunned silence.

"Another important detail you should know," Nour said. "If Maro refuses the legacy, it'll be transferred to the University of Istanbul for medical research. None of it will go back to our family."

Sipping his drink, Nour observed them all with detachment as the hubbub swelled to a crescendo.

The following day he and Nayiri were at Sarto's, an obscure bar up near Columbia, not far from her apartment.

"Sometimes I ask myself what I'm really doing." Nour said.

"You're screwing your sister."

"Half-sister."

"Don't be a wise guy."

Nour remained quiet for a second. "We'll always be together, Nayiri."

"It's not that simple."

"Simple or not, I'm *you*, Nayiri. And you're me."

"Nour." Nayiri took a deep breath. "I love you more than you can imagine. I'd like to marry the man I love so much, bear his children."

The word *marry* hit Nour in the face. "That's impossible."

"Damn it, Nour, I know that. I'm not stupid."

"You don't have to tell me that." Nour smiled. "You know—there was this moment in Maro's office the other day. My thoughts suddenly turned to my father. As if all past evils against your family, your people could be summed up in him. And I still have another mystery to solve. If I don't, the entire Kardam reputation is at risk."

"I'm happy to listen if you want to tell me."

He did. He was glad to pour it all out. He told her about the predicament he was in: with the company, his older brothers and, of course, Altan.

Nayiri listened to him without interruption. When Nour was

finished she said, "Wow. If you can only track down that bloody Ebenezer. I hope this guy Burto can find him for you."

After a fourth whisky sour they were both a little drunk. They couldn't remember whose suggestion it was, but they ended up in a cab to Nayiri's apartment.

"Do you think Lehman is still following us?" Nour asked.

"Was he?"

"Sure he was."

"Why didn't you point him out to me?"

"Because we were kissing."

"Hey! Do you look at other people while you're kissing me?"

Nayiri fumbled with her key. The two of them giggling, Nour took it from her, dropped it, picked it up, and opened the door.

They went directly to the bedroom. They made love for hours, constantly seeking new positions. They tried it standing up, hanging over the edge of the bed, sitting down. Many of their experiments ended in giggling failure. It liberated their minds and freed them to live out all the desires they had hitherto refused to realize.

# 27

$\mathscr{A}$t Nour's insistence Altan went to Ankara to see his brother Touran, the Assistant Deputy Director of Turkish Air Command. The discussion was brief. He hadn't been able to conceal his disdain, and when he left he slammed the door, hard, behind him. He knew that his two unruly brothers were capable of criminal actions of the worst kind, and he was persuaded that Touran and Ramazan shared responsibility for the unrest at the tobacco plants in Bafra—a situation that could turn nasty. The reputation of the company and the family were at stake, the destruction of a name whose power and reputation stretched back to the beginning of the nineteenth century. For the people of Antep and the Black Sea coast, the Kardams were synonymous with security for their families, prosperity for the region, and economic progress for the country.

"You'll be sorry you accused us," Touran warned him before he left. There were no cabs at the taxi stand, so Altan kept walking. There was some kind of festival going on, and the loud voice of a young man, amplified by a huge loudspeaker, announced the matinée performance of a new Turkish Houdini. Altan was watching, glad of the distraction, when a voice beside him said, "Altan Bey, Altan Bey, your brother would like to see you. He's waiting in the car." It was Levent, Touran's chauffeur.

Altan turned away angrily. "If he has anything to say, tell him to come himself."

Levent hesitated a moment, then crossed to the other side of the street. Altan saw him return to Touran's car, and a few minutes later the black sedan pulled up beside him. "I've got something important to tell you, Altan," Touran said. "Please get in."

"Why should I?"

"You need to hear this."

The chauffeur opened the door and Altan got in, sitting on the fold-away seat across from Touran. His brother was, as usual, dazzling in his colonel's uniform, and the car smelled of French cologne.

"Wait for us outside, Levent," ordered Touran. The driver shut the door obediently and walked over to look in the shop windows.

Touran's took a cigarette from his silver case and lit up without offering one to Altan. "Our brother Kenan phoned. The news is bad. The Bafra tobacco workers have gone on strike."

There had been unrest for some time among the tobacco-processing workers. They had been complaining lately about alleged wage differences between them and the shipping crew. Altan knew there wouldn't be any strike if Touran and Ramazan hadn't given the shipping workers bonuses for hiding contraband inside the tobacco bales, but he said nothing.

At that moment, a young policeman approached the car and, touching the black plastic visor of his cap, saluted Touran. "You can't park here, sir. You'll have to move."

Touran exploded, "You'd better learn how to address an officer. This is my car and I'm on official duty. Get the hell out of here."

The law-enforcement officer excused himself and left.

Touran pushed his head out of the car window and called Levent. "Your place is next to the car, not miles away from it. I don't want to be bothered by these idiots. Do you understand?"

Levent was used to his boss's sudden rages. He returned and stood next to the car like a well-trained sentry.

Altan watched the incident and sadly reached to open the door. "You know how I feel about this, Touran. I've said everything I had to say. I'll fly to Samsun to take care of the strike."

Touran's eyes sought reconciliation, but Altan wasn't prepared to drag out another useless conversation. He saluted his brother with a curt *hoshcha kal* and got out of the sedan.

The following afternoon Altan and Erol were driving along the sea, by the white, foam-fringed rocks, to Bafra—a lavish agricultural hinterland. Anatolia's two great rivers, the Kizilirmak and the Yeşilirmak, emptied into the sea there, one on each side of Samsun. They had built up fertile deltas, now planted with corn and tobacco crops amid bucolic surroundings. The entire coast was lush and verdant throughout the year, with plentiful rainfalls turning the filbert and tobacco fields a permanent green.

Despite the late afternoon sun and clear skies, the heavy rain of the night before had partly flooded the road. The mud was thick as molasses. Altan was seated pensively next to Erol in the open jeep.

Erol, much younger than Altan, depended on his brother's advice and experience. His brother Kenan, who worked with him, wasn't capable of comprehending either the mentality or the language of the workers, who were mainly of Laz extraction.* Altan found himself going to Bafra once a month to supervise the shipments, inspect the plantations, and check the books and the quality of the crop, which varied from one harvest to another.

The coast road to Bafra, with its digressions inland to various villages, was more interesting than the town itself. Altan's favorite little province on the coast, though, was the tea country east of Bafra; he always enjoyed his trips to Rize to inspect the family's tea plantations. He loved both the people and the scenery. The green was ubiquitous: the dark sheen of the tea plantations on the lower slopes blended with the forest above, and behind it stood the peaks of the Pontiac Alps—the real country of the Laz.

"That's where the new warehouse will be. It'll be the largest in the country," Erol said, and proudly pointed to a vast green expanse. It stretched to the hills in the distance.

"Father would've loved to see it realized," responded Altan.

"He wasn't terribly keen, though, at the beginning."

"Because he thought it was dangerous to expand the business so widely."

"There's no danger in expansion, Altan. The danger's always our two brothers."

They were driving alongside a tributary of the Kizilirmak. On the other side of the brook were the tobacco-drying barns. Altan's eyes swept over them absent-mindedly. He was busy calculating the cost of the wage increase he would have to offer. As the jeep slowed choirs of gnats whizzed frantically over their heads.

---

*Lazuri-speaking population on the southeastern shore of the Black Sea. The Lazes are an ethnographic group within the Georgian people.

"They're intolerable at this time of day," Erol remarked
"And bad for the crops."

The passing vehicles—mostly trucks of all sizes, including eighteen-wheelers—splashed muddy water over the jeep. The brothers were used to it, and barely noticed. They drove into the dying sun until they reached the first station, a boundless expanse of pale yellow and deep green flowers. Workers were busy removing the suckers, or auxiliary shoots. The first station contained the plants that had been transplanted in February. In the second station, only five miles away, the peasants were completing the last priming, removing two to four ripe leaves at a time.

Even from a distance Altan could feel the wave of heat spreading over to the road. Inside these small, insulated barns the green leaves were hung over long sheet-iron flues that carried heat from furnaces around and under the floors. Once it was dried, the tobacco would be trucked to plants to be cleaned, sorted, and redried, then moistened slightly and packed for storage. It was there that the trouble had started. According to the strikers, some of the workers were receiving extra pay, even though they were all performing similar tasks and working the same number of hours a week.

When the brothers arrived, it wasn't yet six o'clock. The men were still hard at work, stripped to their waists. Their bronze torsos gleamed with sweat.

Altan thought about the unpleasant consequences of the last New York shipment. He was convinced that the alleged bribes were connected to the shipments.

"I can't see anyone missing because of a strike," said Altan.

"They're working alternate hours. They work an hour, they stop for an hour. If we don't respond to their demands by tomorrow, they'll bring the plant to a complete standstill."

The southern sky was slowly turning purple. The muezzin's chant sent echoes across the open fields: *Allahu Akbar*—Allah is Most Great—*Allahu Akbar*... There is none worthy of being worshipped except Allah...

It was a noble call, a divine appeal in the stillness of dusk. The distant call brought the peasants out of the barns to pray. The grass was still wet.

They spread their prayer *kilims* on the ground. They turned toward Mecca and the Kaaba,* and began to recite their prayers, adopting the successive postures with an impressive simultaneity.

When they finished praying, the five burly peasants in charge of security ran panting up to Erol and stopped all at once. Seeing Altan beside him, they bowed deeper and lower than usual. Then one said hastily, "They're getting ready to fight."

Altan spotted groups of peasants collecting their weapons: heavy sticks, thick branches, rakes and spades with long wooden handles. They began to congregate outside the barns. The women also assembled. They would spur on their men with wails and chants of lamentation.

"Trying to attract attention," Erol told his brother.

"Let them," he replied calmly.

"*Efendi*, please, do something," one of the peasants asked Altan. "They'll kill each other."

"Let them," Altan repeated, though he was deeply concerned. He saw that Erol was on the verge of exploding. "Stay calm," he said.

The angry crowd grew as the sun sank behind the hills. The hubbub grew ever louder. Three battalions of makeshift weapons moved into offensive formation, ready to confront the enemy—pitchforks and spades first, iron rakes next, and then clubs. Brandishing their weapons, they advanced toward the processing plant, which was within shouting distance.

Altan hopped into the jeep and drove full speed into the teeming workers. The rustic troops parted to prevent themselves from being run over by the speeding vehicle. They recognized the head of the Kardam family. Silence fell, minutes passed. Altan had planned the entire strategy like a seasoned field marshal before an offensive.

Altan stopped the jeep in the midst of the crowd and climbed onto the hood. "My kinfolk," Altan cried. "I've been told about your grievance, and I've come to settle it."

The workers chanted, "*Chok yasha, Chorbaji*, long live the boss! Long live the boss!"

Altan's bony features lit up in a smile, and he raised his hand for quiet. "I know you're all peace-loving brothers and sisters. Choose six

*The Muslim shrine at Mecca, toward which believers turn when praying.

people and send them over to my office tonight. I'll listen to your complaints. Then I'll decide what to do."

The chanting grew louder. Women joined the men. Clubs began to beat time on the empty oil barrels. The rhythmic shouts of "long live the boss" resounded high and loud.

Altan had a hard time freeing himself from the mob to drive back. Erol was watching the scene with a satisfied smile. Kenan had returned from his inspection tour and joined his brothers. He expressed his gratitude in his own way: "I watched the whole thing. You handled them like a real pasha on the battlefield."

The remaining hours of the evening were given over to negotiations between management and employees, in Erol's office on the second floor of the administration building. The six representatives of the tobacco workers were adamant in their demands: they wanted more money. Their chief spokesman, a slim, muscular man with a pronounced Laz accent, explained: "Only a few are receiving higher wages. Here are their names." The man produced a list of about fifteen names, written in a childlike scrawl. "They deny that they're paid better than the rest of us. We've been told that they're spending and buying much more since the last spring flood."

"You're all intelligent people, Ali. You should know better: people talk; people speculate, even without any evidence," said Altan.

"But Seyfi the grocer says he's had to order more white cheese, twenty extra gallons of olives, and another huge block of *halva* to meet the increased demands of these people."

Erol chortled. "Maybe he's improved the quality of his cheese."

Bald Hamdi, now forty-six and surprisingly knowledgeable in village gossip and rumor, disagreed. "I heard Ibrahim bought his wife a gold bracelet, Jaundiced-Muammer got a new carriage, left-handed Hafiz now has four cows and two horses, and Guerilla Kadir bought himself a machine gun. My list is long. Would you like me to continue?"

"Any idea why they're paid better wages?" asked Altan.

"Because they're packing opium instead of tobacco," replied the same man.

There was a long silence. "Excuse us for a moment," Altan said, and he and his brothers moved to the adjacent office to continue the discussion in private.

They knew that higher and more equitable wages were inevitable, but they also knew they had to find out the source of those generous gifts to some of the workers. When they returned to the room the six delegates were arguing about Fazil, the plant watchman, and his new teeth. Ali swore he had managed to pay for two new gold teeth. Others insisted that he only had one—a large one in front, which had been there a long time. Gold teeth were status symbols, displaying prosperity and a rise in social status within the rustic brotherhood.

Altan interrupted. "As I promised you this afternoon, we've decided to increase your wages by twenty *kouroush* an hour."

"May you live long, *Chorbaji*. We'll pass the news on to our brothers and sisters." They were jubilant. With an extra twenty *kouroush* an hour they would be able to buy many extra loaves of bread and packs of second-rate cigarettes.

It was a triumphal achievement for Altan. When the meeting was over, he hadn't only settled the strike, but obtained necessary information thanks to a worker who seemed to have a personal grudge to settle without even asking for compensation. There was no reason to doubt the details the man had furnished, for Altan had investigated everything. It was a little too early to act; he was still waiting for a few more details and had to be very cautious with the police to avoid complicating things. Besides, the police might very well have been accomplices.

As for the crates stacked in the warehouse instead of being delivered directly to the shipping department, nobody seemed to know much about them. Finally, one of the warehouse workers admitted that the foreman who had ordered them put there had died in a mysterious accident a week later.

Since the nationalization of alcohol, tobacco, and poppies, the new government had banned the private exportation of opium but not its cultivation. The Turkish monopoly controlled the sales. Only part of the annual harvest was shipped to legitimate European and American clients; the rest left the country illegally. Much to his dismay, Altan could no longer doubt Nour's suspicion that the Kardam tobacco shipments had turned out to be a front to cover other activities— supplying opium to the Independent Tobacco Company in New York.

# 28

$\mathcal{M}$aro's face beamed with joy at the sight of her son, and she hugged him close. Her buoyancy was effusive, as if to make up for her husband's resentment.

It was Nour's second meeting with the Balian family that week, and this time Vartan would be present. There was a short reception line waiting for him, including Uncle Noubar with his wife, Sirvart, and Sona, one of their two daughters. From his bent posture, it was evident that Uncle Noubar's arthritic pains were bothering him, but he spoke warmly. "I'm Noubar," he said. "I couldn't believe it when I heard the news."

"By God, it's wonderful to have you among us," Sirvart added. Sirvart was a female version of her husband. With white hair and furrowed cheeks, she looked ten years older than her sixty-two years.

Their pretty daughter Sona had black curly hair, black eyebrows and high cheekbones. She said playfully, "So you're my uncle!"

Nour smiled. "Apparently I am, if that's all right with you?" He shook their hands gratefully.

Nayiri came in, went straight up to him, and gave him a hug. Nour looked over her head to see Magda and her husband, wine glasses in hand, talking to a tall, distinguished-looking man standing in the entrance from the hall to the living room. Nour knew immediately that it was Vartan. His white hair, classic gray business suit and polo tie enhanced his imposing air.

Nayiri took Nour's arm. "Come meet my father." Maro came over to join them. "Meet my husband, Vartan," she said, and they stood before him. "This is Nourhan, my son."

Vartan managed to utter, "I'm glad to meet you," and they shook hands stiffly. Nayiri said, "Does he remind you of anybody, *Hayrig*?"

Vartan observed him carefully. "Yes, of course, the anchorman on WNYV."

Nayiri laughed. "Exactly." There was no sign of the rancor toward her father she had voiced at their last family meeting.

Vartan forced a polite grin. "Don't worry, young man, you've just been compared to the most eligible bachelor in New York City."

Maro took a deep breath of relief. Vartan's antagonism was not in evidence, and she knew he was making a tremendous effort not to hurt her.

Jake came up to Nour, and they greeted each other happily and fell into a conversation. Nour felt a genuine liking for his new half-brother. He looked like a football player, but when he began discussing business his intelligence was obvious.

"I'd love to have a talk with you about something," Jake said before Maro interrupted them.

"Jake's our financial wizard."

"Mother, stop exaggerating."

"Exaggeration is part of being a proud mother. Now come and eat."

In the dining room, the long table was garnished with glistening hors-d'oeuvres, Oriental and Middle Eastern dishes. Magda and Araxi moved continuously back and forth between the kitchen and the dining room, bringing out steaming casseroles and platters. Nayiri stayed with Nour. Maro was watching them carefully.

Except for Tomas and his wife and children, all the Balians were there—a mere handful, Nour thought, compared to his enormous family back home. He shook hands with Roberto, Magda's husband, whose face had the flushed look of a good Italian overly fond of pasta and red wine.

"*Per Bacco*. We've already met!" cried Roberto.

Conversation stopped instantly and Magda moved closer to her husband in case she had to cover one of his usual bungles, which were always more likely after his second drink.

"In the lobby, at the Waldorf... the clockmakers' convention. That's it." Then, turning to Nour, he said: "You remember, of course. I explained where the big clock, the one in the hall, came from."

"Oh yes, yes, of course. The clock." Nour didn't say that he remembered this potbellied Italian's disconcerting familiarity more than his lecture on the Waldorf clock.

Vartan approached, and taking advantage of a brief pause in their chat he asked Nour: "When did your father quit politics?"

Nour realized the implication of his question. "After the war."

He saw Vartan's face muscles tense. "I guess the old guard didn't survive Kemal's purge," Vartan said.

Nour weighed his words carefully before answering. "That's right. The majority of them disappeared, most of them assassinated. My father considered it wise to retire from public life and administer his estate."

"I believe he was quite rich."

"According to Turkish standards, yes, but in terms of American standards maybe less so."

Vartan cut straight to the point: "Do you know why he left such a considerable sum of money to my wife?"

"It seems to me that my father wanted to be absolved of something."

"Some people think that money can buy everything, even absolution," Vartan went on.

"My father never placed such importance on money. I don't think he considered his bequests a means of insuring the eternal rest of his soul. To me it was a goodbye gift, without any other implication. But I suppose he had a precise intention when he appointed me to execute his will."

"To send you back to your mother," Vartan said bitterly.

"I'm sure he wanted me to know that I had a mother, besides my adoptive one. And blood ties with a community different from the one I grew up with."

Maro stood nearby, relieved to see that the two men were speaking equably. "He's beginning to accept it," she said to herself, smiling at her husband.

Vartan said, "He waited a long time to divulge the truth to you, didn't he?"

Vartan's openness astonished Nour. "Perhaps he thought I wasn't mature enough," he said mildly.

"Then he could have investigated it himself."

Nour hid his impatience. "My father got in touch with a law firm, but his attempt failed because of some rather ugly circumstances, and he didn't persist after that. He must have thought that it was not his job to do so and passed it on to me."

"If you say so, young man."

Nour saw that Vartan was reluctant to call him by his name. He also realized that Vartan had referred to Rıza simply as "he" during their conversation.

"Let's start in on the buffet," Araxi urged. "Everybody is starving."

Nayiri glided between the two men, taking their arms, and the three of them went up to the table. Maro handed them plates, then looked up. "I think that's Tomas's car."

Tomas's children dashed joyfully into their grandparents' arms. His wife, Anna, was a tall blonde woman who looked as if she spent her time at spas, hairdressers, and manicurists. Nour had a hard time taking his eyes from her vertiginously low neckline when Maro introduced them.

Roberto said in a low voice, "Marilyn Monroe in *Gentlemen Prefer Blondes*. Don't you think?"

The two men winked at each other, and Nour smiled: after all, clock-making wasn't Roberto's only interest.

Apart from small talk, Nour and Vartan didn't have any further exchanges, and as the evening went on the atmosphere gradually relaxed. They were all enjoying themselves when Maro suddenly asked for their attention: "I asked all of you to think about what I should do with the inheritance. And no one has said anything about it. Tonight I'm going to tell you what I've decided to do."

There was dead silence.

"I'm going to accept it, but not for myself and not for the family. You'll all agree that the money should serve a good humanitarian cause, especially one within the Armenian community, which needs it badly. It seems to me that we Armenians have suffered too much at the hands of the Turks to refuse this manna as restitution for past bigotries."

She turned to Nour and continued with a majestic smile, "Pardon me, Nourhan, for my crude words against your people. But they had to be said. My children's generation is innocent of the crimes committed by their elders. In the meantime, it's the duty of the older generation to impress upon them the message: 'Never again!' So I'd like to donate the money to the Holy Savior Armenian General Hospital in Istanbul so it can build a new cardiology wing. I'm sorry for delivering such a pompous speech on such a joyous occasion, but I just wanted to explain the reasoning behind my decision."

Jake let out a cheer and everybody joined in. Nour was pleased. Maro had accepted the money, and the scheming of Ramazan and Touran had been foiled. His father was the victor. He would have been smiling from ear to ear if he had been there.

There were a few disappointed faces. Roberto wasn't going to get a cent to renovate his pharmacy, and Anna wasn't going to buy her dream Cadillac convertible. But Maro was relieved. Her daughters seemed to be happy with their mother's resolve.

"Imagine. I have six children," she said for everybody to hear. "This is a miracle! For the first time, all of them together. Who could have foreseen such happiness? Many thanks to you all of you for sharing my joy this evening."

She looked at Tomas, who had remained quiet throughout. He nodded to her with a meaningful smile on his face.

Roberto took out his camera to record the happy occasion. Nayiri went to drag Uncle Noubar and Vartan into the group picture. Then she paused next to Nour, placing her head on his shoulder. Nour thought that the scene would make a wonderful sepia print.

*Part* four

# 29

Seeing that the doorman was busy, Charles Burto quickly crossed the street and entered the glittering lobby of the MacGregor Apartments. The doorman gave him a cursory glance and returned his attention to the young woman who was asking him to get her a cab.

The mailboxes were in an alcove at the rear of the lobby. Jonathan Ebenezer lived in apartment 7B on the third floor.

Burto took the elevator. He rang the bell and knocked on the door, finally pounding. At the commotion, a couple of neighbors stepped into the hallway, and Burto questioned them.

The first neighbor assured Burto that he didn't know any Ebenezer. The second heatedly declared he wanted nothing to do with Ebenezer, who threw rowdy parties, and suspected that the old lecher engaged in perverse orgies. The only firm information came from the woman in number 7C, a seasoned whore who could have turned a trick and talked to him at the same time. She was made up in a way guaranteed to single her out: green eyeliner, heavy mascara, scarlet lips, and straight platinum hair.

"Mr. Ebenezer? A real gent, a real charmer. Where else would he be, at this hour? At work, of course. Unless he's at his Long Island mansion. You should've known that yourself, instead of pestering us with your silly questions." As if regretting her reproachful tone, she smiled. "Not that I mind being disturbed by a handsome man like you."

Burto had no time for play, even if he had found the offer inviting. "I appreciate the compliment, Madame, but I'd really appreciate if you could just tell me where Mr. Ebenezer works."

She shrugged disdainfully and went back into her apartment, slamming the door. Burto chuckled. "Let's try the doorman," he said to himself, and went back to the elevators.

The solidly built uniformed doorman recognized him as he approached.

"Are you looking for someone?

Burto introduced himself and shook the man's hand, palming him a freshly folded ten-dollar bill. With a broad grin the doorman slipped the money into his pocket. "Do you know where Mr. Ebenezer works?" Burto asked.

"No I don't, sir, but a chauffeur-driven limousine always picks him up when he's in town."

"And when he isn't?"

"He lives somewhere on Long Island."

"Do you know what business he's in?"

"Not exactly, sir." The doorman sounded apologetic for not being able to supply ten dollars' worth of information. "He was here two nights ago. He left with a suitcase this morning. I think on a short trip, judging from the size of the suitcase. Maybe he was on his way to his Long Island house."

"Do you know what nationality he is?"

"I know he speaks with an accent. I don't know his nationality, but I think he's Jewish, because he wears a skullcap sometimes."

"You wouldn't know where he comes from, either?"

"That I couldn't say, sir, but he receives foreign magazines and newspapers."

"What language?"

"Sorry, sir, I couldn't tell you. You should've been here yesterday. I had some of his newspapers but I gave them all to him before he left. Are you some kind of a detective or something, mister?"

"A company investigator, but let's keep it between ourselves."

The man pinched his lips. "I've never met you, mister. Let me know if I can be of any further help. Any time."

"As a matter of fact, you can help me right now," said Burto. It was the opportune moment to get to the tough part of the bargain. "Do you know the superintendent well?"

"Yes, of course."

Burto lowered his voice. "Can you get me the key to Ebenezer's apartment?" He was aware that this was a dirty request. "Would you like to add a twenty bill to your collection?"

The doorman's face beamed, but he sounded hesitant. "You're asking too much, mister."

"All I want to do is find his Long Island address. It won't take a second."

"Are you sure that's all you want?"

"That's it." Burto said it so convincingly that he almost persuaded himself. He reached for his Camels, offered the doorman one, and lit one himself. "Can you manage it or not?"

He could see the doorman was tempted, contemplating the brand-new twenty-dollar bill, when a blue sedan drew up in front of the entrance and an elderly woman got out. She opened the door and beckoned imperiously. "Jason, can you give me a hand with my suitcase please?"

"Coming, Mrs. Decker." Then he turned to Burto. "I'll be right back."

Alone in the hall for a few minutes, Burto decided to call Nour. As the doorman passed with the woman's luggage, Burto went to the telephone on the small counter beside the entrance. He dialed the hotel number and asked for his room. It rang several times, but there was no reply.

By then the doorman was back. He gazed at Burto's troubled face, which looked weary all of a sudden, and whispered, "I went up and opened the door, mister. Can I have my money?"

Burto pulled another bill from his money clip, gave it to him, and walked to the elevators. What the hell, he reflected, if I'm lucky I'll find something interesting; I must be crazy to get into such a mess, bribing the doorman, breaking into Ebenezer's apartment, running after clues like a desperate cop...

He quietly turned the knob of the door to apartment 7B and opened it. The curtains were drawn. He looked for the nearest light switch and, when he found it, powerful spotlights, fifteen or twenty of them, turned the four-room apartment into a greenhouse drenched in tropical sunlight: the plants included two artificial palm trees with artificial parrots perched on the branches. There was a combined living and dining room, giving access to a modern kitchen. The bedroom was

altogether another territory. It looked like an expensive sex shop: porno-
graphic pictures, nudes of both sexes, decorated the walls; the ceiling
was covered with huge mirrored panels, and the bed, which looked
more like an upholstered landing pad, was a mess, suggesting recent
occupancy. Gaudy electric candles were dimly reflected in the mirrors,
and a door led to a bathroom with a sunken tub large enough to
accommodate three people side by side.

Burto hurriedly began turning out desk and dresser drawers,
examining papers, tossing things aside and picking things up with a
complete lack of self-control. There wasn't a single scrap of paper that
even hinted at the man's identity. He even went through the pockets
of the suits and turned over the toupée that lay neatly on the dresser,
but all in vain.

Then, in the hall, he saw a partially used book of matches on the
floor. It was from Sophie's Bar, at the corner of 99th Street and Seventh
Avenue. He put it into his pocket and walked out before he had a
chance to get depressed. A twenty-dollar horror movie. It might even
have been enjoyable, had it not been for the absence of the protagonist.

While Burto was on his way to Sophie's Bar, Nour and Jake were
having lunch at the Waldorf restaurant.

Jake was an altogether different person from the cheery half-brother
of the day before who had yelled hurrahs and applauded Maro enthusiastically. Today, in his well-cut suit, he was a serious, well-informed
young businessman.

Jake didn't mince his words, but got straight to the point. "I'm
thinking of a wholesale grocery import business, and wanted your
opinion. I can also import a great deal from Turkey. What I have in
mind is probably extremely small by your standards, but it's a start."

Nour listened to Jake's ideas. The venture was, perhaps, a little
remote from his immediate interests, but Nour was touched by Jake's
frankness and initiative. "It's an excellent idea, Jake," he said. "But before
we say more I have something to ask you. I'm seriously thinking of
transferring one of our holdings to New York. Instead of exporting
tobacco to American companies, it would be much more profitable if

we could export our tobacco and cotton to a Turkish-American enterprise based in New York City. If that happens, I could use your help."

"Wow. Yes. I'd be glad to help." Jake kept his eyes fastened on Nour. "What do you need?"

The appearance of Nicole in the doorway prevented Nour from explaining the rest. She waved and came over to their table, her face flushed with excitement. "I'm sorry to barge in like this, but I have important news for you." She looked at Jake and hesitated to go on.

Nour saw her uneasiness, and said, "Please—sit down. This is my brother Jake."

Nicole was confused. "A new brother?"

"I've suddenly found myself with three more new half-sisters and a couple of half-brothers."

"You come to New York to execute a will and find a whole new family. That's wonderful!" She smiled. "Well, I've been trying to reach you. I called your room three times but you weren't in. I didn't want to leave a message and decided to take a chance and come to the hotel. Burto says he's on Ebenezer's track. He wants to meet you here at five o'clock."

Nour shrugged. "I'll be there. I just hope he's got something for me this time."

"I think he does." Nicole stood up. "I'm in a rush. I have to get back to the office before Mr. Sherman leaves." She bid them goodbye and dashed off.

Jake was dizzy: Nicole, Burto, Ebenezer, not to mention a possible business opportunity in the big leagues, selling tobacco instead of olives and okra...

Nour pulled his chair closer and said, "Jake, getting back to my project—"

"Before you tell me the rest, Nour, may I ask a favor?"

"Of course."

"Can you give me Nicole's telephone number?"

Sophie's Bar was smoky and crowded, its decor reminiscent of Ebenezer's pad: red velvet banquettes, walnut and bronze partitions, soft lights, and a thick red carpet. Skimpily dressed waitresses, flashing lots of flesh and permanent smiles, carried trays of drinks. The jukebox played a Nat King Cole song.

Burto preferred to sit at the bar, next to an exotic black woman with hazel eyes. Her dark curly hair was pulled back and hung almost to her waist. She gave Burto such an inviting look that he instantly struck up a conversation.

"I'm Burto."

"I'm Charlotte. I'm a hostess here."

"Can I buy you a drink?"

"Thank you." She called the barmaid. "Lisa, a pink champagne, please."

"And a scotch for me," Burto added.

After a bit of small talk and rubbing of her legs against Burto's, she leaned over and whispered into his ear: "We have rooms upstairs. I'm sure you'd be more comfortable there, sweetie," and she kissed him on the cheek before straightening up. She wore a white top, cut very low and barely covering her breasts, which were large, out of proportion with her skinny body. Her long, brightly colored skirt was slit to the waist, exposing everything when she crossed her legs.

"I'm sure I would be. We'll go up shortly, but I'm waiting for a friend." He put his hand on her shoulder. "Maybe we can make a four-some, if you have another friend as gorgeous as you are."

"I hope your pal's as nice as you are."

"He is. You might know him: he's a regular here." Her long eyelashes froze and her eyes widened with curiosity. "His name is Jonathan."

"Which Jonathan, the old guy?"

Burto laughed. He was heading in the right direction. "Don't call him the old guy, he won't like it."

"What do you want me to call him? Rock Hudson?" She blew her cigarette smoke into the air and whispered again in Burto's ear. "To tell you the truth, he's a bit weird. He makes us do all sorts of strange things. Once he invited us to his country place in East Hampton. You've probably been there. God, what a nightmare! I hope you're not like him!"

"Don't worry, I know what you mean. I'm as straight as you can get. I love long kisses, dark nipples, and sleek, slender legs." He paused for a second to see what other attributes would be appropriate for his companion. "Long lashes, green eyes, and dark velvet skin."

"Stop, stop, I get the picture. You're the kind I like."

Burto pulled her toward him and covered her full lips with his mouth.

She didn't shy away.

"I wish he'd get here soon, I'm getting a hard-on already."

She smiled and, taking a handkerchief out of her purse, rubbed her lipstick off his mouth. "Jonathan's a wealthy man. Are you in the same line?"

He ordered a second round of drinks. "Yes, I am."

"Oh, another tobacco man. You must be filthy rich too." She moved closer, rubbing her hand along the inside of his thigh.

Bingo! At last he had the information he had been seeking all afternoon. How lucky he had found that little matchbook. He glanced at his watch: it was twenty to five. He left a ten-dollar bill for the barmaid.

"You're driving me crazy. Let's not wait for the old guy."

Charlotte wore a triumphant smile. "Okay, honey, let's not."

"I'll just phone to tell him I'll be upstairs with you." He had seen the public telephones at the bar entrance. "I'll be right back."

He walked right past the telephones, opened the door, and left the bar so fast he barely avoided falling over a hot-dog cart parked right in front of the entrance. He hailed a cab and asked the driver to take him to the Waldorf as fast as he could through the rush-hour traffic.

# 30

Pat Herrera and Charles Burto parked their car along the curb about a hundred yards from Ebenezer's country house. The road was deserted and looked like a private thoroughfare. The clouds had moved in after a humid day, signalling an imminent downpour.

The lighthouse on the opposite side of the bay blinked about every ten seconds. Burto restlessly timed the intervals between the flashing by counting in his mind: one-two-three, one-two-three, light-light-light. Herrera was all attention, his eyes fixed on the black Mercedes parked in front of the three-storey house. Just then the front door of the house opened and out came a short, slim older man in a beige suit.

"That must be him," both men uttered at the same time.

They waited while the chauffeur, who resembled a bodyguard more than an ordinary driver, opened the back door and the man climbed in. As the car began to pull out of the curved driveway onto the road, Burto zoomed in so close that there wasn't enough room for the chauffeur to swerve, and he ran into Burto's front bumper.

The chauffeur jumped out of the car, swearing furiously: "Shit, man, why don't you look where you're going?"

Burto leapt out. "Sorry, friend, it's my fault."

"Fuck you!" The man lurched forward, clutching Burto's throat.

Before Herrera could come to his rescue, Burto met the attack, rammed his knee into the chauffeur's groin, and he crumpled against the car door. Profiting from the sudden skirmish, Ebenezer opened the door to get out, but Herrera slammed it so violently that the tiny man was knocked flat between the front and back seats. When the driver tried to get to his feet Herrera delivered a sudden uppercut, and the man was knocked cold instantly. Herrera opened the door, grabbed the old man and, without looking at his face, dragged him into their car.

"Hop in and let's get out of here!"

Burto jumped into the car, and pressed the accelerator to the floor. The arrest, or rather kidnapping, had taken no more than a couple of minutes.

Burto's unexpected telephone call that night delighted Nour.

"What do you know about the man?"

"His name is Jonathan Ebenezer, born in 1882 in Jerusalem to Judah and Belva. He immigrated to the United States immediately after the First World War, determined to seek his fortune as a merchant like his father, who ran a modest citrus-packing house in Palestine. He's been well known to the police for some time. We got his pedigree just before his arrest. Nicole was more than helpful in obtaining it."

"I'll be there first thing in the morning."

The news was most welcome after his heartbreaking conversation with Nayiri, announcing his impending departure for Istanbul.

Nayiri, whose depression had at last lulled her to sleep next to him, was now wide awake. "What's going on?" she asked, thinking the worst—an emergency call that would force Nour to leave right away.

"They've arrested the son of a bitch."

"I told you they would." Then she said optimistically, "You may have to stay in town longer to interrogate him."

"I'll find out in the morning. "

Nour was pressed for time; he had to leave in a few days to be present at the pending trial and defend Kardam International against the charges laid by their long-standing American customers and expose the fraudulent transactions of Metin Bey, the company's marketing director. The latter was a delicate case that could damage the company's reputation if it wasn't handled right.

Nayiri understood the situation and cursed the harsh restraints of their genetic ties, but she kept repeating, "Let me come with you."

"Not this time, Nayiri. I'll be back soon."

She looked stupefied, incapable of imagining herself without Nour by her side.

Nour was equally distressed. Wordless, he watched Nayiri's face. Then he kissed her and said, "Let's try to get some sleep."

Mat Herrera's office was on the second floor of the Seventh Precinct. With its numerous filing cabinets, stacks of legal pads, newspapers, an old-fashioned coffee percolator, and cups scattered on a wooden table, the room looked more like a supply room where the staff took their coffee breaks than the office of one of the principal police lieutenants in the precinct. His small desk and the tiny table he used mostly for conferences were a mess, but Mat Herrera knew every piece of paper cluttering his workspace and could have put his hands on it even in the midst of a blackout.

Dressed in a navy-blue suit, Nour's classmate Irving Leonard was sitting behind the little oak table. Burto, Nour, and Chris Garcia, who had suddenly showed up as Ebenezer's lawyer, were still standing, sipping coffee.

Chris Garcia was smooth and believable as he explained how their firm had been favored by Mr. Ebenezer's business and had had the honor of representing him on various occasions over the last fifteen years. Nour didn't interrupt. Having no credentials as an attorney in the United States, Nour had retained Irving Leonard to represent the Kardams.

Garcia assured them that his firm would be pleased to turn over Ebenezer's files before any charges were laid against his client or the company in question. Irving didn't have to be told that Garcia was not a neophyte and would never produce documents that would incriminate Ebenezer—and would certainly never hand over files containing the evidence that Ebenezer had paid him half a million dollars in cash and had promised another half a million following the successful customs clearance of the incoming tobacco shipment.

When Irving Leonard brought up the subject of his suspension from the bar, Garcia explained uneasily that he was there simply as a customs broker and wanted to witness the interrogation, and wouldn't be representing his client in court if the case came to trial.

Listening to Garcia's endless falsifications, Nour found it difficult to contain his fury. Evidently Lieutenant Herrera was losing patience too. He pressed the intercom and asked his men to bring Ebenezer in. The door opened and, flanked by two officers, Jonathan Ebenezer walked in, his face dark and somber, his hair combed straight back, resembling a shrunken apparition from the underworld. He gazed at Garcia like a little boy looking to his parents for protection.

Herrera was chain-smoking. He said to Garcia, "I'm charging you, Mr. Garcia, with the illegal practice of law. You have no legal right to be here. I have no intention of continuing this interrogation unless you leave my office immediately. But before you leave, tell me, did you also represent Morrison Tobacco before Ebenezer bought it?"

"That was a long time ago."

"Did you or didn't you, Mr. Garcia?"

Garcia, unprepared for a confrontation with Herrera, who was known for his merciless tactics and ruthless queries, was caught off-balance. "No," he stammered. "I didn't."

"Get the hell out of my office, Garcia," Herrera said, and Garcia left, muttering incomprehensibly.

Nour had been looking closely at Ebenezer since the officers brought him in. Ebenezer kept his eyes lowered, not meeting Nour's gaze. Nour got up and approached the old man, leaning over until his face was inches from his. Then Nour reached up and pulled off the man's toupée in one swift movement, exposing a shiny, tanned skull.

"Well, well! Look who's here! Metin Bey, the old bastard! It seems the dead have risen from the grave. May Allah roast you in hell." He turned to Herrera and Burto, who were watching them, astounded. "Gentlemen, allow me to introduce you to the head of marketing for Kardam Exports, the *late* Metin Bey."

Metin gazed at Nour entreatingly, trembling. "Give me a chance to explain, Nour Bey." It was strange to hear such meekness sobs from this tiny, insignificant man. He no longer dared to taunt Nour by addressing him as *Küchük Bey*, as he had persisted in doing in the past.

"You're the lowest form of scum." Nour said nothing else.

Nour studied the profile of his former marketing director in the sunlight that flickered through the dirty Venetian blind covering the only window in the room. It was the kind of face that could only belong to the city that he had left behind, with all its tangled frauds, imposters, and intrigues.

"I refuse to be interrogated without the presence of counsel," Metin Bey managed to say.

"We don't need to interrogate you" Herrera answered. "We have enough evidence to send you straight to jail."

"You're mistaken about my identity," he said as a last resort.

Burto stepped forward. "We're mistaken about nothing."

"My name is Jonathan Ebenezer."

"Not while I'm around, Metin Bey," Nour said calmly.

The old man's dejected face reminded Nour of his late father, whose conduct had baffled him so much. There he was, Metin Bey, sitting before him in disgrace, like a miserable mobster.

"We won't bother you with any further questions," Burto assured Metin Bey. "Instead, we'll gift-wrap you and ship you back to Turkey."

"You have no right to do any such thing to an American citizen," Metin objected.

"If you don't shut up, I'll send you back in a casket," Herrera interjected, and the remark was greeted with loud laughter. He spoke into the intercom, and the two officers appeared again. "Take him back to his cage."

When the meeting ended, their course was clear. Irving Leonard would get a search warrant to investigate the Garcia files and obtain an indictment. The police would keep a close eye on the incoming tobacco shipment to penetrate the smuggling operation, and Nour would immediately fly to Istanbul to ask the Turkish authorities for Metin's extradition to stand trial in Istanbul.

Nour met Nayiri that afternoon at Central Park. "How was the meeting?" she asked. "What's the latest?"

"You couldn't guess, even in your wildest dreams, what happened."

"What? Tell me."

They started walking, and Nour told her the whole story about Metin Bey, the toupee, Jonathan Ebenezer's real identity, and the tobacco scam.

Nayiri was completely astonished, but she was also subdued. Nour's imminent departure had crushed her. She didn't know how she would ever do without him.

Their walk ended up at her apartment.

After they made love, Nayiri lay face down on the bed. "Have you ever been in love before, Nour?" she murmured.

"More or less."

"What do you mean, more or less?"

Nour kissed her neck. "I mean not seriously. And you?"

She said, "Yes, more or less." She turned over and looked at him. "Nour, are you really leaving?"

"I'm afraid so. I should be in Istanbul before Metin's extradited."

"I knew you'd be going, but not so soon."

The silence in the room weighed more heavily than their thoughts. Nayiri took his hands. Her lips trembled. "You can't leave without me."

"I won't be gone forever, Nayiri. I'll be back very soon."

Her sobs choked her voice. "I don't have the courage to wait for you." She was quivering. Nour caressed her hair, trying to calm her. Tenderly, he kissed her eyes, her face. He wished he could keep her in his arms forever.

# 31

$\mathcal{N}$our was heavy-hearted as he stepped off the plane at Yeşilköy International Airport in Istanbul. After a month of extraordinary developments and emotional turmoil, he was back on his native soil to append a bitter chapter to the saga of the Kardam dynasty.

He spotted Altan from afar, waiting impatiently for his brother to arrive. Nour quickened his steps to hug him. "Good to be back."

"Let's get going before the traffic gets worse." Altan grabbed one of Nour's suitcases to carry it to the parking lot.

They took the shore route to the city, which was already jammed.

"This thing with Nayiri," Altan said. "You really frightened me."

"I can't get her out of my mind, Altan," Nour confessed. "The moment I got on the plane, I regretted leaving her behind."

"That bad, eh?"

"I know, it's insane."

Altan sympathized with his brother, who seemed ignorant of the consequences of such a scandalous affair. He didn't wish to burden Nour with added guilt, so kept his thoughts to himself.

"Esin phoned to find out when you'd be back."

"I don't feel like seeing anybody."

"I didn't tell her when."

"I need to be left alone. I'll retreat to the *yalı*."

"Leila is there, waiting for you," Altan said.

"Oh no!"

Altan shrugged helplessly. "Melek and Ilhan are there too."

"I'll be happy to see your wife and son. But Leila... "

They remained silent until the traffic started moving again.

"Metin's arriving next week," Nour said. "I have things to settle before they deliver the shit bag."

"Had it ever crossed your mind that he might still be alive?"

"Never. You?"

"Of course not. And those fuckers Touran and Ramazan, pretending to mourn, cursing you for causing Metin's death."

"I hope the Haydars are getting ready to celebrate their father's resurrection."

Rıza had been dead for almost three months. It was remarkable how little Leila missed him. She hadn't been able to forgive her husband for his notorious will, which deprived her of her son.

Tonight she was waiting impatiently for Nour, not so much because she had missed him, but to hear all about Maro. She had asked the cook to prepare fresh lobsters, Nour's favorite dish.

It was late in the afternoon when Melek arrived. "I'm exhausted. I haven't been shopping in Istanbul for ages!" she said happily before kissing Leila.

Her son, Ilhan, bowed, kissed Leila's hand and touched it to his forehead. Altan watched him proudly.

"Let me see, Ilhan, if you've grown since the last time I saw you," said Leila tenderly.

Ilhan stood upright, almost on his toes, in an effort to look even taller. Leila sized him up. "Yes, you've become a giant," she said, and wrapped him in her arms.

Apart from his blue-gray eyes, Ilhan was the spitting image of his father. His broad shoulders, tanned face, and curly hair were certainly characteristics of the Kardam lineage. And like his kinsmen he was a real firebrand, never still for a moment.

"Where is Uncle Nour?" asked the boy.

"He'll be here soon," his mother replied.

Melek was in her late thirties, with hazel eyes and an oval face. Although not beautiful, she was a warm and peppery person. Some members of the family, especially Safiyé, didn't appreciate Melek's outspoken character, and consequently she remained outside the net, never part of the clan, and always refused to participate in the family's crucial decisions. Whenever Altan insisted that she show more interest in Kardam concerns, she turned it into a joke. "Remember," she said, "I've not yet been initiated into the inner sanctum."

Leila talked about the coming reception at the French Embassy. Altan and Melek made an effort to show some interest and tried to find a good excuse not to attend. Ilhan was playing with the white Angora cat when they heard Nour's footsteps.

"My dear mother."

Leila jumped to her feet and dashed to embrace Nour. "*Shekerim*, I'm so delighted to see you back safe and sound." After kissing and hugging him twice she stood back and examined her son. "I think you've lost weight. Didn't they feed you in America?"

"Only hotdogs, *Annejiim*."

The word *Annejiim* melted Leila's heart, making up for the times Nour had hung up on her while he was in New York.

"We heard so much in the press about your conquests of those gorgeous Americans," Melek said.

"Stupid gossip," Altan said irritably. "Just rubbish written by equally rubbishy reporters. They're simply trying to portray Nour as a low-down playboy, trying to stop him from running the Kardam holdings."

"Who are *they*?" asked Leila, frowning.

"People who want to take over if Nour is put aside," Altan replied matter-of-factly.

Leila changed the subject. "How is your mother?" Her tone was a mixture of derision and envy.

"Maro, you mean. Considering the shocks she's lived through in the last few weeks, she's fine."

Leila didn't appreciate his reply. She sensed a tinge of protectiveness, or even compassion, in Nour's tone.

"She sends you her greetings," he said.

"That's very generous of her." Leila couldn't prevent herself from asking: "Tell me, is she still beautiful?" Nour's silence displeased her. She attempted another variation of the same question. "Do you consider her as attractive and desirable as she was before?"

"How should I know what she looked like before, Mother?"

"Don't try to evade my question."

Nour couldn't help thinking how different Leila was from Maro. Both were delightful in appearance, but Leila was the embodiment of Ottoman standards and traditions and Maro was more European. Leila was impulsive, ostentatious, and vain; Maro was reserved, cautious in her remarks, and certainly much more educated.

He sighed. "Mother, I didn't go to New York to judge Maro's beauty."

"Excuse me for asking," she said coldly, and left the room. Melek followed her, taking Ilhan, leaving the brothers to talk freely.

Altan noticed Nour's frustration. "Forget it, Nour, you know she'll never change."

Nour changed the subject. "Tell me, Altan, did they find out who assassinated my star witness?"

"He was shot in a store by an unknown assailant."

"No suspects?"

"According to Rahmi...'

"Which Rahmi?"

"The cross-eyed Rahmi in Bafra, Erol's man."

"Yes, yes."

"He's insisting that Metin Bey was very close to a gypsy chief called Left-Handed Bekir, well known for his deft criminal arrangements. I'm sure Rahmi is right. The police are aware of the relationship between Metin and Bekir."

"Sons of bitches!"

Altan lowered his voice." I brought the memoirs with me, the book I found in the mystery drawer. Nobody else has seen it. I'll give it to you later, but don't read it tonight if you want to sleep peacefully."

The sun was about to plunge into the Bosporus. The straits shimmered first gold, then crimson as a roaring bonfire. In a moment it was dusk, the serene hour in Yeniköy. The lights on the Asiatic shore came on one by one: yellow, orange, red, and blue. The traffic on the Anatolian shore was gradually reduced to a parade of steadily moving dots of brightness.

Despite Altan's caution, Nour couldn't resist opening his father's memoirs that night, and what he had already gone through was nothing compared to the painful ordeal of reading them. His father's appointment as the regional head of the deportation of Armenians was a puzzle to him. What could the government hope to gain by employing a man like Governor Rıza? And what could Rıza himself hope to achieve by allowing himself to be so employed? His father must have been acting on deep convictions to be able to carry out such brutish acts. But that wasn't all; in the end he had played Pontius Pilate, washing his hands of the matter and blaming the state for everything. No one would ever know the full magnitude of his crimes, which had been committed with the silent complicity of the Allies.

When Nour finished reading, he sat there in shock. His father had begun writing his memoirs after handing over his seals of office to his successor. Why should he leave such incriminating evidence instead of smothering the sickening past? A cathartic exercise, perhaps? Or simply the defiant action of an obsessed criminal.

Nour recalled what his father had told him once: "He who saves one life saves the whole world." Did he really mean it? The lives he saved were those of Maro and her son. Governor Rıza's atonement for his sins.

In the second half of the journal Nour skimmed over the vivid, gruesome details of human suffering and concentrated instead on his father's love story, a total contrast to the rest. The pages devoted to Maro were a fragmented, internalized exaltation of a woman, a detailed crusade of love, almost Dante-esque. They covered the years 1915 to 1918, until Maro's departure for Constantinople—no more entries after that. Rıza's love had fled.

Following a sleepless night, Nour went down to breakfast in the crystal gallery overlooking the sea. Kerim bowed as he greeted Nour and delivered a message: "Leila Hanim left for the city. She asked me to tell you that she won't be back before supper."

"Thank you, Kerim."

Nour, narrowing his eyes, gazed absent-mindedly at a Soviet tanker moving toward the Black Sea. What he had read was sufficient to destroy any war criminal. Vartan would have loved to get his hands on these pages and, with great satisfaction, take them before the International Court of Justice to obtain a posthumous conviction. But Nour felt a novel urge to somehow vindicate his father.

After he had his coffee, he picked up the phone and asked the operator to connect him to Nayiri's number in New York.

# 32

$\mathcal{I}$t was Kurban Bayrami, the Festival of the Sacrifice, the most important religious and secular holiday of the year, commemorating Abraham's near-sacrifice of Isaac. Most of the stores were closed, and the people in the streets were in their best finery. Turkish flags decorated the storefronts and buildings, and herds of sheep were driven through the streets. According to Scripture, Abraham sacrificed a ram in Isaac's stead, and it had become a tradition on the day of the *bayram* for every head of household who could afford a sheep to sacrifice one and distribute a sizeable portion of the meat to the needy and to donate the hide to charity.

The Bureau, better known as the Second Division, was housed in the Sanasarian *khan* on Mimar Kemalettin Boulevard, not far from the Sirkeci train station. The offices were located around an inner courtyard, and the quaint marble fountain in the center was paradoxical for a building where no one was able to sit and enjoy the refreshing sound of the water as it trickled slowly into a large basin.

The police at the Second Division were known for their unconventional methods of making people talk. They continued to borrow the brutal practices of the *bastinado* and other tortures from the Ottoman past. For them, fear was the only effective interrogator. They knew how to coax the truth out of even the most stubborn criminals. It wasn't unusual for them to torture people to death or to the point where they voluntarily jumped out the window and committed suicide.

Metin Bey, accompanied by two American plainclothes policemen, had arrived at Yeşilköy International Airport via Frankfurt at noon and been handed over to the Turkish police. He was due at the Second Division any time.

Outside, in front of the drab structure of the Second Division, a young butcher with a sharp knife in one hand grasped the head of a sheep with the other and cut the animal's throat. Onlookers crowded around the dying animal as the bright red blood welled over the cobblestones. This was a symbolic sacrifice orchestrated by the staff of the Division.

Nour was speaking with Constables Mehmet and Fehmi, experts in international drug busts, while he waited for the police van to arrive. These two showed no mercy to felons like Metin, who had made a travesty of Turkish national security with his lengthy criminal activities.

"He's a filthy rich scumbag," said Fehmi.

"A rotten swine," added Mehmet.

Nour refrained from adding other adjectives to their list of Metin's attributes.

A boy of eleven or twelve hustled up and down the building's hallways, delivering coffee, tea, and Turkish delights from a couple of suspended copper salvers, which he swung with astonishing dexterity.

A policeman appeared and announced that the van was approaching the building. The news spread quickly. The people in the courtyard dashed out to witness the arrival. The appearance of the old-model khaki prison van always drew a large crowd. First an armed officer climbed out and then Metin Bey: he descended slowly, as if every step caused him agonizing pain. He was handcuffed. He looked so thin and exhausted that the onlookers wondered whether he would reach the gate of the building or collapse on the pavement. He kept his hands buried under his jacket in an effort to hide the handcuffs— a spectacular scene of humiliation, rolling out in slow motion. The security officers pushed the man to make him walk a little faster. Another one prodded him with the butt of his gun to spur him on.

Sabri, Metin Bey's son, stepped out of the crowd, Özkoul beside him. "Stop it. Can't you see he can't walk?"

"Stay back," the officer said.

Sabri inflated his barrel chest. "You people have no idea who you're dealing with. This man deserves consideration."

Özkoul pointed at Nour. "See that bastard? He's the one who should be charged, not this innocent soul."

Immediately a large group of reporters surrounded Nour.

"Kardam Bey, Kardam Bey, would you care to make a statement?"

At that moment the two plainclothesmen showed up out of nowhere, hemming in the Haydar brothers.

"You two are under arrest."

They had been snared without warning.

"My offering for the *bayram*," Nour said to Sabri, and a broad grin lit up Nour's face. He felt as though he was righting an ancient wrong, committed not only by the marketing director but also by his own father, who had falsified Metin's true colors as carefully as he had concealed Nour's true identity.

Nour had already given a long deposition and furnished the police with a copy of the tape of his conversation with the Haydar brothers in his office two months earlier. The National Security Division was aware that opium was being smuggled out of the country tightly compressed and hidden in tobacco bales, and the Kardam enterprises had been under close surveillance for some time.

Mehmet, the plainclothesman, walked over to talk to Nour. "Mr. Kardam, we're informed that the last shipment has already arrived in New York. We'll hear from the Americans shortly."

Nour refused to answer the reporters, who were swarming around him like green flies in a butcher shop.

"Look, mister, you'd better not stick your nose in what's none of your fucking business," Mehmet told one of the reporters who was still pestering Nour for a statement.

"I'm a reporter."

"Not when I'm around," Mehmet exploded.

An angry sound, half roar, half hiss, rose from the crowd: "They should be hanged."

Nour recognized the voice of Hilmi Sabah, a well-known workers' syndicate leader; he had been the stevedores' local branch representative during their recent strike. Nour had talked to him on two separate occasions before forwarding a subpoena to the retired customs officer, who had at last agreed to testify at the trial, the one who had been taken out by the Haydars.

Nour went to silence the syndicate leader. "Trust me, Hilmi, we'll take care of all of them. Please don't talk to any of the reporters."

Hilmi Sabah was a stout man of forty. He silenced immediately and looked at Nour with trust. Nour offered him a cigarette, then lit one for himself. He held on to the moment, pressing it like a gift into his jam-packed memory.

The intercom blinked: it was Nour's secretary. "Kardam Bey, Dr. Ozan's here; she'd like to see you."

"Tell her to come in," Nour said, sighing wearily. Esin! He had been in Istanbul for more than a week without giving her any sign of life.

She came in and stopped a few steps away before approaching him. "I came to find out if you were still alive."

"Esin, I'm so sorry, I've been terribly busy: the family, the trials, company problems..." He invited her to sit without kissing her.

"You look exhausted. Late nights, undoubtedly," Esin said, sarcasm lightly embodied in her voice.

Nour didn't like her attempt to make him feel guilty. "Not for any reasons you may have in mind."

"It's Altan who revealed the secret because I pestered him so much. When I saw the pictures and read the articles in the papers I was madly jealous. I realize we've been lovers for such a short time and you've promised me nothing. What hurt me most, though, was that you didn't tell me you were coming home."

"It wasn't a pleasant trip. It's a long, complicated story. I've got a great deal on my mind concerning the company, and had a very bad night... Let me take care of my problems first. We'll see each other in a few days. I promise, Esin. I'll call you soon."

"I'm sorry I dropped in without warning." she said coldly. "I won't kiss you— you haven't shaved. I know the way out. *Ciao!*"

Nour stubbed out his cigarette nervously. He had no desire to see another woman. He wished to become a faceless exile in his own city and detach himself from family, friends, acquaintances, trials, arrests, reporters, the police. He thought about the New York shipment, the pending arrests, Metin Bey, Irving, Burto... No matter how they looped around, his thoughts always came back to Nayiri. Their daily telephone conversations were not enough; they couldn't embrace, they couldn't kiss. Never had he experienced such passion. He was scared, as if the filaments attaching him to his work, to his existence, to what he was, had torn loose.

It was three p.m. when Leonard phoned to inform Nour that the tobacco shipment had reached New York via Genoa and Marseilles aboard the *SS Rotterdam*, a Dutch vessel. The news couldn't have been better: Mat Herrera, the heavy-handed law enforcer, had masterminded the operation in collaboration with the customs authorities and the FBI. The tobacco bales had first placed on special barges near Pier 47 and then trucked by Ebenezer's tobacco company to a warehouse on the outskirts of Newark. In the afternoon, as employees began to unload the trucks, ten unmarked police cars surrounded the premises and carried out a raid, seizing firearms and a ton of hashish. The company crew, in an attempt to escape, had opened fire on the police from inside the building and caused two casualties: a policeman, and a truck driver who had been caught in the crossfire. The warehouse was equipped with a sophisticated narcotics lab for the manufacture of heroin destined for the American and Canadian markets. The information was made public immediately after the raid. Among those arrested were Garcia and his associates—three veteran customs officials who provided the company with easy customs clearances.

Before ending their conversation Nour said, "Irving, the more I think of it the more I'm convinced that Metin sent the Grade-A tobacco to Ebenezer instead of to our longtime American client because somebody along the line had made a big mistake. They must have hidden the narcotics in the Grade-A bales instead of in the inferior-grade tobacco that Ebenezer was supposed to receive."

"Mistakes sometimes are sheer blessings, Nour."

Ramazan and Touran, anticipating the eventuality, had already handed in their resignations and vanished. Their sudden decision took the Ministry of Defense by surprise and opened the door to all sorts of suppositions. Despite Nour and Altan's efforts to save the Kardams' reputation, the scandal began to spread in the press.

Touran had disappeared without informing his family, and no one knew where he was. Ramazan had left for Marseilles, hoping to obtain refugee status in France. When Safiyé learned the scandalous reason for her sons' resignations, she was distraught. "It's the highest treason for a high-ranking officer to run away like a vulgar criminal," she cried. "I don't ever want to see them again."

Contrary to expectations, Leila remained undisturbed by these events, even though her friends ignored her at receptions, and she felt that she was being observed like an unusual creature at cocktails and other events to which she was invited. She preferred to stay at the *yalı* and let her cats keep her company.

Pigeons invaded the cement courtyard of the Second Division, their cooing overwhelmed the noise of the endless traffic outside.

Stretched in the armchair, Altan was absorbed in gazing at the ceiling and counting the innumerable black fly specks. He was glad to be relieved from his demanding role as acting director of the company during Nour's absence.

"Gentlemen, we cannot thank you enough for your precious collaboration. We'll keep you informed with regard to your brothers," said the division director. "We've already requested Interpol and other international security organizations to keep an eye out for them and to arrest them if possible. I'm terribly sorry about this but..."

"No one is above the law." Nour completed the director's sentence.

The place, the circumstances, the long discussions, even the foul smell of stale tobacco in the room had a depressing effect on Nour and Altan, and they were glad to leave.

Once in the street, Nour turned to his brother. "Altan—are you sure about your decision? Are you sure you want to return?"

Altan had decided to finish his years on the sun-filled plantations. "I told you, I'm not a man to live in a city, Nour. I'm going back to my land." Altan hugged his brother and then hid his emotion by turning briskly away. "I'll see you later."

Heartbroken, his hands in his pockets, Nour accelerated his steps. When he reached his car, he drove directly to the Admiral Bristol American Hospital, where Esin worked.

"Dr. Ozan finishes her shift in an hour," said the receptionist at the pediatrics department after checking the chart on the wall.

"Thanks. I'll wait for her outside."

Nour had finished smoking his third cigarette when Esin showed up. Her face lit up when she spotted Nour resting against her old gray Studebaker.

"This is a surprise! What's going on?" Esin hadn't heard from him since their uncomfortable encounter in his office.

He kissed her on both cheeks. "I came to take you out to dinner."

She immediately forgot her anger. "Oh, the way I'm dressed. I had a horrible day. Can we pass by my apartment so I can change? I could use a shower too."

When they stopped in front of her building, she said, "Come on up. Much more pleasant than waiting in the car."

He flipped through magazines while she was in the shower, and when she came out of the bathroom wrapped in a towel, he got up and put his arms around her. Pulling her body against his, he kissed her for a long while, and they went into the bedroom.

Naked and interlaced, their bodies slowly rediscovered one another. Nour needed to erase from his skin the traces of his distant love, but there was no fire in his embrace, and he felt her resistance. He yearned for Nayiri's audacious, delicious passion.

After they made love, he said, "I want to apologize. I know you were furious because of the write-ups in the American press."

"Simply jealous," she replied. "I love you, Nour."

She wanted him to say it too, but instead he kissed her in silence. Then he sat up and lit a cigarette.

"I'd like to tell you something," Esin said. "I had a fight with my parents."

"Over what?"

"A letter I received from Bellevue Hospital in New York. I'd applied last year, and now they're offering me a two-year internship in pediatrics."

"That's fantastic," Nour said, with surprising fervor.

"But I'll turn it down. I don't want to be separated from you."

Nour's enthusiasm waned. Things were advancing too fast: first her declaration of love, then her announcement that she was willing to forego a rare opportunity that most medical graduates would die for— refusing it because of him.

Esin was waiting for his reply. "Are you upset?"

"I don't think you should say no to New York, Esin."

"You'd like me to leave, wouldn't you?"

"No. Let me explain. I'm in a complete dilemma myself. I've been planning a new business venture in New York." He paused, then blurted out, "Accept the offer, and we'll go together. If you don't mind marrying into a family with a complex, scandalous past."

Esin was so overwhelmed that her hands were trembling. "It's you that I want to marry, not your family," she said. "I couldn't give a damn what your brothers have done. Whether you're a Turk, an Armenian, a Christian, or a Muslim; I'll go to the ends of the earth as long as I'm with you."

All Nour wanted to do was extinguish the image of Nayiri, but he couldn't. He knew he was a liar, a hypocrite, with an uncontrollable, bigamous craving to screw his own sister. He pulled Esin violently toward him, and covered her mouth with his.

# 33

*E*ver since Metin Bey's arrest the battle lines had been drawn: on Nour's side were Altan, Erol, Kenan, and his sisters, and against him, of course, were Touran and Ramazan, who always tried to snatch whatever they could without bothering about the family's reputation. Their sudden disappearance, though, had eased Nour's conscience. They would simply be unavailable for trial. Turkey couldn't ask France to hand over Ramazan, since there was no extradition treaty between the two countries. As for Touran, his whereabouts were still unknown. The only troublesome question now was how to handle his father's case posthumously and disguise his own involvement.

As for the possibility that the Haydars would lay charges against Rıza Bey as a war criminal, long years had elapsed since the end of the First World War. It would now be practically impossible to present evidence and subpoena witnesses. Furthermore, the Turkish authorities continued adamantly to deny that the Ottoman government had perpetrated any premeditated atrocities against its Armenian minority in 1915.

Nayiri had recently quit her job at Macy's. She had squabbled with her colleagues, and had an unpleasant wrangle with her boss. "This lousy job hardly pays my subway fare and cigarettes, so what's the use of continuing?" she yelled at her boss one morning, before slamming the door in his face.

Lately, she was finding family dinners tiresome, and skipped them regularly. "She doesn't even bicker with Father anymore," said Araxi. Magda attributed Nayiri's sour temper to the fact that she had ditched Greg. "We never hear her mention his name. She must be regretting what she did."

Maro was deeply concerned. Never had she seen her daughter in such a state. There was no trace of her bubbly personality; she never smiled and didn't even care about her appearance. When Maro tried to talk to her, Nayiri just said, "Leave me alone, Mother."

Jake had other preoccupations. Since his first encounter with Nicole, the two had been seeing each other regularly. They were so much in love that their world consisted only of themselves.

When Maro talked to him about Nayiri, Jake—a born optimist—tried to persuade Maro that she had nothing to worry about. "Nayiri's often whimsical. As soon as she goes back to college she'll change."

What people didn't know was that Nayiri hadn't even registered to complete her last term. All she did was smoke and wait for the telephone to ring in hopes of hearing Nour's voice. At the beginning, their conversations were focused on remembering their happy moments together, their lovemaking, and ended by planning their next meeting.

Just talking to him made Nayiri feel aroused and increased her passion for him. As the days went by, though, she became bitter, and Nour's daily telephone calls were no longer enough. To her Lucky Strikes, she added a few glasses of bourbon, in an attempt to encourage the phone to ring sooner.

Nour was engrossed in his business problems and social obligations. He wasn't aware of Nayiri's fragile state, although some of her behavior troubled him. When he reproached her for not going back to college, he triggered a flood of tears. She grieved even more when she suspected that Nour was trying to distance himself from her.

The children exhausted all their persuasive powers trying to convince their parents to go to Istanbul for the groundbreaking ceremony of the new cardiology wing of the Holy Savior Armenian Hospital. Maro and Vartan told them they needed time to prepare themselves before revisiting a past that had long been relegated to the dim corners of their minds. Maybe they would fly over to inaugurate the new wing when construction was completed. Unable to convince their parents, the children proposed to send Nayiri to Istanbul to represent the family at the ceremony.

"It'll do her a lot of good," Tomas said.

"Maybe it will cheer her up," Araxi agreed.

Maro wasn't convinced; she was conscious of her daughter's feelings, suspecting her relationship with Nour.

When Tomas and Maro were alone, Tomas confessed that he knew what was on his mother's mind. "I'm not blind, Mother, I can see what's going on. But considering Nayiri's frail condition, it's better for her to go than stay here."

The suggestion came from an intelligent brother and an experienced medical man. Although not totally persuaded, Maro decided to take the risk.

Nour was alarmed when Maro called him and said that Nayiri was very sick. He could never have imagined that she was so depressed.

"I'll take care of everything," Nour promised. He realized immediately that it was a risky solution but refused to let his rationale deprive him of putting his arms around Nayiri.

Exactly two days after Maro's distressing call Nour found a hand-written note while checking his mail. It was from Howard Lehman, the notorious *New York Times* reporter who had caused him so much trouble. It was a polite request for a brief meeting, enclosing his room and telephone number at the Divan, one of Istanbul's first-class hotels. Nour crumpled the note angrily and threw it into the wastepaper basket. A minute or two later, regretting his hasty reaction, he picked it up, checked the hotel number, and dialed it.

Dressed casually in jeans, Howard Lehman was having a drink at the hotel bar. The place was deserted in the early afternoon. Nour arrived twenty minutes late, grabbed a stool next to the reporter, and asked the barman for a local beer.

The veteran journalist looked tired and jet lagged. "Thanks for agreeing to meet me, Mr. Kardam," Lehman said, punctuating each word with an irritating nod.

"You've got a nerve, Lehman," Nour retorted coldly.

"To be honest I wouldn't be surprised if you punched me in the face. I took the risk. I wanted to explain everything to you personally, face-to-face."

Lehman confessed that he filled the daily gossip column simply to secure a steady income and benefit from his press pass, which opened many doors.

"I'm sure cheap write-ups, trashy gossip, and slanderous accusations pay well."

"I'm truly sorry, Mr. Kardam. I apologize."

"Tell me how the hell you got involved in this mess."

"It's a long story. I wasn't involved, not really." His smile was constrained. "I was approached by our learned friend Chris Garcia years ago with a scoop on an illustrious public figure. The whole idea was to destroy the man's image. As soon as I finished my story, the journalist in me impelled me to investigate Chris Garcia himself. I smelled trouble. He didn't sound very kosher to me—a conniving character, to say the least. Fred Goldwater & Associates didn't seem to be a typical customs agency. To cut a long story short, I asked my boss to authorize me to investigate the firm. The *Times* informed the police of my intent, just to be on the safe side legally. After fairly complicated negotiations they finally agreed, provided I'd report everything suspicious to them."

"And did you, Mr. Lehman?"

"Please, call me Howard."

"Sure, Howard. Did you?"

He frowned. "No. I couldn't risk any leaks, because I was determined to be first with the story."

Nour smiled. "Fair enough."

"Because I played their game, helping them with the media, Garcia and company trusted me more and more. I was getting a handle on many extraordinary developments. In no time I became an expert on contraband deals. In the meantime, three or four days before your arrival in New York, I was asked to write a scandalous piece on you. Again it was Garcia who asked me. And the moment you stepped off the plane, I became your shadow."

"And a conspicuous one."

"I know: I'm not terribly good at that."

"But fairly successful."

"And the rest you know."

"Did you know Ebenezer? Metin?"

"Had heard of him, that's all—just a mystery man."

"And did you tell the police about the mystery man?"

"No. Things didn't fall into place until you reported Metin Bey's false identity. I can assure you, I had no idea who the man was."

"Tell me, Howard, do you mean to say that you crossed the Atlantic just to tell me this?"

Howard noticed Nour's exasperated tone. "To be honest, I don't regret my short pieces on you. That's my profession. What I'm most sorry about is the fact that I was used by a bunch of drug dealing criminals." He grinned suddenly. "Of course, it'll make a fabulous scoop!"

"Wait a minute, Howard. Not so fast. You're not going to write any damned story, not even a line, without my consent."

"I won't. But I'd also like to do a long piece on you for the paper, if you agree. That's really why I'm here."

Nour made a rapid calculation. His impulse was to refuse, but for once this man could be a real help to him. "Maybe," he said. "But I have a few conditions."

"Yes? I'm sure we can come to an agreement."

"First, you'll write absolutely nothing about my personal life without my approval. Second, you will agree in writing to testify at the trials."

"Consider it done." Howard beamed. "But what about the story of the entire operation?"

"That one I'm keeping for myself. I'll write it when I retire."

# 34

$\mathcal{T}$he corporate head office of Kardam & Sons International Tobacco
Company was situated not far from the Galata Bridge that spans
the Golden Horn. The seven-storey gray limestone building glittered in
the midday sun. The traffic on Rihtim Caddesi, along the cobblestone
quay, was congested with cars, trucks, transport vans, and horse-drawn
carriages.

The company chauffeur parked the black Mercedes in front of the
building and opened the door for Nayiri, who was stylishly dressed in
a fuchsia cotton suit. From her looks no one could imagine that she
had been suffering from serious depression, or that she had been
travelling for the last eighteen hours. The receptionist showed her to
the company library.

"Mr. Kardam is in a meeting. He'll be out shortly," she said in
perfect English.

Nayiri examined her surroundings: trade books placed neatly on
long mahogany shelves, magazines on a long conference table, samples
of different grades of tobacco preserved in a glass showcase. She picked
up one of the magazines and turned the pages mechanically, without
seeing a thing. Twenty minutes passed. Nayiri couldn't stay still. She
went out to see the receptionist.

"Big meeting, I suppose."

The way the receptionist looked Nayiri over made her wonder if she
had said something wrong. "Yes," was all she said. "May I get you some
coffee or tea, Miss Armen?"

"No, thanks. I hope it won't be much longer."

"It's been a hectic day for Mr. Kardam."

Just then a pair of giant doors opened and Nour emerged with the
president of the Ottoman Bank. After shaking hands with the man and

saying goodbye to him, he rushed up to Nayiri and embraced her. "I missed you so much," he whispered into her ear.

They walked to his office and he locked the door. "I can't believe you're here."

They kissed for a long while. Nayiri started unbuttoning his shirt. "It's been months since I touched you. Make love to me, Nour."

They undressed frantically, and made love on the carpet, their climaxes quick, carrying them back to the beginning of their affair.

"I can't exist without you," Nayiri said, and turned her head to hide her tears.

After a while, collecting themselves, they dressed, and Nour unlocked the door. Nayiri went over to the large picture window. "What an amazing view! And what an amazing feeling, to be with you again."

"I've planned an itinerary for you, Nayiri. Your first visit to Istanbul should be a memorable one."

"I don't need anything else to make it memorable. I only want to be with you."

"You'll be staying with me at the *yalı*. Your room connects to mine," he added. "The chauffeur will bring you to the city whenever you wish."

Nayiri smiled. "Until today, the only time I had a chauffeur was when I took a yellow cab in Manhattan."

"Leila, my stepmother, is at the *yalı*," Nour said. This was the first time that he had referred to Leila as his stepmother. "When I told her you were coming, she was upset, I think. Two minutes later, she was thrilled that she was going to meet Maro's daughter. You know what she calls Maro?" He paused with a smile, as if hesitating to say the rest.

"What? Tell me."

"Her matchless rival. Beauty means a lot to Leila. It's her primary obsession."

Nayiri laughed. "My mother told me a little about her after you left, and also about your father."

Mention of his father changed Nour's mood instantly. "It's a sad but fascinating story. My mother is an incorrigible romantic."

By the time they climbed into Nour's Jaguar, the chauffeur had already delivered Nayiri's suitcases to Yeniköy.

The ride through the city was a dizzying experience for Nayiri. Compared to the tangled, confused transport system of Istanbul, Manhattan's traffic now seemed child's play. She was fascinated as they drove through the financial and business districts of the city: merchants, businessmen, artisans, a battalion of cars, trucks, buggies, and an endless flow of people.

They were soon in the city's modern residential area, Harbiyé, where Nayiri's parents had lived before leaving for America; Şişli, where her mother's cousin Lucie still had her apartment; then the Armenian cemetery, the setting for the hostage exchange where her father had at last ended his long, frantic search for his wife and had let Rıza Bey go free. Even the place names on the old tram route brought back fragments of her parents' past. She had always been stirred by the hope that one day she would visit Istanbul, or Constantinople, as her mother called it, and bring into focus the obscure images that had crammed her mind.

Nayiri's thoughts skipped between the past and the present, a past that was only a quaint narrative for her and a present that overwhelmed her with its extraordinary squalor and opulence. Nour gave a running commentary, like a professional tourist guide, on the landmarks and history of each neighborhood they drove through. Once they were outside the city on the Maslak Road, the car accelerated. They made a handsome pair in the gray sports car with its top down, the wind sweeping through Nayiri's hair, sunglasses hiding her beautiful eyes.

She felt drugged by the sights, the scents, and the dusk pervading the tree-lined road. And Nour... She could reach out and touch him whenever she wanted. She could bend close and hear his heart beat if that was what she wished. They drove in silence, until they came to Istinyé and began to glide down toward the dry docks and the Bosporus with its choppy waters was before them.

On the morning following her arrival, Nayiri came down with Nour to the Crystal Room to find Leila already there, waiting with great anticipation for the answers to her two questions: first, if Nayiri would find her attractive, and second, if she would remind her of Maro, whose face had remained in her memory, painfully alive and unchanged all these years. Leila was dressed for the occasion: heavy makeup to cover every real or imagined wrinkle on her face, a pair of expensively tailored Bermuda shorts to expose her shapely legs, and a clinging blouse to show off her full breasts.

Nayiri wore a pair of jeans and a strapless top. She looked completely rested after a ten-hour sleep and a bath in the marble bathroom, which reminded her of the tales she had read about the Ottoman harems. Nayiri was enjoying the palatial life her mother had lived under the roof of Rıza Bey years ago in Aïntap.

Leila had frequent dreams that Rıza Bey had risen from the dead to make love to her, and each time she suddenly realized that the woman he was making love to was not her but Maro. His passionate moans and irresistible caresses, even in a dream, were an unpardonable act of unfaithfulness to Leila, and she was tormented by memories of many similar humiliating defeats.

Nayiri's appearance eased her exhausting anticipation, in spite of the tinge of envy Nayiri's youthful physique had aroused in her.

"My dear girl, there you are!" Leila welcomed her warmly.

Nayiri went up to Leila and embraced her.

"It's about time I got to know you!" Leila spoke slowly, to give herself time to find her words in English. "I don't know how many times Nour's told me how nice you are, how beautiful you are!" Without giving Nayiri a chance to respond, she continued: "I see that he was right. You're gorgeous: a ravishing specimen, capable of seducing and conquering an entire company of men. You're the spitting image of your mother. Is she still as beautiful as ever?"

Nayiri jumped in quickly. "Not as youthful as you are, Leila Hanim. I've heard so much about you from my mother, and I see that she was absolutely right."

Nour, totally astonished, stared at Nayiri and found himself unable to react with anything but a smile. Nayiri had done her homework well, and conquered Leila's heart.

Leila went on more freely: "I was so intimidated by your mother when we were young. She was more educated than me. In fact, she was my first tutor in French and English. She spoke eloquently, carried herself gracefully, as if she had been born to tempt the opposite sex. I was so jealous of her that I often retreated to my room and cried."

"Mother, stop exaggerating," Nour interrupted in Turkish.

"No, my dear son, I'm not exaggerating," she replied in English. "The Balians are dangerous. I see from Nayiri's eyes that she could steal any man from any woman. Be careful."

Despite her chuckle, Nour and Nayiri weren't amused by the remark.

"I've no intention of stealing anybody from anyone." Nayiri was too much her mother's daughter to have any interest in this kind of talk.

"Don't get upset, my dear child. What a sweet name Nayiri is. It sounds like Neyyir, a beautiful Turkish name." Leila poured Nayiri some tea, without asking if she'd prefer coffee. "You must understand, my child," Leila began to explain calmly. "I'm still recovering from the shock of losing my son after all these years."

"Mother, please, stop it. You haven't lost anybody."

"You know I don't like sharing, my son. I'm most selfish when it comes to you."

"I wish you would drop that nonsense about sharing me, sharing your husband."

Leila got up and drew herself haughtily to her full height, preparing to leave, But Nour made a sharp gesture in the direction of her chair so Leila sank down again and changed the conversation to the *konak*s, the ancient mansions that Nayiri and Nour were going to visit after breakfast.

At the ceremonies at Holy Savior Hospital some days later, Nayiri proved herself a worthy representative of the Armen-Balian family. Her speech in English and Armenian, her genuine conversation with the guests and hospital staff, her congenial manners were all reported in the press the following day. They even enthused over her dress, a simple light pink, which the two principal Armenian dailies in Istanbul found singularly appropriate for the occasion.

She was enjoying her stay tremendously, visiting all the historical sites, museums, and mosques, meeting with her mother's cousin Lucie, and getting closely acquainted with the Kardam entourage. She spent precious moments with Nour, nights of impassioned sex tinged with sadness.

One evening when Nour went to Nayiri's room to accompany her down for supper, the door was ajar. He pushed it a little to see if she was there. When he saw her come out of the bathroom he halted. Nayiri scurried to shut the door and stood naked before Nour. Her tanned skin accentuated the white parts of her body that were usually hidden by her two-piece bathing suit.

Nour lifted her up and carried her over to the four-poster bed. It was as if he had never felt such desire. He undressed quickly, and they covered each other's bodies with kisses, rubbing, reaching, touching... He kissed her nipples, her stomach, her inner thighs. She let out a long moan...

When she opened her eyes Nour's eyes were glistening. She cupped his face in her hands. "I love you, Nour, more than anybody in this world."

"I love you too, very dearly, Nayiri."

"I don't have the courage to be parted from you again. Keep me here next to you all the time."

Her appeal tormented Nour. What about Esin... New York... the trials... His life had been gradually falling back into place in Istanbul. He cursed himself. He cursed his fragility toward Nayiri. Their voracious passion frightened him. In New York he had been free, but in Istanbul he wasn't the same person, and he was totally responsible for the plight troubling him. Nayiri was unaware of Esin's existence.

"I've got something important to tell you," he said.

She looked hard at him, surprised by the sudden change in his voice.

"I have a friend here, a woman who..."

"Bastard!" She leapt up from the bed, her eyes flashing with hate. "I'd have been dead if I hadn't come to see you. And all that time you were merrily fucking some other woman, whoever the bitch is. And in this bed, I'm sure."

"It's not what you think."

His answer infuriated her even more. "I'm sure you love her too. You love all of them—right? Me in New York, her in Istanbul, another in who knows where—"

"Nayiri, calm down, let me finish."

"Get the hell out of here this second. If you don't go, I'll scream."

As he shut the door quietly, he heard her sobs. He knew it was time to put an end to this.

$$\mathcal{H} \quad 35 \quad$$

*H*ave you seen the paper?"

"I'm reading it now." Maro's jubilant voice couldn't hide her pride. It was as if she were the protagonist of the entire article, reported so beautifully.

"I've read it twice already," Vartan said, equally pleased. "Tell me, when did you and Nourhan have your picture taken in front of our house?"

"Search me, my dear. This Lehman man is apparently the best investigative reporter there is. I wouldn't be surprised if he was nominated for a Pulitzer."

Vartan's appreciation was genuine. The fact that the article exposed the details of Maro's captivity by Rıza Bey was a plus for him. He had at last been able to put aside resentment and had become aware that Maro's son wasn't an ordinary individual who could be categorized, analyzed, or measured with a conventional yardstick.

Maro studied the picture of Nayiri and Nour, taken at the entrance to the Topkapi Palace. The photo revealed her daughter's happiness. She was pleased that she'd sent her to Istanbul.

The telephone didn't stop ringing. Jake called, sounding as though he had become the chairman of the board, replacing Nour Kardam. Araxi was equally delighted. Magda was apologetic; she told Maro time and again how wrong she had been to treat Nour so coldly.

"Forget about it, Magda. I'm sure he has forgotten it already."

Tomas was at a loss. "I feel like flying to Istanbul and hugging him. But I also feel a bit guilty, Mother."

"What on earth for?"

"For the years we neglected him. Now we discover that he's an international magnate, and we welcome him with open arms."

Maro's heart gave a twinge. Tomas's words were a painful reminder of what she had secretly reproached herself with so many times.

Nour also received many phone calls. They were all from overseas, since very few people in Istanbul had read the *New York Times* Sunday magazine. Besides Maro and the rest of the Balians, the callers included Nicole. She sounded ecstatic, and said she was enchanted with her new job at Irving Leonard & Associates. At one point she burst out laughing. "Do you know, Nour, Jake is my handsome payoff for the Ebenezer operation. We've been seeing each other ever since."

There was a boyish satisfaction in Nour's voice: "I'm so happy for both of you, Nicole."

He was sure that, in addition to calling him to congratulate him, Maro would mail him one of her long missives. Her letters were dispatches of affection and personal confession about the past, about the Balians, about the feelings she had nurtured for him over the years. They were also her lifelines, firmly attaching Nour to a period when he hadn't been aware of his own identity.

The Asiatic shore glowed with the warm colors of twilight. Nayiri and Nour walked through a narrow alleyway leading to an area of rose and tulip gardens divided by an oval marble pond. There was a dinner table set beside the pond. Kerim appeared with a tray decked with fried red snapper, grilled shrimp, and lobster.

The storm had gradually lost its ferocity after two tumultuous weeks following Nour's attempt to explain his relationship with Esin to Nayiri. They both knew that nothing was going to be as it had been before. Nayiri refused to meet Esin, not even out of curiosity. She was jealous. Esin would always be her prime rival, as Maro had been for Leila.

Nour picked at his food silently. Nayiri didn't say much either. Then she reached over and put her hand on his. "I'll miss you terribly, Nour."

"I'll miss you too, Nayiri." He wanted to kiss her, but he sensed they were being watched by Leila from the second-floor sitting room.

Nayiri bit into a shrimp and wiped her mouth. "I know that you met Esin before me. But all the same it angers me to leave you with her."

He leaned closer to her. "Let's be realistic, Nayiri." He stroked her cheek, oblivious now of Leila, who was indeed watching them from the sitting-room window.

"I can't help it," she said. "I love you with all my soul, with all my body."

"I told you I'll come to New York. I told you I'm opening a new branch with Jake's help. Give me time to set it up."

"You will, you will... When?" Nayiri felt vanquished and it frustrated her even more. She knew that she would become an understudy, a standby, and would wait for the lead actress to give her a chance to take over. "Why can't you have more than one wife, like your father?" She laughed bitterly.

Nour didn't bother to answer her. They were in no mood to appreciate the seafood, which had been delivered fresh to the *yalı* only a few hours before. Nour poured more wine from the pitcher on the table. It was then that he suddenly noticed Leila, dressed in a high-buttoned ivory silk gown, walking toward them. Kerim, seeing Leila from afar, bowed deeply. She bestowed an approving glance on the old servant. Nour stood up to pull out a chair for her.

"What are you two plotting together?" She didn't expect a response from either of them. "Please, continue your supper. I hope you'll excuse me for not eating with you this evening. I ate with Yilmaz and his wife." Yilmaz, a retired admiral, and his young wife, Aysel, were Leila's inseparable friends and lived four houses down, in another ancient *yalı*. "They've heard about the *Times* story and asked me to congratulate you, Nour."

"It's nice of them, *Annejiim*."

There was an unfamiliar melancholy in Leila's look. "You two are alone this evening. Where's Esin?" Her question was certainly not a manifestation of curiosity but an expression of dissatisfaction.

"She's busy at the hospital," Nour replied.

"She's a sweet person, and comes from a very good family," Leila continued. "I hear she's got an important job in New York. You'll have lots of opportunities to see each other."

For a moment Nayiri felt like fainting. The bastard: he takes her with him to New York and doesn't have the guts to confess it. She would have left at once if Leila wasn't with them. Nour could hardly swallow, but he was pleased that his mother's presence had saved him from another hysterical scene. Afraid of Nayiri's unpredictable reaction, he immediately brought up something that he had planned for Nayiri even before her arrival.

"*Annejiim*, I have a suggestion."

Leila looked at him inquisitively.

"Nayiri is leaving in two weeks, and—'

Leila was genuinely sorry to hear this. "Not so soon, my daughter, you must stay longer. I was hoping to take you to Antep to show you the region and introduce you to the rest of the family."

"Thank you, Leila Hanim, but I have to go back."

"Unfortunately, she can't postpone her departure," Nour explained. "But I'd like to organize a *mehtap* for her before she leaves Istanbul."

"What a delicious idea, my son, I haven't been to one for ages. A delightful suggestion."

Nayiri was lost. "I've no idea what you're talking about."

Mother and son looked at each other like conspirators. "You'll see," said Nour, and stood up. "I'll walk my mother to her quarters."

Leila took her son's arm, flushed with pleasure. She couldn't imagine that as soon as they were alone Nour would announce his engagement to Esin, offering her the greatest happiness of her life.

# 36

*A* week before Nayiri's departure, Istanbul's elite were ready to assemble aboard the *Savarona* for a *mehtap*, a moonlight festivity. The luxurious yacht was more of a cruise liner than an ordinary yacht. The government of Turkey had bought it from a wealthy American for Mustafa Kemal's private use and for state receptions. Shortly after the president's death, the boat was given to the Heybeli Naval School of Istanbul for use as a training ship, and it was rented out occasionally, with a complete crew, to prominent citizens when needed.

The night was perfect for a cruise reception, warm, with a full moon. The marble quay of the *yalı* was barred with moonlight and shadow, like a giant elongated zebra. Waiters passed around trays of canapés to the crowd of two hundred guests. Young waitresses in native Turkish costumes served drinks and canapés. Following cocktails, everyone would go aboard the *Savarona*, which was anchored along the pier. It glittered like a multi-level nightclub, festooned with hundreds of bulbs, colored lanterns, and sparkling silver streamers. The band was playing near the shallow lily pond and would soon move on board and play alternately with another group of musicians, one for Oriental and the other for Western tunes.

The guests were a true reflection of the racial mosaic of the city, most of them longtime friends of Nour and the family. Altan and his wife, Melek, were also there for the occasion.

Nour ran back and forth in his white dinner jacket introducing his half-sister to the guests. Esin greeted Nayiri with a huge smile. Nayiri forced herself to pronounce a few polite words. When everyone had passed along the reception line, Nayiri let out such a long and loud sigh of relief that Leila frowned at her reproachfully.

212

The yacht was entering the Sea of Marmara; a breeze stirred about the people on board and the sea broke into long undulations. Leander's Tower, standing on a tiny rock, was only a few hundred yards off shore. Esin leaned against the railing, suspended between heaven and earth.

"You look exhausted," she said to Nour. "And worried."

"I'm tired," was all Nour said.

He had been worried about Nayiri ever since the beginning of the reception. Nour had spent sleepless nights, blaming himself, trying to come up with a solution. He knew he had acted selfishly, unable to master the extraordinary passion that constantly drew him toward his half-sister. At last, incapable of manipulating the situation any longer, he had come to realize that Esin would make a perfect wife and mother.

Altan signalled to his brother discreetly that Nayiri was drinking too much. Nour asked her to dance, and all eyes turned on them as they glided onto the dance floor to the melancholy melody of an Argentinean tango. Other couples joined them. Hülya Taner, a blonde in her twenties who had followed Nour like a shadow all evening, was dancing with an older man, her eyes fixed on Nour and Nayiri. She was the daughter of the former Turkish ambassador to Washington. Her inseparable friend Süreyya, another of Nour's admirers, was also on the dance floor. She turned out to be more audacious than Hülya. She led her partner closer to Nour and wiggled her body with exaggeration. Unmindful of Nayiri, she said to him, "I hope I'll have the pleasure of dancing with you, Nour, before the party is over."

"It'll be my pleasure, my dear Süreyya," Nour answered uncomfortably, for Nayiri was clinging to him like an aching paramour. Despite his polite efforts, pushing and retreating, Nayiri didn't move away. Nour relaxed when the orchestra shifted to a Glenn Miller swing tune, necessitating a more acceptable distance between them.

The dancers were then asked to clear the floor so that two young Middle Eastern dancers could start their show.

Sara was renowned as one of the best belly dancers in Turkey. The other, Sabah, equally renowned, was a young Libyan immigrant. The Oriental band played a lively Middle Eastern tune, and the two of them began to dance. Curvaceous hips undulated, long fingers clacked brass castanets, and graceful arms beckoned, as though soliciting people to participate in this fairy tale brought down from the summit of Kaf, the imaginary mountain that surrounded the world. The dancers responded to the unanimous encores by dancing two more numbers.

No *mehtap* could be considered complete without the nostalgic sound of the *oud*, and the sudden appearance of *Oudi* Hrant, an internationally famous player, brought the audience to its feet.

Leila, who was next to Nayiri, drew closer. "You seem rather sad, my child. Allow me to share my happiness and let you in on a secret. Our Nour is getting married."

Nayiri felt dizzy, nauseated. The lights were still out, except for the spotlight projected on the *oud* player. Leila stood up with the rest of the guests to applaud when the *oudi* stopped playing and let the musicians take over.

With an effort Nayiri got up and left the table.

As the yacht neared Sedef Island, an exquisite show of fireworks began: colorful, radiant sparkles scintillated under the dome of the night. Rhythmic blasts and crackling spurts of dazzling light, brighter than stars, spread in the darkness.

Nour still had to thank his guests. He walked to the stand. The orchestra stopped. Heads turned to him as he grabbed the microphone.

"My dear friends, I'm quite aware that no one is in the mood to listen to speeches after such a long night. I'd simply like to thank you all for responding so enthusiastically to my last-minute invitation. My mother tells me that the last *mehtap* the Kardams organized dates back to prewar days."

Heads turned toward Leila. She cherished all the polite glances directed toward her. "I only hope that it won't be another twenty years before the next *mehtap*," she said.

Some applauded, others whistled, and a few called out, "Let's make it an annual event."

"What triggered this reception was my sister Nayiri's first visit to Istanbul. I wanted her to have a taste of some of the ancient traditions that have been totally neglected in recent days. She'll be leaving us next week, but with a firm promise that she'll come back as often as she can."

His eyes wandered to find Nayiri, but she was no longer at the head table. Altan came up and whispered to Nour, "Nayiri suddenly got up and left the table. She'd been drinking way too much, and Melek thought she was going to throw up. She ran after her, and a good thing too—otherwise she would have fallen overboard."

"Where is she?"

"Melek is with her in her cabin. The doctor on board gave her a sedative. She's sleeping. There's nothing you can do. Just take care of your guests."

Premonitions of dawn were already in the sky as they crossed the darkness of their festive night. They entered the Bosporus to head back to the *yalı*. A few stars were still visible.

When Nayiri woke up the following morning, the yacht, the reception, the guests, the music, the drinks, and the rest were like a blurred nightmare. She decided to leave that same day. There was no way she could stay for another week.

Nour tried his best to change her mind. Even the doctor suggested a few days' rest before taking such a tiring trip, but to no avail. Leila was the culprit. He had intended to tell Nayiri with tact, appealing to her reason. If need be, he had even thought of reminding her that his marriage would make it easier for them to carry on their relationship. Leila, however, had ruined everything. Finally, as it wasn't possible to find a flight leaving for New York the same day, the trip was postponed to the following afternoon.

Her plane left immediately after lunch. At the airport, right before boarding, she kissed Nour on the lips, more like an incensed sister than like herself. When Nour told her to look after herself, she replied, "What for? I'm already dead."

Maro smiled joyfully when she saw her daughter come out of the arrival gate. Her happiness was short-lived, however, for she soon noticed Nayiri's sallow complexion and the dark rings under her eyes.

Nayiri restrained her tears as she put her arms around her mother. "Thanks for coming, Mom. Take me to my apartment, please."

All the way home, Nayiri refused to answer her questions, and when they got to the apartment she told her mother to leave her alone.

"Out of the question," Maro replied firmly. "Now you tell me what happened. You come back looking unhappier, more miserable than before. What's happened that's so terrible you can't even talk about it?"

No reply.

"I won't leave until you tell me."

"Nour's going to marry her."

"Marry who? Esin?"

"Yes. He's a good-for-nothing liar."

Maro let herself collapse on the sofa. She suddenly understood: her daughter was hopelessly in love with Nour. The brusque disappearance of Greg, the glances exchanged between Nayiri and Nour... I've been an idiot, she thought: those feverish eyes, not the eyes of a brother and sister.

"You're in love with him, aren't you?"

"I love him to death."

It was all Maro's fault. She had agreed and even arranged for Nayiri to go to Istanbul, dispatching her into her lover's arms. She held Nayiri by the shoulders. "My dear daughter, listen to me. You and I have loved men we shouldn't have loved. They were not for us. We were not for them. I pulled through, and you will too. I know it's hard, I know it's cruel. But you must. Trust me, please."

# 37

$\mathcal{B}$ ekir's swift and stealthily planned murders were well known to the Turkish police, but despite tireless efforts they had been unable to put him behind bars. His crimes were either carried out by well-trained second or third parties or executed under such singular circumstances that there was never sufficient evidence to arrest him. Bekir, also nicknamed Lefty, was a gypsy chief and lived in a shanty neighborhood when he was in town. Nobody knew where he came from. His crony, Rahmi, said that whenever Bekir came home drunk, he would beat his wives so badly that they remained incapacitated for days. Regardless of the situation, nobody dared stick his nose in his business to try to stop him. His criminal competence enhanced his reputation, as did the monetary rewards earned by each contract. As long as he was paid, Bekir would take care of any troublemaker. That's how he earned his second nickname: the Terminator.

Rahmi, Bekir's partner in crime, was sharpening his knife on a round whetstone that he turned with his foot, dousing the blade from time to time with a few drops of water. His bird-like figure, elongated nose, pale sunken irises, shaggy eyebrows, and shaven head gave him the look of a Biblical prophet, and people referred to him as the Hermit, as he lived a solitary and ascetic life.

Bekir had come to discuss the details of a new contract. He watched his friend sharpen his long knife.

"Good job," the old connoisseur said. "Get it ready for tonight."

Rahmi glanced at him without uttering a word. It wasn't wise to question Bekir.

"Do you remember the guy who lives in that corrugated metal hut at the foot of the hill on the way to the port? He's got his friends into trouble, spilled secrets that he shouldn't have."

That was more than enough for Rahmi. He would receive his share, and that was all he cared about. He expressed his agreement with a mumble.

"There's also another character," added Bekir, lowering his voice. "A big shot, who shouldn't have listened to what others told him. I'll pick you up this evening."

On his way back from the plantation after a long day in the office, Altan parked his jeep near a corrugated metal hut. He smoked as he waited for the occupant's return. He didn't remember the man's name. For Altan he was "the thin man from the strike" who "got his friends into trouble and spilled secrets he shouldn't have," and refused to be paid for the information he had divulged to help Altan hunt down the traffickers. He must need money, Altan had thought. All tobacco workers needed money. As their boss, Altan valued the tough work these people were doing day in and day out, twelve months a year, bent over, sweating under the scorching sun, taking care of the tobacco plants. Altan wanted to try again to give the thin man from the strike some money.

After a second cigarette, Altan grew impatient. "Where the hell is he at this hour of the evening? Perhaps an extra job for a few *kouroush*," he said to himself.

The thin man didn't know Altan was there. He was, at that very moment, inside the hut, lying on the floor with his throat cut, bathed in a pool of blood. "You dirty swine," Rahmi had mumbled while cleaning his knife after carrying out the first contract. Then, hearing the approaching jeep, he and Bekir had run into the woods.

A cloud veiled the moonlight. Altan was ready to leave, but Bekir, agile as a cat, slid quietly into the back seat of the jeep, tightened his grip on the bone handle of his knife and, with a quick motion, planted the long blade into Altan back.

By the time the moon reappeared, Bekir and Rahmi were a long way from the hut, were sharing the banknotes they had found in their second victim's pocket. In the calmness of the night, his chest resting against the steering wheel, Altan looked like any tired driver who had pulled over for a nap before getting back on the road again.

Until the end of his days good old Kerim bowed whenever he entered Nour's room. He did so again when he burst unexpectedly into his master's office at the *yalı*, eyes bulging, tears running down his hollowed cheeks. He seemed so distraught that Nour made him sit on the couch.

"What is it, Kerim? Tell me."

"Altan Bey... the police... downstairs... "

Nour hurtled down the stairs two at a time and recognized Commissar Mehmet on the doorstep. Nour grabbed the police chief by the arm and, unable to formulate the words, questioned him with his eyes instead. Nour didn't even hear the officer's polite words of greeting—only those dreadful words, each syllable reverberating in his head: "Your brother, Altan Bey, has been assassinated."

Later that day, Nour flew to Samsun to see Altan's lifeless body. Only then was he able to accept the tragic reality.

Altan's wife insisted on a private funeral for her husband in spite of his mother's objections. In the end the family decided to respect Melek's wish. The funeral took place at the family mosque adjacent to the mansion, and then the body was carried to the family plot to be buried next to Rıza Bey's grave.

Nour stayed in Gaziantep for a week following the funeral. He tried to sort out all the legal matters and comfort Melek and Ilhan, his favorite nephew. Regardless of his efforts and his sensible reasoning, Nour was unable to convince Melek to return to Istanbul. It would have been easier for them to cope with the cruel void created by Altan's tragic fate, and much better for Ilhan: he would attend good schools and be exposed to the amenities of the big city. But Melek was adamant; she preferred to stay in the family mansion and take care of the plantations, at least for the time being. "It'll keep me closer to my husband," she insisted; "I'll have to prepare Ilhan to take over his father's responsibilities." Under the circumstances no brother or sister bothered to suggest a family gathering to decide who the new head of the Kardam family would be: Nour was their tacit choice.

For Nour, Altan's death meant unremitting torment and chaos. He went to his office only to take care of urgent business. He had abandoned his office on the company's top floor and moved to another one on the same floor. While Nour was in New York Altan had occupied the premises and sat in Nour's chair, behind the sumptuous desk, keeping everything intact until his brother's return. Nour couldn't see himself working within those walls any more. The lavish president's office had now become "Altan's office" for good and was locked up, with all the memories of a beloved brother.

Upon his return to Istanbul, Nour asked the minister of justice to oversee the case personally, with a close eye on the inquest. He pressured Commissar Mehmet to do his utmost, without foregoing outside help when needed. Nour called him every day to ask about progress, but there were no encouraging leads, and the police were still in the dark.

The police had difficulty discovering what the top man of Kardam International was doing in such an out-of-the-way place at night. Was he there to visit the man who was found lying in a pool of blood with his throat slit? Or was he making his usual round of the plants? And, if so, why so late in the evening? Some attributed the crime to prowlers attracted to Altan's vehicle and wallet.

Commissar Mehmet ignored all speculations. The region was known for sheltering a rough crowd, quick with their knives, but it was difficult to see any logical connection between a wealthy landowner and a poor guy who sweated at the plantation, slain in close proximity.

"Exactly," said Mehmet to Nour, "it doesn't make sense. It simply stinks."

"The Haydar brothers?" asked Nour.

"We interrogated them under pressure. No, it wasn't them, but they're not scot-free either. They're incensed to see their corrupt schemes go down the drain. Wait and see if..." Lost in his thoughts, the commissar didn't bother to finish his sentence. He sat up, however, when he heard Nour offer a fifty-thousand-dollar reward for anybody who provided information leading to the arrest of Altan's killer —cash to be paid by him personally.

Despite his efforts, nothing could console Nour. He couldn't accept his brother's death. He locked himself in his room and mused for hours, thinking about their younger days. Altan had taken him under his protective wing when Nour was young. Nour remembered how the two of them used to fight Ramazan and Touran, and Altan's patient smile as he listened to his young brother's crazy adventures. Nightmares woke him up in the middle of the night, and he woke up exhausted. Then he felt wiped out for the rest of the day.

Maro and the rest of the family conveyed their condolences and expressed their concern by constant calls and in writing. Maro's frequent letters to Nour wishing him strength and courage didn't bring him much solace, but he appreciated her sincere feelings. Nayiri's silence before the tragedy was converted to an outpouring of affectionate concern and frustration. She wrote about her revulsion at the cruel reality of life, hoping, in the back of her mind, that Nour would at last comprehend the savage ferocity of losing a loved one.

Esin was always present, staying by his side to share his pain. She asked him to change the date of their wedding, insisting that they couldn't hold such a festive event while the family was still in mourning. Finally it was decided not to have the grandiose wedding that Leila had been dreaming about. By staying in Istanbul, though, they couldn't avoid inviting the entire array of relatives and friends.

But that all changed one good morning when Nour asked Esin to confirm her acceptance of the internship at Bellevue Hospital. "We'll get married in New York," he said, "and settle there for good."

Despite Commissar Mehmet's inventive methods of making people talk, the Haydar brothers had denied any involvement in Altan's murder. The police transferred them to the most notorious penitentiary outside Istanbul, known for its ferocious interrogation techniques, hoping to crack them before the trials. The prison conditions were so harsh that the majority of the inmates preferred to be shot by the guards while trying to escape rather than prolonging their stay in a hell on earth. Finally the prison director placed an informer in the Haydars' cell.

After a few weeks, Sabri, the older brother, began to show signs of weakening and started blaming Özkul for their predicament. "They'll soon make us talk," he groaned. "If they get hold of the gypsies we'll be fucked. If not we'll croak in this shit-hole."

As expected, the commissar eventually managed to make them confess. Sabri and Özkul denounced the head of the gypsies, Lefty Bekir, and his accomplice, Rahmi the Hermit, as the criminals responsible for the double murder. Nour heard about the arrest of the cut-throats while he was in New York, finishing the formalities of opening the overseas branch of Kardam International. He flew back to Istanbul immediately.

Nour was astonished when he saw Commissar Mehmet waiting for him in the arrivals area, just before passport control. He took Nour aside from the rest of the passengers. "Your brother Touran gave himself up to the police yesterday. Apparently he couldn't live as a fugitive any longer. He confessed everything. He insists that he has personal grievances to settle with a member of the family."

Nour's astonishment was mixed with incomprehension. "Whom?"

"Ramazan. He puts all the blame on him. He swears that it was Ramazan who ordered Altan's execution. He's the mastermind, he says. He's the one responsible for the trafficking." The commissar looked at Nour, disconcerted. "I'm truly sorry, Mr. Kardam. I realize it's a difficult situation, to say the least."

"It's not difficult, it's mortifying." Nour had never thought highly of Ramazan and Touran, but it never crossed his mind that they could be so vile.

"I'd like to see him," Nour said.

"Not for the moment, Mr. Kardam. He's in police custody. By the way, he also asked the family's forgiveness for his perverse behavior."

"I can never forgive him."

Mehmet nodded, then changed his mind. "Come to my office. You can talk to him face-to-face. I'll assume responsibility.

Touran looked utterly dejected as he sat in a rickety chair in the center of an empty room at the station. His hands were untied and the handcuffs were still dangling from one of his wrists. Nour examined him through a one-way glass window before going in. In a wrinkled suit and stained shirt, his face unshaven, he was hardly recognizable. He didn't notice Nour enter. His eyes were fixed on the dusty floor. In a way Nour pitied the ex-colonel, who had always been so smartly dressed and lived so elegantly, surrounded by servants.

When Nour placed his hand on his shoulder, Touran made a defensive gesture and gazed at him for a few seconds before recognizing his brother.

"I didn't do it. He forced me," Touran stuttered. "I beg you to forgive me. I'm so sorry. I never wanted this to happen."

Touran blubbered as he wiped his tears with his sleeve. The sight was too real, too wretched. Nour couldn't look at him. He could easily have strangled him with his bare hands.

"Please get me out of here, Nour. I'll give you everything I have."

His plea revolted Nour even more. Not a word about Altan, no mention of his mother or of his family. After taking out a contract on his own brother, he was begging to get out of prison.

Nour left the room in disgust, without bothering to say a word.

A week later, Nour walked down to Kardam International and took the elevator up to his office. Shahané and Erol, his half-sister and half-brother, were already there, waiting for him. As it would be impossible to run the business from New York, he had decided to pass the management of the company to Erol without relinquishing his own post as president of the Board of Directors. Shahané, who had an interest in politics, would help him as an adviser. She never liked to be in the forefront, but preferred to be the power behind the throne. Their meeting didn't last long. Nour had planned everything to the last detail.

Following a brief leave-taking, Nour took the elevator down to the ground floor and told his driver that he would prefer to walk. It was one of those rare occasions when he let himself be absorbed by the unending rush of the streets, the traffic, the pulse of the city that he loved so much. Regretfully, he realized that he had reached the end of a splendid era. How strange that the Kardam dynasty now rested on Erol's shoulders. Five years earlier, nobody dared imagine that this man, perhaps a little drab, would take command of the company. Likewise, nobody had ever thought that Ramazan would be on the run, Touran in jail, Altan stabbed to death, and Nour about to start life anew in America, with still so much unresolved on his mind.

# *Part* five

# 38

$\mathcal{N}$our and Esin could never forget the turmoil caused by Leila's first visit to New York almost a year after their wedding. She arrived with twelve Lancel steamer trunks packed with clothes, shoes, and all the rest, which didn't pass unnoticed.

First she had refused to travel, insisting that a dignified wedding worthy of the Kardams could take place only in Istanbul: a grandiose ceremony, surrounded by all the members of the immediate family, close and distant relatives, friends, government officials, diplomats, and celebrities. However, realizing that her appeals fell on deaf ears, she said that another acceptable contingency would be to have the wedding in Monaco, with chartered planes to carry the wedding guests to the nuptial ceremony and reception. When the couple insisted on having a very private wedding, Leila refused to cross the Atlantic. Finally, after months of squabbling, coaxing and convincing, she agreed to visit the newlyweds provided she could stop over in Paris on her way to New York and renew her wardrobe before the long-dreaded encounter with Maro.

Maro had stirred Leila's imagination for so long that at one point she believed she was visiting New York mainly to contend with her, to find out who would prove the more seductive, who would be the darling of all the men at the reception. Maro's superiority had always frustrated her: not only had she demoted Leila from her position of favorite in the past, but even today she called into question Leila's role as Nour's mother.

Leila came from a modest Anatolian family. Since her marriage to Rıza Bey, she had made serious efforts to educate herself in the grand Western fashion, to become a polished woman. Her genuine thirst for refinement, though, soon turned into ostentation. Despite her age she still didn't realize that excessive makeup, expensive clothes, and ostentatious jewelry were no match for a strong personality like Maro's.

At seven-thirty on a Saturday evening Leila set out on the most anxious journey of her life: the ride from the Plaza Hotel in Manhattan to Maro's residence in Forest Hills, Queens. Nour and Esin accompanied her. Getting out of the car, she discovered a tight knot of apprehension in her chest. When she reached the door, she hesitated before ringing the bell. It would have been better, she thought, to meet Maro at her hotel or in a restaurant, on more neutral terrain. She was still undecided when the door opened and she found herself staring into Maro's black eyes.

"My dear Leila, such a splendid moment!" Maro's outreached hands encouraged Leila to rush forward and kiss her.

"It's a dream come true, Maro, my sweet soul. How marvellous to see you after all these years."

Nour and Esin beheld them incredulously. In the heat of her excitement Maro had forgotten about them, and they waited patiently for the welcoming ceremony to end. Maro turned to kiss first Esin and then Nour, and they all went inside.

"How exquisite, how wonderful you look," Maro said. "You've not changed at all since I last saw you."

The compliment immediately lifted Leila's mood. Her anguish evaporated. She regained her self-assurance, and, to demonstrate her multilingual efficiency, she switched from Turkish to English. They sat in the living room and at once started reminiscing. Images were recalled, a few peculiar incidents revived, emotions surged, and they kept wiping away tears.

Nour wished that the visit could be short, but there was a lavish table in the dining room awaiting the arrival of the other family members. Was Nayiri going to make an exception and show up to greet Leila? He knew that she had been to few family gatherings since her return from Istanbul.

Esin listened to the two women attentively, for everything she heard was new to her, especially when they switched to Maro's last months of pregnancy in Gaziantep. At one point Rıza Bey became the principal subject of their conversation.

"He was very special," Leila agreed. "He was capable of handling a dozen women, but there was only one who totally invaded his heart for the rest of his days." Leila's eyes were focused on Maro, who fidgeted uncomfortably in her chair. "And that was the Armenian woman who loved him with discretion—made delicious love to him, like a goddess, from the bottom of her heart."

Maro flushed.

"Don't feel embarrassed, Maro, that's exactly what he told his wife Safiyé."

Nour excused himself to go to the kitchen for a glass of water. Maro was enjoying her talk with Leila about bygone days, no matter how cruel and how unpredictable Rıza had been. But Nour's obvious discomfort was enough to make them change the subject.

Later, when the crowd arrived, Leila felt ill at ease. She couldn't take her eyes off Maro as she chatted with the other guests. She was convinced that Maro looked younger than she did, and that her simple light gray wool dress was more appropriate for the occasion than the expensive Worth suit she herself was wearing.

She took Maro aside and said, "I wouldn't have worried half so much, Maro, if I'd known you'd receive me so warmly. But you were always generous to me. I hope you'll come and visit me in Istanbul."

"That'd be nice."

"And I hope you approve of the way I brought up your son, Maro."

Maro was caught off guard. "Leila, Nour will always be *our* son." She smiled and covered Leila's hands with her own. "And you've done a fantastic job as a mother."

Maro and Vartan had put aside their old quarrels. As Perg had said to the staff, seeing them arrive together every morning, "It did them good to have a fight. They're much closer now than before."

Owing to his advancing age and the anguish caused by his brother Noubar's death, Vartan had reduced his workload and stopped lecturing completely. He was at the stage of final revision of the third and last volume of *The Armenians Within the Ottoman Empire*. Occasionally, when the news was worth commenting on, Vartan would write an editorial, but he hated having to do it simply because he always had, and to fill a space in the paper.

"Somebody has to take over," Vartan said to Maro. They were at the press.

"You can't carry on like this. It's high time you rested and spent more time with your grandchildren. You'll miss seeing them grow up."

Maro felt disheartened. "We can't depend on Perg anymore. She's even older than we are."

They had both lost their old enthusiasm. They could foresee with bitterness the end of the *Armenian Free Press*.

"This is not even a profession," Vartan said. "It's like the priesthood. It's a vocation. Who'd want it in this day and age?"

"I almost regret the success of our children sometimes," she said jokingly. "Tomas a successful surgeon, Jake in business with Nour, Magda and Araxi with their own professions."

Nayiri remained the only possibility. Maro seriously considered passing the torch to her one day and asked her to assume responsibility for the paper more often than before. In the beginning Nayiri looked on it as she would any other job, but gradually the work filled the void she had experienced since Nour's marriage. Vartan complained that after all her years studying psychology she was going to end up running a newspaper, but deep down the idea of his daughter taking over the *Armenian Free Press* delighted him.

# 39

$\mathcal{I}$t had been a long and difficult winter, especially for Nour, who spent his time shuttling between Istanbul and New York in order to follow Altan's dragging murder trial, to close trade deals, and to contest the Turkish Ministry of Transport's decision to expropriate an enormous chunk of the Kardam cotton fields for a new airport on the outskirts of Adana. The trial had its peculiar moments, in particular when the prosecuting attorney began to defend the offenders instead of denouncing them. Nour's last trip to Turkey, however, had an altogether different nature. Ankara had offered him the opportunity to become Turkey's next ambassador to Washington. Considering his reputation and background, they could think of no one better qualified, But Nour wasn't interested; he would never agree to play the dirty game of politics. He looked for a way to turn down the offer without affronting the Turkish government. After long hours of thinking, he managed to persuade them that his work in New York, promoting trade between the U.S. and Turkey, was far more important and profitable to the country than an ambassadorship, for which he had neither the credentials nor the inclination.

Over a span of seven generations the Kardam family had generated many prominent political figures, but Nour and his brothers smashed the mold, and preferred to expand the family enterprise instead of wasting time on political phantasms. Within four years Bali-Kardam International had placed itself, according to the *Wall Street Journal*, among the fastest-growing business ventures in the United States.

Almost all members of the Kardam and Balian families had now been offered a role in the direction of the new Kardam holdings, either managing company branches; establishing trade affiliations, both local and international; or expanding their public relations, mostly outside the country via Turkish affiliates. Even Vrezh, the young Armenian-American law student who had shared a pizza with Nicole, had been awarded a junior press attaché job, but he still had to pass the New York bar exam, having failed it twice already. The only ones who weren't directly implicated in the corporation were Esin and Tomas, the two physicians; Nicole, now a junior partner at Irving Leonard & Associates, and Nayiri, who was busy editing the *Armenian Free Press* full time.

Nour's relations with Nayiri were still unsettled, like a dragged-out lawsuit with frequent interruptions, mostly because of Nour's business trips and attempts to cool the affair, followed by surprisingly impassioned submissions. Jake's marriage to Nicole had been another occasion of serious conflict. Nayiri refused to attend both the ceremony and the reception.

"You'll be with *her*. I can't stand it. It'll make me sick."

Using all his persuasive skill, Nour had been able to change her mind. Immediately after the vows, however, Nayiri had dashed to the bar and downed a couple of quick bourbons, and had to be driven home by Araxi before the wedding feast had even begun.

Nour was tired of her demands for his exclusive love. It was impossible to save a decaying apple, he thought. Esin suspected there was something between her husband and his half-sister, but she made the enormously difficult decision to wait and let it end by itself without quarrels and scandal.

One evening in early April, most involuntarily, Esin prompted the rupture between Nayiri and Nour. She dashed into her husband's study, where Nour was reading the evening paper.

"I have a present for you," she said, showing him the results of a pregnancy test. "I'm going to have a baby," she exploded with delight, and threw herself into his arms.

A smile lit Nour's face. "At last, an heir to the Kardam dynasty!"

"It could be a girl, you know," she whispered.

"What difference would that make?"

Nour made up his mind that evening. Even if the parting was tragic and painful, he was going to end his relationship with Nayiri for good.

The following morning he called her at the paper and told her that he would go around to her apartment after work.

Nayiri was wearing a silk kimono and had her hair down. As soon as Nour sat in the armchair, she said, "Okay. Tell me what's up."

"I don't know how to begin."

She braced herself. "Just say it."

"Esin is expecting, and I think..."

She cut him off dryly. "I'm in the way, is that it? One too many, I suppose."

He hesitated. The speech about the next generation that he had formulated seemed totally absurd to him now. "I didn't say that."

"But you're thinking it so loudly that I heard it. Your wife is going to furnish you with many more descendents. You'll care for them. You'll make sure they go to the best schools, the best colleges, and take over your empire one day. And there's no role for me in that scenario." Nayiri started to cry.

"We'll always be good friends."

"Of course, I can even become your children's godmother! Goddamn it, I love you, Nour, and instead of loving me too, you're hurting me. I knew you'd leave me one day, but I hoped—" The words stuck in her throat.

Nour knew she was right: there was no role for her. And, despite her unconventional love for Nour, Nayiri was an intelligent woman. She knew it was impossible to continue. She realized it was inconceivable to keep Nour to herself for the rest of her life. What she didn't know, though, was that in the back of her mind she harbored an iron determination: to create a giant invisible obstacle in Nour's heart that would prevent him from ever being able to love Esin completely. Somewhere in the back of her mind was the desire to tarnish Nour's absolute devotion to his wife.

"I know you still want me," she said. "Let me touch you. Let me feel your desire. Come, take me one last time." Tears ran down her cheeks; it was impossible to hide her pain.

Nour closed his eyes and made a tremendous effort not to give in. He couldn't trust the passion that would be generated the moment his lips touched her skin. He stood up. "I can't," he whispered, with a lump in his throat, feeling guiltier than ever.

As he closed the apartment door, he heard Nayiri shriek like a wounded animal.

Another blizzard shut down New York in February, the second serious pounding of the winter. At midday, the snow plows at Idlewild Airport stopped operating because the swirling snow made it impossible to see the runways. Two million schoolchildren saw the silver lining and had the day off. By evening, when the snow finally stopped, more than two feet had fallen. Snow ploughs began digging the city out. Nour appreciated the unexpected holiday, even though he was on the phone all day, talking to clients and taking care of the recent mistakes made by the insurance brokers in charge of the secure shipment of cotton and tobacco from Turkey.

It was three o'clock in the morning when the shrill ring of the telephone woke them. Esin answered, and the conversation was short.

"Take her to hospital. I'll be there immediately."

She got up and dressed hurriedly. "Nour, please call me a cab. One of my patients is in critical condition. I have to go."

Nour offered to drive her, but she refused. "Go back to sleep," she said. "I won't be gone long."

Nour hated these late-night telephone calls from the hospital or from patients, who could always rush to the emergency room instead of calling his wife. Esin made herself available around the clock, seven days a week. "I'd feel guilty if anything happened to any of my patients," she always said.

By the time she had put on a pair of wool pants and a sweater, the cab had arrived. "I'll call you the moment I get there."

"If you don't phone within half an hour," he said, "I'll call out the police."

Esin had already left.

Nour did try, but he couldn't get back to sleep. He went downstairs, poured himself a cup of coffee, lit a cigarette, and went to the main living room. It wasn't the first time that Esin had had to leave in the middle of the night. He had expressed his disapproval once or twice, but he couldn't say more than that. It was evident from her reply that she didn't appreciate his intrusiveness.

"Either I work as a doctor or I become a housewife," she told him. "There's no in-between."

About an hour later the doorbell rang. Nour wondered who it could be. She probably forgot something, he thought.

When he unlocked the front door and pulled it open, he was face-to-face with two police officers. "Yes?"

"Are you Mr. Kardam?" the younger and the taller of them asked.

"Yes, that's me. What's the—"

"I'm Officer Harding, and this is Officer Santos. We're from Station 1 in Queens. We'd like to talk to you."

Nour stepped aside to let them enter. "Please tell me what's going on."

"I'm sorry, Mr. Kardam, your wife has been in an accident," Santos said.

Nour's voice quavered. "Nothing serious, I hope."

"Your wife was hurt."

"How badly?"

"Badly injured. She was taken to the hospital immediately. The cab she was in collided with a truck. Please come with us. We'll drive you there," Harding said quietly.

Filled with panic and dread, Nour said, "I'll get dressed."

Up in the bedroom, he dialed Tomas's number. "It's me, Tomas. Esin has had a serious car accident on her way to the hospital. Can you meet me at the Queens Center?"

Nour was unable to answer Tomas's questions about the nature of Esin's injuries. When he came back downstairs, Officer Santos spoke quietly. "Mr. Kardam." There was uneasiness in Santos's voice. "I should tell you that your wife was unconscious."

Nour's stomach lurched. He should have driven her himself.

They sped along the expressway to the hospital, Nour repeating to himself: Let her live. It's all my fault. I should have driven her. Let her live.

He was greeted by a doctor. "Mr. Kardam, I'm Dr. Peterson, Chief of Surgery. We need your permission to operate on your wife."

Tomas arrived before Nour had time to ask if an operation was absolutely necessary. He talked to Dr. Peterson for a minute, then turned to Nour. "Sign it, Nour," he said, sounding alarmed. "She has severe head injuries. It's the only way to save her."

"Can I see her?"

"Yes, of course."

The chief of surgery took him to the emergency ward. A policeman was standing guard. Esin lay unconscious, a tube in her mouth and another one stuck into her arm, her head wrapped in a blood-stained bandage. Two male nurses were encasing her right leg in a cast, from the toes to the hip.

The accident had occurred as the taxi was making a left turn off the Long Island Expressway onto Kissena Boulevard at a traffic light. The truck driver, heedless of the weather conditions, was speeding and ran the red light. The taxi driver, losing control, collided head-on with the truck, and both drivers were killed instantly. Besides her head and facial injuries, Esin had broken several ribs, her right femur, and her right ankle.

The nurses came to wheel her up to the operating room. Nour walked with them to the end of the corridor, his eyes on Esin's face, and then he was stopped. Tomas was already in his light green surgical scrubs, waiting for the nurses to bring her in. There were three other doctors, all clad in identical uniforms, only their eyes visible between their masks and their operating caps.

Nour sat on a bench and recalled their conversation about the baby's religious upbringing. How silly of them to make an issue of such a trivial matter even before the baby was born. Esin had always been selfless in her love for him. If only she lived, so that he could reciprocate her sacrifices and make her realize even more that nothing in his life was more important than she—not even Nayiri. His young wife, whom everyone considered the luckiest woman in the world, was now fighting for her life, and Nour could do nothing to help her. He got up and walked to an area where he could light up a cigarette.

He was in the hospital solarium, starting on a second packet of cigarettes.

"Nour," Tomas called softly.

Nour turned and stared at his brother. Tomas was still in his greens. After waiting five hours for the surgery to be over, he found he couldn't ask the obvious question. Tomas walked over and placed his hand on his shoulder.

"They've done everything they can. She's in stable condition. Now all we can do is hope for the best."

"Thank God she's still alive."

"The next forty-eight hours will be critical."

"What are the chances?"

Tomas patted his shoulder gently. "I don't like to make predictions," he said, but his tone indicated that they weren't very good.

"And the baby?"

"She miscarried."

It was to be expected. He made no comment. Esin's image still hung in his mind: rushing madly, slipping into her warm clothes to dash to hospital to save a little girl's life.

"She's in the recovery room."

"When can I see her?"

"As soon as they take her to intensive care."

Nour stared gratefully at Tomas. "Thank you."

"I'd better phone Mother. I don't think we can keep it from her."

Another hour passed before Dr. Peterson came to talk to Nour. "The surgery went well. Now all we can do is wait to see if she responds to it."

"Thank you, Doctor."

"She's out of the recovery room. You may see her briefly."

Nour entered the intensive care unit and shut the door quietly. She was asleep beneath a plastic sheet, tubes in her nose, mouth, and both arms. Her head was encased in white gauze. He stood very close and looked at her damaged face, talking to her quietly without expecting a response.

The nurse came to remind him that he should leave. Outside, the corridor was quiet. All he could hear was the clamoring of his own thoughts. He went to the elevators and pressed the down bottom.

238

"Nourhan."

It was Maro, and Tomas's wife, Annie.

"You should have called us," Annie said.

"I'm so sorry," said Maro, who couldn't restrain her tears. "I know she'll come out of it, my son."

Annie and Maro began asking him questions, and he answered them as best he could. Then Jake and Nicole came in. Nicole took Nour's hand, as though trying to communicate her distress through her touch.

"Let us take you home, Nour," proposed Jake. "You'd better get a little rest."

"I'm not ready," Nour said. "I want to stay a little longer,"

By then Tomas had come in to talk to them. He insisted that Nour return home and rest. They wouldn't let him back into intensive care until the next day in any case.

"I'll call you the moment there's any change," he said.

Nour bowed his head and followed the family.

Three days after the accident, Esin still lay unconscious in the intensive care unit. The two top neurosurgeons in North America, one from Los Angeles and the other from Montreal, were brought in for consultation. They agreed that it was a serious concussion, and that the surgeons had successfully removed the haematoma caused by the impact. From there on it was a matter of stimulating the patient's responses with drugs and by constantly talking to her, preferably someone whose voice she might at one point recognize.

Nour remained at her bedside, whispering to her, holding her hand, talking about their future plans, about the day's news, the weather... Esin's parents were devastated. During their long telephone conversation with Nour, his in-laws never stopped blaming him.

"If you'd stayed here, none of these things would've happened," Esin's mother kept saying.

The news of the accident had been much harder on Vartan than anyone would have expected. With the passing of time he had grown closer to his stepson, and had accepted Esin as his own daughter. He began spending hours in the seventh-floor waiting room, expecting

Nour to come out of the intensive care ward with good news, but her condition remained the same.

Annie, Araxi, and Magda came to relieve Nour from time to time, but he was adamant about staying there, like another sophisticated machine attached to his wife's body. He sat close to her bed, keeping watch over his wife and talking to her.

Letters and telegrams were pouring into the office, expressing concern and sincere sorrow at his wife's accident. Jake prayed night and day for Esin's recovery; if she didn't make it, he doubted Nour would ever regain his enthusiasm for life. Altan's murder had already ravaged him, and now this.

There was no sign of Nayiri. Although he thought about her from time to time, Nour didn't mind her silence. Her voice would only have added more pain to his grieving mind.

Nour arrived at the hospital early every morning and left late at night. He watched his wife so carefully that he would have been able to perceive every minute change in her breathing and facial expression, but both remained unchanged: eyes closed, cheeks as pale as whitewash, lips separated by the tube stuck down her throat. Nour tried to imagine the black eyes behind her closed, swollen eyelids. He was even tempted to lift them to see if she would recognize him.

At one point on the fourth day he thought that Esin responded to his words with a gentle squeeze of his hand, and he was overwhelmed with happiness. But it didn't happen again, and in his disappointment he realized it must have been his imagination. "Listen, sweetheart," Nour muttered, his face almost touching hers. "You've slept long enough, don't you think? I'm beginning to lose patience with you. I want you to open your eyes. Let me see those beautiful dark eyes that seduced me at first sight."

In times of calamity Nour tended to plunge into philosophic intro-spection, examining events, relationships, actions. Life had certainly been tempestuous since his father's death. Money had never been a problem; in fact, it had been the origin of all recent events—his father's will, the inheritance, the discovery of his real identity, Nayiri, his new company in New York, the trials... Yes, the list was endless.

He looked at least a decade older. Every time Tomas came to visit, Nour experienced a brief moment of elation that he hadn't yet given up hope. He greedily thought of what he wished to happen, but her interminable silence widened the chasm between what he wished and her actual state.

"Hang on, my sweet," he whispered to Esin. "Hang on, please. When I look at you I remember how the baby would kick, and you would have trouble sleeping. Now you're sleeping like a baby yourself. Perhaps you're also wondering why you were stricken by this horrible misery. I know I shouldn't have let you go alone that night... I know I've caused you this pain... "

He was exhausted, and he must have dozed off momentarily. He became aware that somebody was standing near the bed.

"Nayiri! Is it really you?"

"Yes, it's me. Tomas told me about the accident. I wanted to see you earlier, but I was locked up in a detox clinic. Now I'm out, and Tomas insisted that I come." Her voice trembled. "I'm worried about you. And I'm sorry about your wife." She stood there without moving, taking in the sight of Esin connected to machines, the tubes, the lifelines, and the muffled thumping of the respirator.

"Thank you for coming, Nayiri," Nour managed to say. "I had no idea—"

"Tomas arranged it. He's been helping me a lot lately." She tore her gaze away from Esim and looked at him. "Nour, I just wanted to say that calamities often bring people to their senses, unite families—and they've made me accept that you're my brother, and to put the stuff of memories behind me."

With that, she tiptoed out of the room.

That evening, Nour finally accepted Vartan's invitation for a family dinner at Café Trocadéro, a small 1930s-style bistro in Manhattan. Vartan and Maro thought it would do Nour good to break his monotonous vigil at Esin's bedside.

Even surrounded by his family, Nour didn't seem to be able to relax his mind, which was elsewhere: Nayiri's surprise visit... her declaration...

her softened face... detox...

Nour was still grappling with all this when he heard his name. He was being paged. He jumped out of his chair. He had informed the hospital where to reach him in case of any change or emergency.

"There's a call for you, sir. You may use the telephone on the bar," the waiter said.

The conversation lasted hardly ten seconds. He bolted back, shouting for the entire restaurant to hear, "It's Esin. She's coming out of her coma. Hurry, Tomas."

Tomas leapt up and they dashed toward the door.

The only people allowed at the bedside were Tomas and Nour. Dr. Paterson was already there when they arrived. Esin's eyelids flickered feebly. No one dared to speak. The movements stopped for a brief second. Dr. Paterson indicated with a nod of his head that she had come a long way. Nour placed his hand on her forearm. It felt so thin and so fragile. He spoke to her softly, trying to encourage her to open her eyes. Another second or two, the same flickers of the eyelids, and then her black eyes opened, focusing on Nour and then on Tomas and Paterson.

It took no more than five minutes for the Balian telephone network to diffuse the good news until every single member of the family heard that Esin had regained consciousness. From New York to Istanbul to Antep, the news of the triumph spread.

Leila was convinced that Nayiri's unexpected visit had triggered the recovery. She insisted that Nayiri was endowed with supernatural gifts. "The moment I stared into her eyes, I knew that Allah had blessed her with something inexplicable, an extraordinary other-worldly gift."

# 40

 our tracked Esin's convalescence attentively, and smothered his
 wife with love. As soon as she was allowed to travel, he took
her to a head-injury clinic in Switzerland to accelerate her rehabilita-
tion. When the doctors pronounced Esin completely recovered, Nour
took her on a long European tour—the honeymoon she'd never had
time to have.

To celebrate their return, Maro organized a party. Nayiri smiled
uneasily when she saw Esin radiant with joy on her husband's arm.
After dinner Vartan stood up at the table and said, "I want you all to
hear this." His eyes sparkled, as he recounted to them all what had
happened the day before. When he got to the office, he had found all
the staff in a festive mood, gathered around Nayiri. The moment she
saw her father, she burst out, "Finally! We've been waiting for you."
Then she picked up the latest issue of the *Free Press* from her desk and
proudly announced, "I have the pleasure of presenting our newborn
child: the first bilingual issue of the *Armenian Free Press*," and handed
it to him.

For Vartan it was a dream come true. Not only had his daughter
taken over the *Press,* but she had also enriched it with a much-needed
English section. Now it would circulate among a much larger and
younger reading public.

Vartan continued, his face beaming with pleasure. "I didn't know
how to thank her. She gave me the greatest gift of my life. I was so proud
of her I couldn't find words to express it. I asked if her mother knew
about it. And what do you know, Maro walked out of her office,
grinning from ear to ear."

Vartan's enthusiasm moved Nour. He was delighted for both father
and daughter.

Vartan kept on talking, "Imagine, Nourhan! In English! I certainly have no intention of stopping writing my editorials now. From now on, one in Armenian and one in English, every week!"

The technical and financial details of the Bali-Kardam Tower in the middle of Manhattan were almost finalized when Nour had a sudden change of mind and stopped the project.

Commissar Mehmet had called him to announce the capture of Ramazan. Ramazan had shown up at the Amsterdam Schiphol Airport under a false identity, and an immigration inspector, much more vigilant than his colleagues, suspecting that the passport had been falsified, pulled the passenger aside while the matter was investigated. The Dutch police instantly discovered the true identity of the fugitive and alerted the Turkish authorities.

Nour knew that even after such a long time, the moment Ramazan joined his brother Touran in prison, a new suit would be filed by the Haydars, generating a series of scandals in the press, and once more the Kardam name would be besmirched with obscenities. Despite his wish to see the culprits punished, with time and after the two gypsies had been sentenced to life imprisonment without parole, Ramazan's arrest had lost its significance and he relegated that sordid episode to an obscure corner of his mind.

"Now our enemies will have the malicious pleasure of stirring up more shit," Nour said. "And there will be nasty consequences. We'll look idiotic, with our glass and steel tower. They'll accuse us of living off drug money. It's over for me."

In spite of his relentless prodding, Jake couldn't convince Nour to change his mind. He didn't want to be disturbed, regardless of the reason. He put off all social and business obligations. "You can't imagine how ashamed I am, ashamed of my brothers, ashamed of our past," he confessed to Esin. "Every time I go out I feel that everybody's pointing at me."

His conversations with his sisters and brothers in Turkey didn't help to lift his spirits. He was going through a sudden deep depression. Erol wanted to change the name of the company to save its mercantile image.

Shahané, crushed under the attacks of her political friends, wanted to leave Istanbul. Leila's reaction caused Nour a lot of pain. "The last time the papers talked about these two bastards it killed Safiyé. She shut herself up in her property in Gaziantep and died, alone with her shame and heartache." Saddened not to be able to frequent the *beau monde* of Istanbul anymore, Leila packed her wardrobe and left for the rocky precipices of Monaco.

As expected, when the new suit was filed, Nour refused to attend the hearings; instead he asked Nicole to fly to Istanbul and follow the trial in an unofficial capacity. Nour would, of course, have no choice but to go if he was subpoenaed, but his lawyers promised to try to take care of everything in a way that wouldn't require his presence.

During the long hearings, the prosecution established a direct connection between the Kardam and the Haydar brothers, thanks to Touran's confession. Furthermore, Ramazan was found guilty of ordering Altan's assassination. Although they escaped the death penalty, they were condemned to life imprisonment without parole, as if to make Metin Bey feel like he was in good company.

For the duration of the hearings, which felt longer than a life sentence, Nour stayed at home, telephone in hand, and refused all visits. In his ordeal he grew closer to the Balians, who tried to ease his pain with frequent calls and occasional visits.

Once everything was over, though, and as it was against his nature to surrender to adversity, he shook himself out of his depression and let life run its course as before. Furthermore, in order to forget the black episode, he told Jake that he was going to let the Bali-Kardam Tower rise as a monument of defiance against all his adversaries.

# Epilogue

ℐt was another busy day for Nour: a board meeting in the morning and a ribbon-cutting ceremony at the new library of the Museum of Modern Art late in the afternoon. Between a long meeting and an inaugural cocktail party, he created time enough to be driven to Irving Leonard's office to review the changes he had asked his friend to make in his will.

Now in his mid fifties, Nour was deeply involved in philanthropic activities and major charitable events. He had become one of the most sought-after corporate executives in America. Many projects—artistic, scientific, educational, business—took account of his opinion and made sure that his name was associated with the campaign.

Esin had reduced the size of her medical practice and accompanied her husband on his travels all over the globe. Their two children, a girl and a boy, were old enough to be left alone with a nanny and Grandmother Maro.

Getting together with Irving was equivalent to a happy class reunion. They always reminisced about their Harvard days, joked, laughed, gossiped about friends, and, in whatever time they had left, talked business.

"And Dave Rappaport?" asked Nour.

"Divorced."

"Smitty?"

"Divorced too."

"And Don Crotty?"

"Bankrupt."

"Heavens! Change the subject."

"Here's the latest version of your will," Irving said, smiling, because he knew that, as business kept branching out and holdings multiplying, he would be asked to make many more changes.

"Thanks. And the special clause?"

"It's in there."

Nour placed the will in his briefcase without looking at it. Before leaving, he reminded Irving of the dinner they had planned with their wives on Saturday evening.

"I'd have to be nuts to forget dinner at your place," Irving laughed.

In the car on the way to the museum, Nour read the amended will, especially the clause he had asked for. It was a precaution in case anything happened to him before the fruition of the project:

> The sum of $1,000,000 (one million dollars) is to be set aside in a special account for a new translation center, affiliated with the Department of Eastern Studies at Harvard University, to promote the dissemination of Armenian literary classics in English. Nayiri Armen-Balian is to direct the center and will also be the sole proprietor of the center and of all its physical facilities. Furthermore, the program is to receive a subsidy of $100,000 (one hundred thousand dollars) annually during the first five years of its operation to accelerate research and the establishment of affiliations with other universities. Another $500,000 (five hundred thousand dollars) is to be put in a trust fund for the *Armenian Free Press*, to enable it to upgrade its facilities with a view to publishing books in Armenian and English.

The driver of the limousine was getting impatient as the traffic on Fifth Avenue crept along at a snail's pace. Nour, however, was busy reading the will one more time to make sure nothing had been forgotten. The moment his eyes rested on the special clause, he was reminded of the past: first, disturbingly, his father's will... then his summers at the *yalı* as a child... Antep... Chicago... New York... Nayiri arriving at the Waldorf in her Second World War jeep... the doorman's stunned look... their sexual workouts at her apartment... Then the frantic chase after Metin... the trial... his solitary evenings in their Long Island house whenever Esin was on night shift at the hospital... her horrible accident... the birth of their daughter, Selma, followed by a baby boy named after Altan...

Playback of two long, sensational decades unfolded before his eyes like a home movie. Nour seemed to be absolutely unmindful of the congested traffic and even more unmindful that he was running late for the ribbon-cutting ceremony.

"We made it, but we're twenty minutes late, sir." The sound of the chauffeur's voice summoned him back. "I'm sorry about that."

"It's quite all right, Ronald, I had a splendid ride. Thanks."

The driver couldn't quite figure out why his boss sounded so pleased about having arrived late.

Nour was unable to accompany his wife to Vladimir Ashkenazy's piano recital at Carnegie Hall that evening. By the time the reception at the museum was over it was already eight o'clock. Esin had left with friends, and they would drive her home after the concert.

Nour asked the maid to bring some coffee to the library while he checked the mail. There was a registered letter from Harvard University. It must be for the annual fund-raising campaign, he thought. He slit open the envelope and found a letter signed by the chancellor. The university senate had nominated him to receive an honorary doctorate at their spring convocation. He couldn't wait for Esin to return in order to tell her.

For a brief moment he was surprised when the young maid returned with a cup of coffee in her hand. Strangely enough, he was expecting to see good old Kerim, with his eternal obeisances, forgetting that the years had finally caught up with the old man.

The maid put another log in the fireplace and smothered the flames momentarily, but within minutes a golden glow bathed the room and the log shot sparks into the four corners of the hearth.

The rest of the mail was of little interest. He put it aside, opened his briefcase on the desk, and began going through a few documents in preparation for the next day's breakfast meeting.

After finishing his reading, he picked up his will to place it in the safe. The forty-page text gave him a feeling of fulfilment. He had changed the will at least twenty times, a word here, a phrase there, adding a comma, deleting a semicolon. It contained benevolent intentions and generous declarations. He didn't wish to create conflicts among his heirs. He refused to reprise that rueful scene generated by one specific clause in his father's will. He felt like an outgoing president or prime minister, making patronage appointments before leaving office.

Nour sat idly behind his desk and let the minutes advance, roaming down memory lane—his favorite pastime recently. His life had been bountiful, excitingly fertile, exuberant in love—impassioned, forbidden, perverted...

"It's not over yet; hopefully I still have many more years to live," he said to himself, and he opened the metal safe, hidden behind the Seurat painting he loved.

He rotated the lock left and right seven times to complete the secret code, then heard the last click. He turned the key in the lock. The safe opened. While putting his will inside, he touched his father's Moroccan-bound memoirs and suddenly remembered: "When you finish reading it, promise me you'll burn it," Altan had said when he gave it to him. "I never want to hear about it again."

Altan's voice rang in his ears. He was sorry he hadn't fulfilled his pledge to his brother.

He carried the leather-bound book to the fireplace where the fire roared, and dropped it onto the flames. While the memories of an infamous past were consumed in an orange and red blaze and burnt to ashes, he walked back to lock the safe before Esin got home.

# Glossary

Note: Except for place names, Turkish and Armenian words are spelled somewhat phonetically to reflect the original pronunciation.

*agha* — form of address for an illiterate person or head male servant in an important man's household
*aghabey* — elder brother
*annejiim* — my dear mother
*anoushes* — my sweet
*bey* — mister
*beyefendi* — gentleman
*büyük hanim* — the senior lady, matriarch
*charshaf* — outer garment formerly worn by Turkish women
*evlâtlik* — foster child
*han* or *khan* — inn or very large building
*hayrig* — father
*hemsherim* — fellow countryman
*hoshcha kal* — stay happy
*ilâhi* — priceless
*jijim* — my darling
*konak* — residence
*küchük bey* — little man (mister)
*mayrig* — mother
*musalla* — funeral stone
*namaz* — divine worship, prayers
*sedir* — Oriental sofa
*yalı* — waterfront retreat (house)
*yataghan* — scimitar or sword